Enchanted August

Enchanted
AUGUST

Brenda Bowen

PAMELA DORMAN BOOKS

VIKING

VIKING
Published by the Penguin Publishing Group
Penguin Random House LLC
375 Hudson Street
New York, New York 10014

USA | Canada | UK | Ireland | Australia | New Zealand | India | South Africa | China
penguin.com
A Penguin Random House Company

First published by Viking Penguin, an imprint of Penguin Publishing Group, a division
of Penguin Random House LLC, 2015

A Pamela Dorman Book / Viking

ISBN 978-0-525-42905-0

Printed in the United States of America
10   9   8   7   6   5   4   3   2

Set in Kepler Std with Neutraface Condensed and Magesta Script
Designed by Daniel Lagin

to Michael

ACKNOWLEDGMENTS

Above all, the author wishes to acknowledge Elizabeth von Arnim, on whose incomparable novel *The Enchanted April*, this novel is based.

Enchanted August could not have been written without the talent and wisdom and kindness of many people, chief among them Pamela Dorman, Seema Mahanian, and all at Pamela Dorman Books/Viking and Penguin; Faith Hamlin, Edward I. Maxwell, Stefanie Diaz, Jody Hotchkiss, Heide Lange; Tim Federle; Betsy Morrell; Lucie Kinsolving; Anne Schwartz, Lee Wade; Donna Bray, Alessandra Balzer; Laura Godwin, Donna Jo Napoli; and most emphatically, my large, warm, loving, beloved, indefatigably supportive family.

Not to mention songbirds; the denizens of the real Little Lost Island; and the state of Maine.

June & July

CHAPTER ONE

*W*hen Lottie Wilkes opened her eyes on the morning of June 13, she congratulated herself on passing the one-year mark without having had sex with her husband.

Ethan sighed softly in his sleep. He turned over, draping an unconscious arm across her forehead. He was so dear in his sleep—the sweet shallow breaths, the familiar humid smell, the flutters behind the veiny lids—Lottie couldn't get enough of looking at him, so soft, so vulnerable. He grunted.

Lottie remembered that it had been a year because almost exactly a year ago—the day before their anniversary—she and her husband had managed to find it in themselves to "log some sack time," as he used to put it. Lottie had felt a little overlooked in that last exercise, as if she could have been anyone, and asked, "Can you kiss me like you used to?"

"Jesus *Christ*, Lottie!" he'd replied, before flinging off the covers and storming out of the apartment. Lottie had forgotten for the moment that he didn't like being asked to do things, and promised herself no sex unless there was kissing. A promise she'd been able to keep.

Ethan opened his huge brown eyes. "Hi, Mommy," he whispered.

"Shhh, sweetie," said Lottie. "Don't wake Daddy."

Ethan would turn four in September. This month he was three and three-quarters. He was precocious with fractions. He was not precocious about sleeping in his own bed.

"Come on, sweetie," she told him in a whisper. "Let's get up."

It was 5:42 A.M., and this June 13 was the seventh morning in a row that would have been better spent asleep. Summer officially started in eight days and yet it was gray, dreary, wet, cold; animals would stay in their dens, birds in their nests, fish in whatever they slept in—reefs? Ethan, of course, was impervious to weather. He could be relied on to wake up between 5:30 and 5:47 every morning, after having gone to sleep—screaming, under protest—somewhere shortly before midnight. And running headlong into their bed between 2:37 and 3:04. Ethan, of course, could take a two-hour nap late every afternoon, and did. Lottie and Jon could not.

Sleep deprivation is what really kills you about child rearing. Not spending time with their little selves or pushing them in strollers or talking, seriously, about whether doorbells are magic. That stuff is gorgeous. The killer is the two- to three-hour-a-night sleep regimen, not just once in a blue moon, but night after night after day after night. Sex was collateral damage. And truly, Lottie's life was easier without it. Less laundry, too.

Lottie led Ethan to the bathroom. He was proud of his Pull-Ups, but not so proud that he didn't soak them just before daybreak.

"Good boy!" said Lottie enthusiastically when Ethan stood pleased and tall next to the potty, emitting nothing. "Good try!"

She adored him, and not just because they looked alike: curly-haired, wide-eyed elves. She was stunned by the words in his little brain. She was struck dumb by the determination of his solid body. She marveled every time he framed a new idea.

"Breakfast, Mommy!" said Ethan this morning, and Lottie was overcome, as she was every morning.

And as they did every morning, the early hours passed in a flurry of bananas and instant grits and Z100 and train videos on YouTube. Jon arose at 7:15 as he did every morning and got dressed in his striving lawyerly suit and boxed shirt and kissed them both on the cheek on his way out to work.

"Bye, little buddy," he said to Ethan. "Happy almost anniversary, hon," he added to Lottie as he headed out the door, almost as if he, too, remembered. But not enough to want to do anything about it. "I'll be home on the late side."

Whatever that meant.

Lottie and Ethan busied themselves getting ready for preschool. Four hours a day and twenty-seven thousand dollars a year. That was the thought she had every morning as she pushed the stroller up the slope to Happy Circle Friends. Twenty-seven thousand dollars a year that she didn't make and Jon did and that neither of them could put toward their college loans. And Happy Circle was the *cheap* one.

This morning the twenty-seven thousand dollars seemed more punitive than usual. It would have been so much easier to do preschool at home. The weirdly warm rain pelted down in sheets from the leaden sky. Lottie didn't have rain boots—or at least she couldn't find them, again, on her way out the door—and her feet would be soaking before they got to Third Avenue. Ethan was kicking against the plastic sheeting of his stroller, loving his power over the raindrops, which he directed into rivulets from within his cocoon.

The parking lot of dripping strollers crowded the vestibule of the former church that housed both Happy Circle Friends and its tonier rival, President Pre. Lottie's purple leggings were soaked from knee to hem. Most of the Happy Circle moms were not her friends, but Lottie tried to be friendly to everyone. She was the friendly type. Her hair was so wet she shook it out like a dog all over Ethan—he loved that— as she said good-bye to him.

"Good boy, Mommy!" said Ethan and patted her like a puppy. "Go now." Once he was at the Lego table he didn't want her around. "Bye, sweetie Ethie!" said Lottie, and even she knew she'd have to stop calling him that soon. She braced herself to start back out into the rain, picking her way through the soggy souped-up Maclaren strollers to the vestibule.

It was really coming down now. What was this, hail? The rain hadn't let up since mid-May. Of course, soon they'd be begging for a little cool rain once the savage heat of August blew in. Lottie adjusted her slicker and put her hands in her pockets. Maybe a large skim latte would help.

As she turned to leave, something caught her eye: a new notice on the old-fashioned bulletin board by the front door. There, among "Our Beloved Nanny Is Leaving" and "Breast-feeding Coach—Beyond Pain to Lactation," was one that read:

Hopewell Cottage
Little Lost Island, Maine.
Old, pretty cottage to rent, on a small island.
Springwater, blueberries, sea glass.
August.

All at once she was aware of a sharp intake of breath just behind her.

"Is that because of the cottage?" Lottie asked. She didn't even know whom she was asking.

"I'm sorry?"

"Was your gasp because of this sign?" She turned to see another mom—so different from her! Tall and Nordic with a square face and superpale blue eyes. This was a President Pre mother, a big-deal President Pre mother: Rose Arbuthnot, an actual genius.

The other mom quickly folded up a letter that Lottie could see was on President Preschool letterhead. Lottie had heard they were always sending parents letters—e-mail wouldn't do for President Pre. President Pre was tough.

"Little Lost Island," said Rose, not quite to herself.

Rose Arbuthnot was married to a writer, Fred Arbuthnot (she took his name!), who was famous in the Slope for being one of their two residents who had won a MacArthur Award. He was the genius, not her. Lottie recalled that he was also a genius at creating found art and running a hospice and weaving tapestries from hemp collected at City Island marinas. Or something. He was a success at everything he tried. Now he was working on a Major Novel, apparently, but certainly it hadn't come out yet. Still, great things were expected of him.

And yet here was Rose, whose face up close looked even paler (her eyelashes were actually transparent), focusing on the note on the preschool letterhead as if it held her fate on its creamy surface.

"Hopewell," Lottie said to her again. "We need to go there."

"Rose? Shall we head back to my space?"

Rose was startled out of staring at the sign on the bulletin board by the dulcet voice of Patience, the aptly named head of school at President Pre. She was glad for the interruption; she wanted to get out of there before she could be assailed again by the other mom. She knew the subtext of every conversational gambit of this preschool parenting crowd. "Are all Ben's teeth in?" meant "When will he stop biting?" "Beatrice and Benedick—what terrific names" meant "Wow, you are pretty pretentious, even for Park Slope." And the ultimate, "How is your husband's book coming?" which meant the thing she wanted most to avoid: "How in God's name do you live so well when neither one of you makes any money?"

"Yes, absolutely," said Rose. She knew exactly why Patience wanted to see her. The Arbuthnot donation to the annual fund, as massively generous as it was, may have been found wanting. The check had been cashed swiftly, though.

The other mother turned to her and extended her hand. The sleeves of her slicker dripped on Rose's wrist. She had enviably curly dark hair and an expressive face. Harpo Marx's kid sister. "I'm Ethan's mom, from Happy Circle," she said. Rose didn't quite understand the sudden friendliness, but this woman was looking at her with sympathy, even solidarity. She was hard to resist. But Rose did. "I have to go," she said.

"I know," said the woman. "I think we should both go."

"What?" said Rose.

"I'm Lottie Wilkes. Ethan's mom," said the mother again, enunciating clearly, as if Rose didn't speak the language, "and I think we should try to go to Hopewell Island. Because we need to get away from this."

"It's *Little Lost* Island. Hopewell *Cottage*." Rose was a careful reader. "But I don't need to get away."

"Rose?" It was Patience.

"I have to go." She followed Patience down the narrow hall covered with cheery artwork and encouraging signs and Purell dispensers. She and Fred had moved heaven and earth to get the twins

8

accepted here. Even with a MacArthur it was touch and go at admissions time, especially as there were the two children. But now that Bea and Ben were here, they'd be set till graduate school. Or so everyone said. She sighed and hoped that Patience didn't pick up on it.

"*Please*, have a seat," said Patience. Rose sat. Patience opened with chitchat about the school's upcoming summer program and its benefits, which Rose was already aware of, as both the twins were enrolled. Then she moved to the miserable weather, vacation plans, the politics of the Park Slope Food Coop. Rose knew Patience well enough to recognize this phase of the conversation as the softening up.

"I'm sorry Fred can't be here," said Rose. Much as she liked the school, she did not care for Patience's oversolicitous social manner. "That woman could sniff out cash in an abattoir," said Fred when they got the note tucked into Ben's stroller last night, requesting their presence in Patience's "space."

"Can you take this one for the team?" he had asked. Rose felt she took a lot for the team, especially where the twins were concerned. Luckily Patience did not grasp quite how much the Arbuthnots were worth, or she'd be all over them to break ground on a new building. This letter had a slightly different tone, though, so maybe Patience had new intelligence.

"I'm sorry too. But I'm sure you know why we asked you here," said Patience.

Rose nodded. "I think I do."

Patience folded her arms, looked her straight in the eye, shook her head, and said, "We're very *concerned* about Ben."

Pause.

She continued to look at Rose, waiting. Waiting for what?

"What do you mean, you're concerned about Ben?"

"We love Ben very much here at President Pre. He has a bright, creative mind and a *very* free spirit. But the academic year is almost over. And he continues to find it *challenging* to settle down." Rose couldn't speak. Patience shook her head again, each back-and-forth freighted with some sorry meaning. "We feel he may have *special* requirements. He is a marvelous boy, but we wonder whether he might need more help *elsewhere*."

The overemphasized words hit Rose like a fist of ice to the face. What was she saying? Rose barely registered as Patience went on to tell her about excellent psychiatrists and highly recommended therapies that could aid Ben's development.

"I can understand that you may not want to separate him from his twin, but we feel that might be the best thing for both Bea"— pause, significant pause—"and Ben."

What was she *talking* about? Separate the twins? They were almost the same person. They didn't *want* to be apart! They were hugging each other when she had the C-section. Maybe if she hadn't had the C-section Ben would have come out different. Better. Her mind raced. He's being kicked out of *preschool*?

Where was Fred? He'd slash this woman to ribbons.

Then Patience deployed her parting shot: "Ben is welcome to stay here for our summer program, which is largely nonacademic." Nonacademic! "But in the fall . . . I'm sure you can understand. It may not be a good *fit*. Of course, with the necessary support systems in place, we could see how it goes. For the first semester, perhaps."

That was it. Meeting over. Patience got up and shook Rose's hand. Rose could not believe that she found herself permitting her to do it. I want to kill you, she thought. You should never go near either one of my children. I hate you. You are a monster.

The strollers were like a barricade of SUVs against the door. Rose pushed through them, deliberately upsetting the oh-so-carefully calibrated hierarchy of whose stroller deserved which space, because everything in Park Slope was based on some kind of fucking self-righteous moral order.

She braced herself for the rain, now sheeting down, and called Fred from the shelter of a doorway. It smelled like cat pee. It took all her strength not to throw up. He picked up right away, even though he hated anyone to call when he was writing. "How'd it go?"

Rose told him. But as she talked, she couldn't stop her anger from shifting. "Why weren't you here? You should have been here." I'm blaming Fred, she thought. Stop.

"You said it was fine for just you to go."

"He manipulates us, Fred, even at three." Oh, God! Now Ben! "We should have done more when he was younger. When he gets out of control it's tough. It's tough on Bea, too. He needs a stronger hand." Was his sister already a victim? Was she an enabler? Ben was a pest at home. Sometimes he was. What must he be like at school?

"Do you think he's worse at school?" Fred asked.

"What do you mean, worse?" said Rose. For Fred to say it was treasonous. "Are you saying he's bad? Are you saying you want your three-year-old on medication?"

"Rose, I don't even think they give medication to three-year-olds."

The rain was so loud she had to shout to hear herself. "She said they do! She knows excellent psychopharmacologists! Is that what you want for him? I don't even want him in the summer program there at this point."

"Then what are you going to do with him this summer?" Fred said.

"What am *I* going to do?"

There was silence for a while.

"Rosie, we can't have this conversation on the phone," Fred said. "Come home. Let's talk."

She didn't want to go home. She didn't want to see Fred and she didn't want to talk. She walked fast and hard in the pounding rain. Why couldn't Ben be an easy child? *Rose* had been an easy child, her mother always said. Bea was an easy child. Teachers called her a joy. Even Patience was satisfied with Bea. Her stupid horse face had lit up when she'd mentioned Bea's name. What had gone wrong with Ben? She should have stayed home with him another year and not gone back to work. Her salary as an itinerate adjunct was practically worthless in their household economy, worse than useless. Had the genius gene been turned on in Fred and shut down in Ben? Why couldn't Ben just be like a *regular* kid?

Jesus Christ. Whose side was she on?

She turned a corner and saw that short woman, Ethan's mom, through the steamy window of Maisie's Coffees & Tease. Rose found herself walking through the glass door, picking her way through the damp sweatshirts and the slick Windbreakers and the burnt-coffee smell. Ethan's mom looked at her with her enormous brown eyes, not at all surprised.

"Please, can I just look at that place in Maine?" Rose asked. "Lottie?"

And without a word, Lottie pushed a steaming latte in front of her, helped her off with her dripping jacket, moved her tablet so they could both see the screen. They sat in silence together as Rose Google-Mapped Little Lost Island and rain fell against the glass.

CHAPTER TWO

*R*ose got home ready for a lot of sympathy from Fred. She called up to him. "Are you here? Can you take a break for a minute? It was really bad with Patience."

She went upstairs. The door to his study was open. He had his earphones on. He wasn't writing. He was watching a video. From what Rose could see, there was a lot of naked skin.

He jumped and turned around. The headphones tumbled off. "Busted," he said.

"You're watching porn after your son was expelled from pre-school?" Her blood surged. Fight or flight.

"He wasn't expelled, Rose. It's not porn. It's a movie. Look."

She didn't want to look. "I was just completely crucified, Fred." She actually felt her head trembling with the exertion not to hit him. "And you're watching *movies*."

"I thought you'd come straight home. Where were you?"

Later, Rose didn't know whether it was that the whole school conversation had started on such a sour note; or that Fred loved his work more than he did her; or that Ben had suddenly gotten worse; or that Patience had made them believe they were a bad couple, so they became one; but by the end of the week, the idea Rose had nurtured at Maisie's, that they would all go to Hopewell Cottage together, seemed absurd. By the end of the month, Fred was sleeping on the couch in his study. And by the first steamy days of July, even though she wanted to fall exhausted into his arms and hear him call her Rosie and say they would work it out together, they'd both agreed that she would quit her jobs and home-preschool the kids as of September. She'd give up her free time in July so he could finish his latest book. She could do whatever she wanted in August. She needed some time away from all this, he told her. She needed some time to think.

Rose found Ethan's mom's number on her phone.

Do you think we could still go?

Lottie texted back. **I think we can.**

It was odd, Robert SanSouci thought, the effect his tiny scrap of an ad had on people. He had never listed his family cottage with a real estate agent—not that one would, on Little Lost Island. He never rented the place out to friends. He just took his chances, and made sure the sign was in a spot where those who most needed it would see it. The Rule of Robert's Sign.

"It has that effect on people," he said, and the woman in front of him at City Bakery turned around. "Not you," he added by way of apology.

He'd learned, over the years, that the only families or couples or women—in fact, mostly women—who would take the plunge to rent

Hopewell Cottage for a month were those for whom the stakes were highest.

He insisted on one meeting face-to-face, he insisted on a month, and he set the price sky-high. It worked: His system had always found him tenants worthy of the place. Most of them adored it, but not in the way he wanted them to. Now he was about to meet Rose Arbuthnot. The name alone sounded as if it belonged on the island. He took his coffee over to one of the uncomfortable banquettes and sat down at a tiny table. From here he'd have a view of the door and could guess which one she was. He'd really wanted to order a pretzel croissant but the crumbs always got in his beard. Some women didn't like beards.

Hardly anyone knew he had a place in Maine. It was crazy that he owned such a place. It was almost a cliché: He got a call from a lawyer in Pittsburgh about ten years ago. An aged cousin "had passed" and her legacy was a cottage in Maine and just enough to pay the yearly expenses for a decade or more. Robert was still in college and didn't even get there for the first two years. Then, when he finally made the trip—five hundred miles to the twisty peninsula, across a spit of water from Big Lost Island, up an exhausting hill to the place itself—he was overwhelmed. Stunned. He was born and raised outside Chapel Hill; his idea of a cottage was most people's idea of a cottage: a snug little place with a fireplace and a tiny elfin bedroom and a thatched roof. The thatched roof he knew wouldn't materialize, but this place? It was a castle. It was huge and—no other word for it—glorious. Also, it looked like it would blow away in a stiff wind.

The three women who walked through the door of City Bakery in a blast of humid air looked damp yet pleased with themselves. He didn't think any of them could be Rose Arbuthnot. None of those women would have texted him, *Tell me what to do.*

"Oh, there she is," said Robert, again not entirely to himself. He knew he was right when a woman not at all like a rose opened the door and swept the place with her pale eyes. She looked like a painting. But which painting? Her eyes lit on him and he nodded. This was the one. This had to be the one.

The woman came over to him. "Mr. SanSouci?"

"Robert," he said, and extended a hand. She had a firm handshake, which he was glad of. Her hands were dry and cool. She looked maybe a few years older than he was. He liked the crinkles around her eyes.

"Why don't you sit down," he said, "and I'll get you something. Coffee? Cappuccino?"

"I'd love a cappuccino," said Rose.

It was when he came back with the coffee that he realized what painting she looked like. She was that woman in the Andrew Wyeth paintings—not the famous one in the cornfield looking at the shack; the other one. The strapping blonde with the pale eyes who was nude half the time. He blushed. If there ever was a sign that someone belonged in his cottage, this was it. "Is your husband going too? Your family, I mean?" Tactless, so tactless! "I'm sorry," he said, wondering if she was divorced, or gay, or desperately single like he was. "You get to take whomever you'd like. That's the rule of Hopewell. Whoever needs to go there gets to go there." He sensed she would appreciate his use of who and whom, which he hoped he had gotten right.

"I'm taking the place with a friend—someone I know—Lottie Wilkes," said Rose. "You may know her from Happy Circle Friends."

"Happy Circle Friends?"

"Park Slope somewhere? Or President Pre?"

"Oh, the sign," Robert said. "I asked the people who rented the cottage last year to put up a notice for me in Brooklyn this year." She smiled, he noticed. "I have a stack of those cards. They've said the same thing for years and years."

"Lost Island," she said.

He hesitated to correct her.

"Sorry. Little Lost Island," she said. "The people from last year . . ." Robert could tell she was tentative. "They didn't want to go back?"

Everyone always wanted to go back to Hopewell. But so far, Robert had had new tenants every summer. Hopeless, deluded, stupid romantic that he was, he was waiting for the one tenant who'd come back from Maine in love with him; one with whom he would want to live there all his life. He was pretty sure he'd found her right now.

"Um, Mr. SanSouci?"

"Robert, please," he said. He was happy she was so formal. It was a rarity. "I like to share Hopewell with anyone who needs it."

Rose Arbuthnot's cheeks flushed the palest pink.

"It's not that easy to get to," he continued. "You can fly to Bangor and rent a car. Or you can drive up I-95 to Route One and down 286 after you pass through Ellsworth. Then it's a pretty twisty route to the landing. Don't follow GPS or you'll find yourself on Lost Road in Dorset. We leave a boat at the dock for our guests."

"It's kind of you to call us guests," said Rose, "when we're renting. I hope you'll write this all down."

"I will," said Robert. "And *guests* is a nicer word than *renters*." Rose smiled as she sipped her cappuccino. She had a subdued smile, which he approved of. "The motor can be a little balky," he said, "but the Whaler should get you over to the island just fine. It finds its own way by now." He gave a little laugh to reassure her. "Or you can take the ferry across if you get there by six."

"Is that how we get the car across?"

"No cars on the island," Robert said, "just the island manager's truck and the new mower." He was delighted that she looked pleased and not put out.

"So it's ours?" said Rose. "The cottage is ours?"

"It's yours," Robert told her. "And your friend's."

She shook her head as if she were remembering something. "Lottie was wondering if it could be a two-week stay."

He wavered for a moment. A month was the rule and the price was the price. He hated to ask so much for the place, but it was the only way he could afford it, now that Cousin Joan's money had run out. One August rental every year or two meant Robert could keep his rent-stabilized place on East Seventeenth Street, pursue his ill-advised early-music career (not much call for lutenists, but as a guitar player he eked out a living), and pay the expenses on the cottage. It was pretty much a money pit, truth be told. Plus he could visit Hopewell once a year, in July, and know that he'd make enough to hang on to it for a while. If he hadn't had a wedding to play over the holiday weekend, he'd be there now.

What if Rose, despite the fact that she looked like she'd walked out of an Andrew Wyeth painting, was not right for the place? "If you think it's not a good fit I can—"

She put up her hand stopped him mid-sentence. He'd touched a nerve. He hoped he hadn't put her off entirely. "No, we'll take it. I'll write you a check this minute." She looked in her leather backpack and took out her checkbook. Robert was surprised she'd brought a checkbook with her.

"We could do a third right now and the rest at the end of the month or even during August," he said.

When she tore off the check, she handed it to him with a flourish. "There," she said. "It's ours. We're the right fit."

It was only after she had gone and Robert was back home and

getting ready to practice the Dowland galliard that he saw that the check was for the entire amount.

And while he was thrilled—he could pay his rent for another year, maybe even put a down payment on a theorbo—he was not completely surprised. Robert mused on Rose's clear pale eyes as he took down his most treasured lute. He cradled it in his arms and picked out an arpeggiated chord. "Hopewell Cottage works in mysterious ways," he whispered, "its wonders to perform."

CHAPTER THREE

"We only came up with two choices?" asked Rose. "One each?"

Rose's big gesture at the City Bakery had practically wiped out the checking account in her name. She wanted to use her own money for this but her own money did not go very far. They had decided to find two more desperate women, which would mean a quarter of the rent apiece, which would mean they could all afford to go. (Lottie had a stock certificate and Rose had told her about brokers.) They both agreed they needed to abide by the Rule of Robert's Sign. Hopewell Cottage: if you need to go there, they have to take you in.

"I know," said Lottie. Now she was ordering double lattes. She had been checking her stock value every day and it was up another four cents that morning. "Maybe we should wait another week. We should have had a ton of people to choose from."

"One of them can't even be for real," Rose said. "Caroline Dester would not be likely to answer an ad she found in a gym. Even if it was in Tribeca."

Rose had put up her sign in the juice bar of an Equinox on Duane

Street. She had gone into Manhattan to pick up a book on early childhood and decoding issues, which they were holding for her at a new kids' bookstore. She'd passed by the place as the record June rain pelted against the steamy windows. Equinox didn't even have a bulletin board, of course, so she put the card on a table in the juice bar and left. All those overarticulated worked-out bodies: she didn't belong there anymore.

Lottie's voice brought her out of her reverie. "Why did you put the sign there, though? I'm just curious."

"The women at Equinox—they all looked so gaunt," said Rose. She remembered them through the steaming, streaming windows. "One of them might need a little lost island."

"Mine flew out of my hands."

"What flew out of your hands?"

"My sign. The note card about the cottage. It flew out of my hands so I didn't really obey the Rule of Robert's Sign."

"That's how you got this Beverly Fisher? I thought you put it up in the Garamond Club."

"I was going to put it in the Park Slope Coop, because everybody argues about everything there. But it sort of flew out of my hands on my way to a job interview—which got canceled, thank God, because if I'd gotten it I would have had to take it and then I'd have to cancel Hopewell"—she actually shuddered—"and someone picked it up and e-mailed me. Beverly Fisher, the Garamond Club."

They Googled her. Not much there—some Beverly Fishers on Facebook but none of them seemed likely.

"Someone my husband knows is a Garamond," said Rose. She didn't want to tell Lottie it was someone from the MacArthur genius club. "Let me text her."

The answer came almost at once.

**BF—yes, for 30 years was unofficially Mrs. Samuel Gorsch
tho very hush. Recently inherited all of Gorsch's royalties
so is now loaded but you'd never know. Harmless, knows
everyone on Bway. could be a fun dinner companion. Why?**

Rose sent a quick reply. "Beverly could be a brilliant addition," she said.

"Beverly could be a grouchy old lady," said Lottie.

"She sounds mysterious," said Rose. "And with Caroline Dester, we'll have quite the interesting household."

"I don't believe this is the real Caroline Dester, though," said Lottie. "I mean I guess she could live in Tribeca but why would she work out at a gym where people could see her?"

"Her phone number is on the text." They both looked at Rose's phone. The number could have been from anywhere. Even Hollywood.

"She says to call her," Lottie said.

Rose tapped in the number. It seemed awfully presumptuous, calling Caroline Dester. She was the American Dream—a leggy beauty from an old New York family and now one of those young Hollywood faces you saw everywhere. "I thought she went to ground after the Oscars," said Rose. It had to be a different Caroline Dester. "It's ringing." They put it on speaker.

Even tinnily amplified by Rose's out-of-date cell phone, there was that throaty, thrilling voice, which they both recognized with the first hello.

"Oh, hello, is that Caroline Dester?" said Rose, more tentatively than she'd wanted to. "This is Rose Arbuthnot." Before Caroline could hang up Rose added, "You answered our little ad." Why the diminutive?

"Oh, Hopewell Cottage," said the tremulous voice. "Yes. I'd like to go there."

Rose couldn't even recall, afterward, exactly what they had said after that. Caroline Dester needed to go to Little Lost Island and they couldn't say no to Caroline Dester.

"She's going to ruin it for us," said Rose once she'd hung up. She could see it—the island overrun by paparazzi, their pictures on some celebrity website. "We're going up there to get away."

"I don't think she will," said Lottie. "Ruin it, that is. She wants to get away as much as we do. Everyone wants a piece of Caroline Dester," she added. "Except us."

It was true that everyone wanted a piece of Caroline Dester. They had since she was very little. She was the Graff jewelry baby in their first, and most famous, conflict-free diamond ad. When as a child she starred in a forgettable remake of *National Velvet*, A. O. Scott called her "almost as beautiful as Elizabeth Taylor." She had a couple of relatively awkward years, during which she was sent to St. Andrew's in Delaware to make friends with her rich-kid kind and score high enough on her SATs to be admitted to Brown. She lasted there a year and a half, after which she starred in a film by Richard Linklater that turned into his biggest commercial success, grossing $408 million in the U.S. alone.

That was the first Oscar she didn't win.

"I hope they are not gawpers," Caroline said to herself as she looked in the mirror before the arrival of her two visitors. She had the kind of face that looks good in every light, from every angle. Her graceful hand brushed a cascade of naturally highlighted hair away from her turquoise eyes. I hate my nail beds, she thought.

There was not a camera invented that could produce an unflattering picture of Caroline Dester. Her skin practically sparkled, as Jean Harlow's was said to have done. Her body was lithe and obedient from years of personal training and just great genes. She'd had no work done and she was already twenty-seven. She was at the top of her game, until this past February.

The first time they'd run her through the traps of an Oscar campaign it was exciting and a lark. She wasn't supposed to win and she didn't. But this time, she was the front-runner. She'd wanted it very much. She killed it on the circuit: she'd picked up the SAG *and* the Golden Globe. And then she lost it on the night. She had played the humiliation over and over on YouTube, contributing to the four million hits it received within two days. "And the Oscar goes to . . ." The elderly, out-of-it has-been who couldn't or wouldn't read the name after he'd fumbled open the envelope. Julianne Moore charmingly running up to give him reading glasses. The has-been squinting at the card with that grin on his face, looking up at the camera and saying, "Caroline?"

Her stomach lurched again thinking of it now. On the night, she got out of her seat and remembered to lift up her hem so she wouldn't trip. "No, it's Charlize! Sorry, darlin'! The Oscar goes to Charlize . . ." She was still hugging everybody until her producer told her to stop. Her face twisted into a grimace and then the tears just would not stop coming. She couldn't get herself back. She leaked tears all through Charlize's gracious actressy speech. It was great television and #crybabycaroline became a meme within a nanosecond. A few people felt bad for her; most ripped her to shreds. Now she was Sally Field in reverse. At least Sally took home the statuette.

She would have put a paper bag over her head, but that was unoriginal and would have gotten her even more press. Instead she holed up in her mother's house and she decided to quit. By the end of June, she started asking the universe for a sign. Then she found one, literally, on a table at the juice bar she'd ducked into because she'd been caught in the rain. She would go to this place in Maine as a regular person. It would be her first regular-person act—no, *action*— since she was a baby. It was exhausting to be who she was.

Lottie was the one who got in touch with Beverly Fisher about whether she'd really be coming to Little Lost Island. Apparently Beverly Fisher did not believe in the telephone, because she never answered texts or calls and she didn't have voice mail. Lottie e-mailed her a couple of times before she got an answer:

> *Dear Ms. Wilkes,*
>
> *I will be out of town till end July, after which time I will join you in Maine. I have reviewed the accommodations and they appear to be satisfactory, though I am not able to tell much about the blueberries and so forth, as I am color-blind.*
>
> *My desire is not to be disturbed and to have one month of absolute rest. You need feel no need to entertain me. I have had enough entertainment for two lifetimes.*
>
> *With some difficulty I have managed to wire the necessary money to the account you gave me. I will look forward to seeing you there, though only in small doses.*
>
> *Yours,*
> *Beverly Fisher*

Beverly had indeed sent a wire transfer to Rose's account, which bought Lottie a little more time. (She hadn't managed to part with her stock just yet.) Rose apparently felt that inspired confidence. Lottie liked the line about having had enough entertainment for two lifetimes, so Beverly was their fourth. The last lost soul of Little Lost Island.

The Beginning
of August

CHAPTER FOUR

*T*he drive to Maine was longer than either of them had imagined. Lottie and Rose had decided on renting a Subaru in a burst of enthusiasm about New England, but now, as Rose pounded along the endless grayness of I-95 North, she felt driving up together had been a very bad idea.

They had crossed the Maine border hours ago. She had done her reading about what to expect during August in Maine—good weather and fewer bugs, apparently—but how big could this state be? Lottie had been mercifully quiet for the past fifty miles—she had put Ethan's bedtime music on the car stereo and honestly it was pretty soothing—so Rose had some time to think.

She thought about the twins, of course. Where had she gone so wrong? She was a lactating cow for the first year, pumping and expressing when she didn't have the two of them latched on. She loved her two babies fiercely, of course she did, but they sucked her dry in every way. And those names—their private nicknames for the two swimming fishes in her womb—had somehow stuck. Now she was a stay-at-home mom with an unfinished, unpublished dissertation in poetry. A husband who was sleeping on the couch. And a problem child nobody knew what to do with, least of all her.

"Don't cry, Rose," said Lottie. "This music makes everyone sad."

By the time they picked up Route 1 it was already starting to get dark. Rose couldn't tell whether it was because there was rain coming or because it was getting so late. They had badly misjudged the time. As they passed the careworn businesses that lined the roadway, Maine didn't look so hot. The sky was threatening and bruised. There was a smell of ozone in the air, even through the air-conditioning. Rose was a rusty enough driver as it was (Lottie had driven the first three hundred miles), and now, if it rained and roads were slick and it got dark . . . She did not want to think about that.

Lightning flashed in the sky in front of her. "How much farther can it possibly be?" Lottie checked her directions, which were hard to read in the struggling light. Robert SanSouci had not done them any favors by writing the whole thing by hand on onionskin and sending it by snail mail. Why couldn't they just follow GPS once they got off Route 1? Was the place that remote? Was the whole thing an elaborate ruse?

"Robert says the exit for 286 is coming up," said Lottie, as if Robert were a close personal friend. "A while more on Route One, then a few miles on twisty roads, through West Dorset and then Dorset and then Dorset Harbor—a lot of Dorsets—and over a bridge to Big Lost. Then a short boat trip from Big Lost to Little Lost, and we're there."

"If we don't end up in Stephen King country," said Rose.

"At least it will be an experience," said Lottie. "I'm glad we told the others they couldn't come till tomorrow. We'll get to claim the place for ourselves. I want to sleep in the round part."

"The turret," Rose said. "Me too." Her back was killing her and she had a literal pain in the ass from sitting so long. Twenty minutes passed in silence. She thought she might scream just for something to do when Lottie piped up, "West Dorset two miles! You've done it, Rose!"

Rose turned off 286 and headed confusingly east to West Dover, and the heavens opened. At least for now they were on a fairly decent road, but the rain was bucketing down and the headlights of the oncoming cars were strafing Rose's eyes. Lottie was a competent navigator but Robert's directions were discursive rather than practical. The windshield wipers' frantic back-and-forth was making them both crazy.

"I can't even see the road, much less a 'yellow farmhouse on a verge with a large oak tree opposite,'" said Rose after one of Lottie's instructions. "Can't we ask directions?"

"There's no one to ask," said Lottie. "Turn here!"

"Don't yell at me!"

"I'm not yelling!" Lottie yelled.

Rose missed the turn and made a hairpin U-turn but she kept her voice even. "Since we missed the ferry, Robert says there'll be a boat for us at the landing." Lottie had insisted on stopping at L.L.Bean. She was almost an hour late to meet Rose in the parking lot. She thought they'd parked in the Muskrat lot, not the Moose.

"A couple of miles on this road and then we go over a causeway . . . that'll be Big Lost Island."

"Where I bet they have a motel," said Rose.

"Then we look for a dirt road next to a really tall lone spruce on the right."

"Every tree in this whole state is a tall spruce," said Rose.

"Now!" said Lottie.

Rose made a sharp right turn and sprayed up gravel on the car. "This car will be wrecked by the time we're done."

"This car is the state car of Maine," said Lottie. "It's supposed to get wrecked. Follow this road for eight miles and we'll be at the landing."

They headed over a causeway and Rose thought of Bea and Ben and Fred all safe together at home. She pictured them eating their Annie's mac and cheese and laughing at Road Runner cartoons online.

"I can't believe we have to take a boat over," said Lottie. "And I still think you said we were in the Muskrat lot."

"There was no Muskrat lot," said Rose.

"Honestly, I think it's supposed to be right here. Bear right again."

At last the Subaru's headlights illuminated a very small, very fragile-looking wooden dock. A hand-painted white sign with black letters read LITTLE LOST ISLAND.

Rose heaved a huge sigh. "We made it" was all she could say.

They pulled into a small field, with a couple dozen hulking cars parked in two haphazard rows. Rose stopped the car. Silence, except for the sound of the pounding rain on the rooftop. For a moment, neither of them said a word. They had not seen another living being for the past twenty miles. They did not see any on the dock. They had missed the last ferry some three hours ago. They had bags and suitcases enough for a monthlong holiday and now they'd have to face going across the water in what Robert called "a serviceable skiff." Rose had imagined she could handle a skiff but now, in the dark, in the rain, in her despair, she could only think of the possibilities for failure. This was supposed to be my time to regroup, she thought. She let her head drop to the steering wheel.

"I think we wait here a little for the rain to let up. It's already clearing," said Lottie, her optimism grating on Rose, not for the first time. "And take it from there."

"I think we just go and get it over with," said Rose. "Let's take what we need for the night. If we don't go there now I am going to turn around and never come back."

She blasted the door open and got pelted with rain in the fifteen seconds it took to get her slicker on. "I'll head down to the dock and check out the boat," she called. She looked back and could see that Lottie was carrying the bottle of Laphroaig they'd picked up in a moment of giddiness at the New Hampshire liquor superstore. We both need a drink, she thought, the second we get there. Maybe even now. I need one now.

There was only one boat that could possibly be called a skiff tied up to the dock, a twelve-foot Whaler, as Robert had promised.

Rose spotted a Clorox half bottle floating in the boat and grabbed it. "I'll start bailing!" she called. "Here, take my bag. Don't get in yet!"

"Do you know what you're doing?" Lottie asked.

"Yes!" Rose had occasionally taken a boat out on Lake Michigan, back when she and Fred were so poor and so happy in graduate school. But Fred did the bailing then.

"Do you know how to get it started too?"

"You pump the gas bulb, make sure it's in neutral, pull out the choke—" She yanked the starting handle twice, hard. Nothing happened. "Come on," said Rose. She looked up to see that both duffle bags in Lottie's care were already sopping wet.

"Don't worry, Rose!" she called. "It'll catch! I can see the Little Lost dock lights from here, I think."

Rose pulled again. Nothing. She pulled again. Still nothing.

"Let me try," said Lottie.

Lottie got into the boat without falling in, which was the best that could be said of her seamanship. They cautiously changed places. "I think I can do this," she said.

"Just don't flood it," said Rose. "I've already—"

Before Rose could finish her warning, Lottie had pulled the cord a half-dozen times. The air was pungent with the smell of gasoline and Rose knew the engine had flooded. Then Lottie pulled the handle a half-dozen times more, just to make really sure they'd go nowhere.

"You flooded it, Lottie. Do not pull it again for at least ten minutes. If it doesn't start, we can sleep in the car if we have to. Or we can go home. We can just go home."

"You need a hand?"

A figure appeared on the landing. The halogen light made him seem ghostly in the rain. He walked down the ramp toward them and Rose saw he wasn't ghostly at all. He was solid and competent-looking, and very male.

"Oh my God, yes," said Rose.

"Sounds like you flooded the engine. I'll take you over in the ferry if you don't want to wait it out."

The male voice belonged to a kid. He couldn't have been more than twenty, twenty-two.

"But the ferry isn't running now."

"It is when I'm drivin' it."

He walked around to the far end of the dock and they heard an engine burble to life with one turn of a key. Lottie gathered her bags and Rose's and clambered out of the Whaler, and they followed him onto the *Eleventh Hour*, a large, generous, stable, covered double-decker boat. They stood clutching the railings, mercifully sheltered as the rain poured down. The water was choppy and the ferry bounced, but it cut through the water as if it knew by instinct how to get to the other side.

The journey seemed endless, although Robert had said Little Lost was no more than two nautical miles from the dock. Nautical miles were longer than regular miles—Rose knew that much, but even if someone had given her the formula for calculation, her brain was too numb to figure it out. The boat slowed appreciably. "We're here, Rose," Lottie said, and the ferry driver drew them up alongside a dock, dimly illuminated by a couple of floodlights, and cut the engine.

"Can we leave our bags? I don't think I can manage."

"Can't leave 'em in the ferry."

If anything, it was raining harder now, yet their nameless helper swept up their bags with a sure hand and carried them up a ramp and along the dock to the island itself. "I'll get you a cart." The way he said it sounded like "caht."

"A Maine accent!" Lottie whispered.

"This is yours," he told them, proffering a large, wet, plasticky wheelbarrow that did not seem quite in keeping with the idea of a precious Maine cottage. "See, it says Hopewell. You stay on this boardwalk, up the hill, all the way to the top. I'll lend you a flashlight." He took a small, battered, rubber-covered flashlight out of his jacket pocket. "When you get to the top of the hill, shine the light and you'll see a sign that says Hopewell and Grundys. Keep on the path for Hopewell. The door's open."

Before they could thank him or even ask his name, he turned and was gone.

It was a long, hard, wet slog up the hill with their heavy bags and they slogged it in silence, sometimes pushing the cart, sometimes pulling it. When they tentatively rounded the last bend on the path to the cottage, Lottie commented that she'd left the Laphroaig in the Whaler. But by then they didn't need a drink; they needed sleep. Lottie steadied the cart at the base of the wooden steps as Rose walked up to the small screened back door. The rain had let up for a moment, and the clouds parted enough for a slender moon to shine through. Rose remembered reading there would be a blue moon this month, which she'd planned to watch rise on the east side of the island. Ha! If I stay that long, she thought. Now, in the darkness, their struggling flashlight barely illuminated a sign that read HOPEWELL COTTAGE, the letters picked out with bleached shells. They regarded the looming house for a few moments from the wooden porch. Then they climbed up the slick steps and pushed open the sticky wooden door.

"We're here," said Lottie. "Our own cottage in Maine." Rose flipped on a couple of light switches but the electricity was evidently not working. The flashlight's weak beam showed them the house was all wood: wood floors, wood walls, wood ceilings. It smelled of old pine, salt air, mildew, dust, wood smoke. They pushed open two of the most likely doors and found a couple of bedrooms.

"Thank God the beds are made up," said Rose. "I'll take this one for now." She dropped her waterlogged baggage on the floor of her room. "Good night," she said.

Before she could close the door, Lottie stopped her. She leaned in close and gave Rose a kiss on the cheek. "I promised myself, the first thing to happen in this house," Lottie said solemnly, quietly, "would be a kiss."

Rose stumbled into her small bedroom. She oriented herself, had a badly needed pee in a tiny adjoining bathroom. Then she peeled off her clothes, felt her cheek for Lottie's kiss, and softly cried herself to sleep.

CHAPTER FIVE

*L*ottie was almost afraid to get out of bed when she finally opened her eyes the next morning. What would she see out the window? A shining paradise or a muddy hillside? But it would be amazing. Whatever it was would be amazing. She could barely bring herself to look.

There were Swiss dot curtains on the windows and a dim light was coming through shutters behind them—was the sun even up yet? She looked around for a clock and didn't find one. She had no idea what time it was. Her cell phone had stopped getting service somewhere north of Ellsworth, and there didn't seem to be a working outlet in her small room.

Lottie felt as if she had slept a very long time—she hadn't woken up so rested in ages. She thought of Ethan. She had been able to connect to Jon and him for a minute on Rose's phone from Bangor. Would they know she was fine? Would they believe she was thinking about them? But what a joy to sleep so soundly, and by herself!

Other than her eyelids, Lottie hadn't moved a muscle since she woke up. She wanted to take it all in. The air was different here. It was thinner and clearer. It smelled sweet—from the promised roses out-side her window? Or maybe from the old pine of the house itself? She hesitated to go to the window and look out. Could the view be as sweet as this little room? She had a double bed, but it was a double bed for very small people, a couple from a different age. You'd have to be very close to sleep with another person in this bed. But that suited her fine.

Her sheets were crisp and white, as if someone had ironed them by hand. Lottie put them up to her face and inhaled. "They smell like sunshine," she said to the room. She pulled off the bedclothes and placed her bare feet on the warm, worn, unfinished floorboards, flinging her arms out and throwing off her T-shirt with a single ges-ture. She was naked in the warm half-light of this tiny bedroom and she could feel everything waking up again—her skin, the soles of her feet, the tips of her ears. She pushed up her generous breasts dramat-ically. "Va-va-voom!" she said, actually laughing.

And then she opened the shutters.

The first things her eyes lit on were flowers, a riot of flowers—orange gold with black centers; delicate white blossoms; full-blown lilies; and everywhere, wild roses. Even though she was on the ground floor of the cottage she was perched high enough to see that the gar-den of flowers soon fell off, and next came a view of the dazzling water, and out on the horizon, the curving edge of the sea. She breathed in the cool, clean fresh air, which smelled like the ocean. The sun hit her skin and she felt as if she could hardly stay inside herself. It was as if she were too small to hold so much beauty, as if she were washed through with light.

Rose, who had risen not much earlier, was seated on a huge flat rock in the cottage garden. The sun poured onto her skin. The sea before her lay asleep, hardly stirring and yet somehow breathing, alive. You could see for miles, all the way out to the Atlantic. Across the narrow bay the mountains—each one a different color—were materializing from the mist, and at the bottom of the flower-starred grass slope from which the cottage arose she saw a great horse chestnut tree, cutting through the deep blues and the heather of the mountains with its canopy of brilliant green.

Her gaze turned to the garden. She had no idea what most of these flowers were called. I'll learn the names of the flowers here! she thought. Black-eyed Susans she knew. And hydrangeas and roses, of course. She recognized spruce trees, or maybe pine trees, but there were so many kinds just in this one spot, this huge old box of a cottage she would call home for one whole month. When Rose had awakened, she had been elated with the view from her room—tall grass, geraniums, a winding path down to what she hoped would be a rocky beach—but she and Lottie were down on the ground floor, and Rose wanted to see more. Usually her first impulse would be to explore the house, but the outdoors called to her.

Just stepping out onto the warm wet grass with her bare feet changed her outlook on everything that had happened last night. Of course it was hard to get here, she thought. It should be hard to get here. And thank God it rained all last night—it made every leaf greener, every branch darker, every fragrant flower more brilliant.

"Rose!" Lottie called to her. Rose turned and saw her haloed by the rising light. Even she could see that Lottie—whom she had only seen burdened by bags, jackets, stroller—was now something different. She was aglow. Rose smiled at her as she ran down the path in her bare feet. "Oh, Rose, can you believe it? Can you stand it?" She was wearing just an oversize T-shirt and her hair was twice its usual volume. She looked like she belonged here. Rose wondered if the place could already have had the same effect on her.

BRENDA BOWEN

"It's like a dream," said Lottie. "Like a dream, but so . . . solid."

"I know!" Rose said. "These flowers. They just *grow*!" She bent down and covered her face in something shocking pink, a flower she would have thought was fake in Brooklyn. Here it looked almost humble compared to all the brightness surrounding it.

"It's so odd to say it," said Lottie, "but I can't wait till Caroline Dester gets here. She is going to be blown away. And Beverly Fisher too. It's heaven here, Rose, isn't it? And nobody doesn't like heaven."

"It's heaven," said Rose. "It's heaven outside. And it's so sweet inside."

"Sweet and sort of huge. I can't believe they call this a cottage."

"We need to explore," said Rose. "The big bedrooms are upstairs. I bet you can see all the way across the Atlantic from the top floor."

Lottie had turned her face up to catch the sun's morning light. "I don't even think I packed sunscreen," she said. "I thought there'd be so much fog!"

"I did," said Rose. "Come on. We'll check out the rest of the house. We should decide which tower we want before the others come." She paused. The sun, the warmth, the color, the light were working on her. "Maybe we should even give the best rooms to Caroline and poor color-blind Beverly. They might need them more than we do."

"Maybe we should!"

Rose's tender feet smarted as they walked along the stone path back to the cottage. They'll toughen up, she thought.

"Can you believe that somebody who plays the lute for a living owns this place?" said Lottie. "I'm not even sure what a lute is."

"It's like a guitar, only an older version," said Rose. "They're always cropping up in sonnets." Maybe while I'm here I'll write about a lute,

Rose thought. Didn't Campion write about lutes? I'll Google it. But then, a rush of anxiety and pleasure: no Google.

"I see you writing here. You should write a sonnet about a lute," said Lottie. "I looked you up online." She stopped to smell a giant yellow-flowering tree. "Gorgeous."

"Whatever you read is years old," said Rose. "And let's give the writing a little time."

"Oh, I think you will write," said Lottie. "I see it."

"You see a lot," said Rose. "Let's go up to the house and check out whether Robert SanSouci laid in coffee for our house tour."

They found their way to the kitchen, which was happily not filled with modern conveniences. Rose had hoped the place would be spare and frugal. It was. Like most summer places, it had an unruly collection of kitchenware: a vast array of unmatched mugs; some chipped Fiestaware; dozens of unmatched silver-plate knives and forks and spoons that had been through the dishwasher. There were too many spatulas and colanders, no sharp knives, rusted lobster crackers, and an elaborate, expensive corkscrew, still in a dusty box. Charmed as she was by the place, she was a bit disappointed not to find a coffee-maker.

"Look!" said Lottie. "Here's a note, addressed to you."

She handed Rose a light blue envelope with her name on the outside. Pleased to see the heavy rag envelope was tucked closed, not sealed, she opened it up. The writing was old-fashioned, with cal-ligraphic *d*'s and *&*'s, and she was fairly certain it had been written with a fountain pen.

Dear Rose, it said. *Welcome to Hopewell Cottage.*

"He says welcome to Hopewell."

"To both of us?" asked Lottie.

"Just to me so far," said Rose.

"I thought so."

Rose blushed a little, and read the letter aloud.

I hope your journey was not too trying, & that you are reading this on the first of many crystal clear days. Please consider this your home for the month. I took the liberty of stocking the fridge with milk & eggs & a few things I thought you might need. I hope it is not too forward to say that I take pleasure in imagining that the house will please you, & that you—& your friends—will return to it.

Yours,

Robert SanSouci.

"He sounds like he grew up a hundred years ago," said Lottie. "And also like he has a little crush on you."

"I'm not very crushable," said Rose quickly. No one had had a crush on her since the twins were born. But standing here, the lady of the cottage, with the light and the air so bountiful, she realized that she might be crushable. Or she might develop a crush.

"I thought that Rule of Robert's Sign meant he never rented it to anyone twice."

"Not so far," said Rose. She folded the letter carefully and put it in the pocket of her bathrobe. "How about some coffee?"

They found instant in a canister on the counter, and there was fresh milk in the fridge. Rose went to fill the kettle with water. The water from the tap was noisy. And rusty.

"It's brown," said Lottie. "Should we drink it?"

"If we boil it, it might be okay to drink," said Rose. "But I can't imagine it will taste any good."

Lottie made no reply. She was deep into a binder called *Cottage Visitor's Guide*, written in Robert's hand.

"This tells everything!" she said. "What the flowers are, where to get groceries—there's a market *boat* every Monday! He also tells how to get the generator going if there's a power outage. Oh, I hope there'll be a power outage!"

"I don't."

"Here's the social calendar. Can you imagine, a social calendar? There's so much stuff going on this month. A cocktail party and a kids' play! Robert SanSouci is adorable. Maybe he's gay?"

Rose remembered how he'd looked at her at the City Bakery. "I don't think so," she said. She reached up to the high shelves to see if there was a hidden coffeemaker somewhere. There was not.

Lottie consulted the book. "'The water from the springs is the water you should drink. There will be springwater in the cooler in the pantry.'" She wandered into a little room off the kitchen. "He's got everything in here. He must have come right before we arrived. Use this water, Rose."

They filled the kettle with crystal clear water. "From our own spring."

"Either he was just up here, or he asked someone to get it all prepped for us. Maybe our mysterious ferry driver," said Rose. That would make more sense than Robert's traveling to Maine to put milk in the fridge, surely. The stove was about thirty years old but the electricity was working again and it ticked to life. Lottie picked at blueberries in the fridge as the kettle boiled. "They're so tiny. Is this what everyone raves about?"

Rose tried a small handful. "They taste like blueberry jam." She picked up the kettle before it started to screech. She could tell it would be an aggressive whistle.

"Come on. Let's go upstairs."

They walked up the wide staircase, mugs in hand. She hadn't drunk this kind of instant coffee since she was in grad school. It was better than she thought it would be. When they got to the top they found themselves in a dark hallway with at least a dozen doors, all closed.

"This is so incredible," said Lottie. "Which one do we open first?" She tried a door at the near end of the hall. "Look, Rose, this is the turret!" she cried. "It's round!"

As she walked through the rounded bedroom, Rose was a little surprised that the bed was so haphazardly made up, especially as her little room downstairs was immaculate. But she forgave all when she stepped onto the room's tiny porch, some six feet by four. This vista was much broader; you could see more islands and a gray obscurity far away—a distant island, or a storm way out at sea? She and Lottie stood there, drinking in the sun, the heat, the scent, the million diamonds on the water. And almost at the same time, they noticed that they were not alone.

"Welcome to Hopewell Cottage," said Caroline Dester.

It was a little disconcerting that Rose and Lottie had burst through Caroline's bedroom and onto her porch without even a knock. But Caroline supposed she could forgive them this once, as they might not have realized she was already in residence. She was surprised to see them looking so much younger than she had imagined them, though perhaps that was just because they were not in Park Slope clothes. In fact, they were barely dressed at all.

Caroline herself was having a violent reaction against beautiful clothes and the tyranny they imposed on her. You don't take your clothes to events in her line of business; they take you. When she got to the cottage, she realized, to her relief, that here she could wear her favorite French linen shift and nothing else. It was what she had on right now. She instinctively turned to catch her best light and the sun etched her elegant profile.

"Gosh, I didn't realize you were *so* pretty," said Lottie.

Caroline shut that line of conversation down. "Our plane was heading this way yesterday," she said; not a lie, since the plane was headed this way, but only because she had chartered it to do so. "So I took the liberty of coming early. It was so thoughtful of the owner not to be here. I chose this room because it has such a charming little porch, don't you think?"

Caroline was laying on the ingenue-speak but she wanted them to know right away who was in charge. Not only did the room have a charming little porch, but it was in one of the two turrets that directly faced the sea. Even with its imposing architecture and tall narrow windows, Caroline thought it must have been a daughter's room, or a maiden aunt's. It had framed prints of roses on the walls and two pink nightstands. She actually had not taken the largest bedroom, on purpose. The other turret room had even more space. She knew Lottie and Rose wouldn't have it in them to kick her out of this room. They could have come early if they'd thought of it.

"We actually thought you might need this room more than we did," said Lottie. "We would have preferred to give it to you ourselves, but now that you've taken it, we're happy."

Lottie was either an excellent liar or was a true naif. Caroline had encountered so many of the former that it would take a lot of convincing for her to believe the latter.

"Are there any other surprises we should know about?" asked Rose.

Caroline hesitated a bit before she spoke.

When she'd arrived in the small municipal airport the day before, she'd had the distinct feeling she was being followed. A couple of charters had landed just before her craft had landed and one of the passengers, an elderly gentleman, followed her to the small parking lot alongside the airstrip.

There were only three cars in the lot, one of which was the Mini Caroline had ordered. Out of another, an ancient champagne-colored Cadillac, stepped a good-looking young man with a competent air. "All set?" he asked, and the elderly gent got shakily into the gleaming old car.

Caroline drove her Mini to the Big Lost landing just in time to make the three o'clock ferry. She was behind the champagne Cadillac almost the whole way.

As she stepped onto the boat, she realized that the young man who'd driven the Caddy was also the ferry driver. He didn't so much as glance at her as she boarded. Unusual, she thought. The driver's elderly passenger was already installed in the boat, taking up almost an entire bench. Not that it mattered, as there was no one else going across. She hadn't brought a lot of luggage, but it was a little tricky getting it onto the boat. She brushed shoulders with a bearded man who was getting off as she was getting on. He was carrying a guitar case and had a tentative air. Please let him not speak.

"Can I give you a hand?" he asked. Caroline acted as if she had not heard him. She pushed her sunglasses up her nose, left her bags on the lower deck, and walked past him up the stairs to the boat's upper level. The guitar player looked after her and mumbled an apology— for what, she was not sure. He had such soft brown eyes and his voice was so deep that she almost replied; then the boat pushed off. As they motored evenly to the dot of land ahead, she barely registered the elderly man from the Caddy, who did not look at her. But she began to notice him when he stood on the dock with her on the other side, consulted a sheet of paper, and walked behind her all the way up to Hopewell Cottage. They both kept a slow pace: Caroline because she kept getting pebbles in her heels; the gent because he couldn't get up the hill any faster. He was dressed for the city too. Nicely cut blazer, khaki pants, white shirt, good collar; pity about the brown tie. When they wound their way to the front steps of the cottage she thought they would surely part ways. She stalled, to give him a chance to walk past her. "I love those purple flowers in the window boxes," she said. "I wonder if you have them at *your* cottage."

He went up the wide staircase to the front door.

"This *is* my cottage. And I'm color-blind," he said, and walked in.

Caroline looked up at Lottie and Rose and smiled. "I think you'll find Beverly Fisher most surprising," she said.

Beverly had heard the clomping up the stairs and had at first ignored it. Then he thought better of it. The last thing he wanted was to be disturbed. He craved peace and quiet and utter aloneness after all he had been through. But he could only tolerate aloneness if there were people around.

To keep the others at a fair distance, he had come to the island a day early, imagining, correctly, that the owner or previous tenants would have vacated it by the time he arrived and that he would not need to use the backup bed-and-breakfast he'd booked. That way he would have the pick of rooms and would be able to set himself up exactly as he wished.

Unfortunately, another one of them had had the same idea, but mercifully the Dester woman was as uncommunicative as he was.

The other two he could hear clattering in the kitchen and chattering in the hallways. He did not care for the sound of their voices. While they were safely downstairs he silently slid the small dresser on its bit of old rug in front of the door to the hallway. Now there would be access only from the porch, which had an outdoor staircase to the ground floor. He could come and go just as he chose, and any visitors would have to make a point of being admitted. His room was en suite, as Gorsch used to say, so perhaps he would never see the others at all.

Beverly did not care much for views, being color-blind, but this one seemed to be decent. Friends had often suggested that he and Gorsch visit Maine. "But of course the love of your life keeps you at home," Gorsch would say to him. Not just about Maine, but about everywhere.

Beverly had known Gorsch would predecease him, and he'd been prepared for it. They had buried a lot of dead, back in the eighties. Gorsch had "lived positive," as they put it so commercially, for a very long time. (Beverly hadn't even known about the HIV diagnosis for the first year. Gorsch was a sly one.)

By the time Gorsch died, he was ready. All his papers were in order. They were able to say good-bye in a hospice, as Gorsch had desired. All very dignified, like saying good-bye to a cousin he'd see again. It was not actually Gorsch's death that had undone him.

It was Possum's.

Beverly couldn't even conjure the name without leaking tears. Possum had been with him through everything. Or almost everything. He had missed the years when Beverly was himself a kitten, in his Beautiful Boy moment. Back when he'd done drugs with a young Tom Ford and danced with an old Andy Warhol. Possum wasn't even there when Beverly was the toast of the high life of the early nineties, when there were so many men—it was raining men! Possum arrived as a kitten, when Beverly reencountered Gorsch and they mated for life.

They had met as teenagers—boys, really—in the club that was founded by Beverly's great-grandfather. The names of three generations of Fisher men were on the golf tournament plaques and Beverly was to be the fourth. Then a band led by a young Sammy Gorsch took the stage for the month of July and Beverly knew his future would not be what his father had planned.

Beverly flashed on his father's open hand slapping his face over and over and over. His nose bleeding on the shirt and tie he had put on for the Midsummer Dance. A pink shirt and a purple tie that Beverly thought were tan and brown. His mother stood helpless in the background, weeping and begging her husband to stop. But he would not stop.

Gorsch had not been allowed into the country club in New Cotswold, Connecticut. Or rather he was allowed in, but only so far. He was the paid entertainment. "We were like *Dirty Dancing,* but nobody got pregnant," Gorsch said, many years later, when it was all behind them, or mostly behind them. "I'll never put you in a corner, Baby." Beverly didn't agree about *Dirty Dancing.* At least that overblown film had a boy and a girl. At that club, a boy and a boy was not just a transgression; it was an abomination.

Beverly and Sammy had made eyes at each other all summer as Sammy played piano onstage. Neither of them knew very much about how to do what they wanted to do, until a night on the dunes when Sammy asked, "Am I too heavy?" and Beverly thought he meant literally, in weight, when what he meant was "Am I going too far?" He couldn't have gone far enough for Beverly. Everything feels good when you are in love.

His father disowned him after that summer he was sixteen. *You are not my son.*

Sammy disappeared after Labor Day. They didn't meet again till Beverly wandered into a benefit for the Art Song Society at an apartment on New York's West Side overlooking Central Park. That was a long time ago. There was Sammy Gorsch at the piano again. They went home together that night and they stayed together till death did them part.

They shacked up in their first apartment, an illegal sublet on Crosby Street, back when AIDS was in its less horrific phase. Beverly sighed deeply: truth be told, it was all horrific. The first deaths, inexplicable; the next and the next and the next, inevitable. How many blood tests had Beverly had back then? Thank God for his great fear of needles. It made going to the clinic a near-fainting experience, but it had kept him off the hard stuff. Perhaps it had saved his life.

He and Possum had escaped, somehow. And Gorsch had survived for longer than anyone thought he would. The payoff was that Gorsch was a big success. All that pain in his own life made him write tunes and lyrics that were upbeat and funny and cheerful. And popular. His biggest fan site boasted that Sam Gorsch was the Irving Berlin of his day. The day Gorsch died there was a song of his at number one: a nostalgic duet featuring a very old Tony Bennett and a very young boy singer, so childish Gorsch had just called him "that baby." They sang "Blue Willow," Beverly's favorite for so many reasons.

Gorsch was willing to take Beverly on when Beverly was not such a beautiful boy any longer, with no real job and "no dowry," as Gorsch told his friends. And Beverly was happy to be Mrs. Samuel Gorsch, host to his friends, gentle critic of his compositions, keeper of his homes, mollifier of his moods, administrator of his meds—endless meds—as long as Gorsch knew that Possum always came first.

Twenty-two years was too long for a cat to live. Even Beverly acknowledged that. But the money Gorsch had left him allowed Possum the best of veterinary treatment. At one point, Possum had live-in help, just so someone was with him every moment of every day. It was too silly and too indulgent, but what else did Beverly have? He barely stirred from the house in case Possum needed him. He let the correspondence about Gorsch's music pile up, and the money too, he supposed. The East Side place was neglected; the other houses hadn't been opened in at least two seasons.

And then Possum died.

Beverly moved a chair in front of the door along with the dresser. He did not want any of those women to find him here. He just needed a little more time.

"Oh, hello," said a voice. Beverly turned around, startled. Behind him had appeared a small, not unpretty woman with voluminous hair. She looked almost like a child. She must have come up through the porch. The one door Beverly had not secured. "I came up the stairs," she said. "Are you Beverly's husband?"

Beverly's name had been mistaken for feminine since he was born. Certainly being called Beverly had been no boon before he recognized that he was "not like all the other boys," and it held only a certain allure afterward. He silently cursed his parents, again, this time for their antiquated Anglophilia.

"I am *Mister* Beverly Fisher," he said. "Many people do not associate the name Beverly with the masculine gender, and you appear to be one of them."

"Oh!" said the woman. "Then it makes sense you're color-blind. Twelve percent of men are, you know. I think Jon may be a bit color-blind. He dresses in four shades of green and thinks they're all brown."

Evidently this untidy woman was what Gorsch would have called "an original." The only way to handle her was immediately to shut her down, and he knew just how to do it: a garrulous soul such as she would not be able to withstand sheer indifference. Beverly decided to get her out, and quickly. He was not in his seventies for nothing. "If it's all the same to you—"

"I'm Lottie," she said, not only not taking the hint but apparently not even recognizing it. "The one whose notice you found at the Garamond." She put out her hand. Beverly did not take it.

"The scrap of paper I picked up like so much litter in the courtyard of the club," he said, "could hardly be called a notice."

"Ah, but you called us, didn't you?" said Lottie. She walked boldly into the room. "What a gorgeous room! Such a pretty old-fashioned dresser. Painted green!"

"I wouldn't know, as I'm—"

"Views on three sides and your own bathroom! You're lucky you picked it." She ducked her head back out to the porch.

"Rose!" she called. "Come see this! The other turret!"

The second chatterer, the Rose with whom he had corresponded, emerged through the porch door. She was tall and regal. She looked thoughtful. Perhaps she would not chatter quite so much once she had settled in.

"Oh!" she said, apparently quite taken aback. "Who are you?"

"I am Beverly Fisher," he said.

"*Mister* Beverly Fisher," Lottie added gratuitously.

"You're a man?" said Rose.

Another ill-bred woman of the modern age, Beverly thought. "Evidently," he said.

"Forgive me." She had some manners, at least. "But you're at the Garamond?"

"A mixed-gender club since the turn of this last century, I believe," he said.

"And his name—" Lottie interjected.

"I think we've covered that," he said.

"And this room. It's gorgeous."

Beverly had to agree. He had felt a momentary twinge when he arrived yesterday afternoon and immediately claimed the grandest room in the house. It was large, and airy and spacious, and it had a small sitting room or dressing room that branched off from the elegantly appointed turret bedroom. There was even a sleeping porch. Certainly it was meant for more than one person, but Beverly felt it would be the correct room for him, as he would rarely actually have to leave it if he chose not to. He'd taken the precaution of barricading the interior doors precisely so he would not have to entertain intruders, though he had missed the one through which these two intruders had entered. He was relieved that the Dester woman had not made a fuss. Good breeding was easy to spot, rare as it was. Madam Lottie was not so well mannered.

"I would have thought you'd wait till we all arrived to choose the rooms," said Rose. She was standing her ground. "It doesn't seem right to me."

"Yes, it's true," said Lottie. She sighed. "We really should have been the ones to give this room up because you need it most. That would have made us feel quite saintly. But we didn't get the chance."

Was she mocking him, or Rose?

"We could sleep up here," Lottie continued. "But we love our little rooms. "They're perfect for us. We don't need all this when we have heaven of our own."

"Nicely put," said Beverly. "Meanwhile, if you'll excuse me . . ." He stood at the open door to the porch, with purpose. Surely they would get the hint now.

"You don't want us here now," said Lottie. "But you will invite us back, as friends, and soon. I see it." She took Rose's wrist firmly in hers, and the two of them walked out the door, leaving him alone.

CHAPTER SIX

$\mathscr{R}$ose tried to decompress as she sat on her rock looking out to sea. The air, the water, the lobster buoys, the osprey whistling its piercing rising song—for the moment, all was lost on Rose. She'd thought that in this house, the house that she had written the check for, the house she (and Lottie) had found—she'd thought that in this house, at least, things would get easier.

It was stupid. She knew it was. So what if Beverly Fisher was a selfish old goat? So what that privileged Caroline Dester exerted her privileges? The cottage was enormous. Rose didn't ever need to see either one of them if she didn't want to. The turret rooms weren't even so great. The windows were narrow, so both rooms would be airless on a hot day. And the furniture didn't fit properly. And if Rose really wanted a different bedroom, there were a dozen more she hadn't even discovered yet. And all she really needed was a place in the sun to think. Which she had right now.

The waves lapped at the rock she sat on. She wished she could enjoy the taste and scent and chill of the salt spray but she was too filled with regrets. Not about the rooms. She knew she should breathe in, acknowledge her feeling, and then let it go, as her yoga teacher would say. She closed her eyes, took a deep breath, and breathed out.

Though Rose's eyes were shut tight, she registered that a shadow had fallen over her. She didn't want to open her eyes right now to anyone. Least of all—

"I thought I'd go for a walk," said Lottie, "to see the island. And the other cottages. Would you like to come with me? We might meet some little lost souls."

"Let me just settle in some more," said Rose.

"Some souls may be even more lost than ours," said Lottie. "But you might just want to keep breathing. I'll see you at lunchtime. I'll make something good to eat. Beverly brought some food!"

Rose didn't care about food. She didn't really care about where she'd rest her head at night. She wondered how the twins were doing. Then she remembered she had come all this way to have some time and space for herself. She breathed in and out, in and out, looking to recover the elation she'd felt just this morning. It worked, a little. A walk might be better.

She concentrated on identifying the different birdcalls, but she didn't know much about birds. They made so many distinct sounds here: a toy horn; a woodwind; the opening two notes of a show tune she knew in the back of her brain. The path was leafy and fragrant, and again her attention turned to the wildflowers that sprang up in patches here and there. Some Queen Anne's lace—that one she knew. Tiny white flowers like daisies. Some cornflower blue ones. A lot of ferns and so much starry moss! She was puzzled by the clusters of twigs and bark she saw at the bases of trees. Were they birdhouses for those birds that stay mostly on the ground? Plovers?

It was only after seeing the fourth or fifth example that Rose realized she was looking at fairy houses. The clue was some rather contemporary glitter on the forest floor, which had led her eye to an equally contemporary fairy cottage that had been embellished by a distinctly modern hand, with a fairy-sized plastic wading pool and a Lego all-terrain vehicle. Fairy amenities, she thought.

She had read about fairy houses before she came up to Maine. They were famous, the websites said, on Monhegan Island, pretty far south of here. Children built them out of twigs and leaves and flowers to invite fairies to visit. She wondered what Bea and Ben would make of them. Bea would build carefully and slowly. She'd decorate her house with flowers. She'd make sure the fairies would have a comfy place to sleep. Then Ben would kick it to pieces.

She shook her head to dispel the Great Preschool Debacle and all that had followed. I'll make fairy houses for them both. She looked at how the other houses were made and felt a little foolish that she didn't know how to do this, and that she was doing it in the first place. But when in Maine . . .

Four sticks were the four corners of the house. Bea's had to be just right, so the sticks needed to be broken accurately. It was very different to be breaking sticks without the twins to tell her how to do it. Sitting here on the somewhat damp ground, the sharp smell of the leaves around her, the rustle of the trees in the breeze—such a different swath of nature than on the playground, even when the park was at its most lush.

None of the twigs she found would do for Bea. She was precise and careful, like her mother. Rose broke another set of twigs, measured, and found them wanting.

The more she looked around her, the more fairy houses she saw. It was a fairy village. As she wondered who had made them, a crowd of children careened down the boardwalk path. Summer kids. Rose had enough presence of mind to get out of their way. They waved to her as they passed, but they were in too much of a hurry to notice her much. One of the boys pushed another off the path as he ran.

"Morning!" came a cheerful voice behind the kids. The voice belonged to a wrinkly man in his seventies maybe, who was bounding down the walk with the springy legs of someone a lot younger. Is everyone fit here?

"Good morning," said Rose.

"Don't overthink it, now. It's just a fairy house," said the wrinkly man. And he strode out of sight.

Fred would tell her that too, she thought, and it would have been funny, before all the crap that happened this summer. She wished he were here instead of writing that next blockbuster. Or that he was writing his next real novel instead of the trash he was writing now. The incredibly lucrative trash.

Satisfied with the foundation beams at last, Rose situated Bea's fairy house in a lush patch of moss. Then she looked for bark for the roof.

At first the thrillers had been a lark, just one more thing that Fred could do. He had a gift for spinning stories. That's why she'd loved him so much from the start. She'd practically worshipped him, really. He knew everything. He could do anything. And when they were poor— so poor!—in graduate school they had needed each other so much.

Rose was a poet, *was* being the operative word. She still wrote under her maiden name, Rose Maier, but no one published her anymore. Not that she had been published so much to begin with, but she'd been on track, on that poet's single-gauge literary track from personal rejections to a sold poem in *Antaeus* to possibly getting a slender volume published by Copper Canyon.

She placed a piece of birch bark on top of Bea's fairy house sticks. It was a touch too Flintstoney, so she walked farther into the woods and found a clump of tall, leafy golden flowers. She pinched off a stem, then pulled when it didn't break easily. Then she set it on top of the fairy house, a kind of flower lantern.

She never did publish anything else, or complete her Ph.D., which is why she was now in the ranks of the adjuncts. She'd had a book contract at one point. She'd gotten no money to speak of—Granite Hill Press was a tiny place—but it was a bona fide offer to publish her poems between two covers. Fred and she had shared an agent then too: the miraculous, manipulative Holly. She'd been as poor as they were back then. But she had a nose for success. Just after she'd made Rose's deal, she said she couldn't keep representing the two of them. "I'm afraid it's a conflict of interest," she'd told them and then diabolically left it to them to decide who would go. Rose knew immediately that what she meant was Fred was going to make money—Holly knew it even back then!—and Rose was not. So Rose went through the motions of talking it through, figuring it out, and of course they decided in Fred's favor. She never could resist Fred. The literary life meant so much to him. And—blame it on what, her background? her era? her inability to internalize her own politics?—she thought it would be better for their marriage if she backed away. And besides, she'd find a new agent: she had her own book deal—until that fell apart when her editor left to get married in New Zealand and the publisher in turn canceled her contract. After that, she didn't have the heart to find anyone else to publish her. So she turned back to her dissertation. But slowly.

And then the MacArthur. The fucking MacArthur.

Ben's fairy house was next. She didn't have to be as exacting with his. She collected bark and sticks, a lot of them. No moss, and certainly no flowers.

At the time, neither of them had an inkling that Fred was even on the watch list for the MacArthur Award. The committee kept it so quiet, until the onslaught of press and praise. The parties! The interest from Hollywood in those bleak, dense short stories. It died down soon enough, but Jesus, it was a fun ride.

Ben's fairy house was essentially a great big pile of sticks, just the way he'd like it. Rose felt a gigantic pang of something close to panic. She had left her kids for a month? But Fred would take care of them. He was better with Ben than she was. She let Ben push her buttons. Fred did not.

Fred had been great when he got the big prize, of course, because Fred *was* great. The only thing Rose couldn't take was the questions that came her way: "Oh, you're working on your dissertation?" The implication being, always, that there was one genius in the family and she was not it.

So Fred overcompensated. Every quarter, when a payment came in, he wanted to give every penny of it away to the hospice in Chicago where he had learned to help people die. He still felt guilty for burning out, and leaving the place. "Then all this money can't touch us," he said. But Rose said they should find themselves somewhere to live, somewhere modest, but a place that would allow them to be independent and have a family. She could teach at Sarah Lawrence, maybe, once she got her doctorate, and Fred could write. For the rest of their lives.

When they bought the parlor floor and basement of a brownstone on the right end of Garfield Place, it had been modest. Rose loved their house. They could do anything they wanted with it! They could put nails in the wall and buy planters for the half-rotted terrace and marvel at their amazing good fortune. There was a second bedroom for a baby. Mrs. Diorio, who lived upstairs, was a lonely, cranky pain in the neck but she was harmless for the first year. Then when

Rose got pregnant before they were ready and she was so sick with the twins, Mrs. Diorio got sick too, but the kind of sick no one recovers from. Fred was there with her to the end. It was a hard, tenuous, sad time in their lives, redeemed by the birth of Bea and Ben. And by the fact that Mrs. Diorio left her half of the house to the four of them.

She ripped up some moss and made it a roof for Ben's house. It looked more like a troll's house than a fairy's, which Ben would like.

That year, Rose stopped writing and even researching altogether. Her genius husband joked that they should turn out some potboilers together, just to get themselves writing again (though he'd never stopped). "I'll do a military thriller," he said, "and you do a bodice ripper." And back then, when things were still fun, he ripped her bodice right off and they celebrated their new idea.

Only a genius could turn out a military thriller with the kind of military precision Fred did. He had obsessed over military strategy when he was a kid and he was putting it all to use now. As a joke, he sent his first manuscript, *The Pentagon Conscription*, to Holly, and she said that if he used a pseudonym she could sell it for six figures. She sold it for seven.

Were the twins Rose's way out of producing something equal to her husband's output? She never did write that bodice ripper, needless to say. With twins, you don't have time for anything. So now Fred Arbuthnot, certified MacArthur genius, was turning out thrillers under the pseudonym Mike McGowan. They were a little disappointing in terms of sales at the beginning; then the first in the series was picked up by Hollywood and rushed into production. It starred Christian Bale and almost bagged Keira Knightley her Oscar. Now they were casting the third installment, *The Benghazi Contraction*, this time with a colossal budget. All the book promo was done by texts and social media by Mike McGowan's team—Holly had hired them all—and what made the movie tie-in edition even bigger was the fact that no one knew exactly *which* literary genius Mike McGowan was.

Apparently Jonathan Safran Foer was furious that everyone thought it was he.

Rose stood up and regarded her two creations. A good day's work. And I didn't overthink them. She hoped she'd see the wrinkly man again.

Fred Arbuthnot reluctantly pointed his cursor to **Turn AirPort Off** and almost clicked. He had watched almost an hour's worth of movie clips already, and was in danger of wasting his entire morning yet again. He was still adjusting to the household without Rose. As bad as things had been with them, he'd felt a giant ache when she wasn't beside him last night. He had gathered up pillows and wedged himself into a feathery fort to get to sleep. Very childish.

He only had to babysit the twins for a few more days before he took them up to his sainted sister-in-law's house. Thank God. He was so in love with Bea and Ben but they were merciless. He had a break now—they were at the three-hour "day camp" across the street, run by two enterprising overachieving students from one of the local charter schools. He'd already completely revised the new manuscript to give the female foil more lines, more scenes, more depth. She was the only character in the book who was actually real to him. He'd better watch out or he'd get good reviews on this one.

His new film deal included "meaningful consultation" on casting (after the misstep of Kate Upton as the cross-dressing scientist in the last film—luckily just a cameo), and at first he was willing to leave it all in the new director's hands; Sam Mendes rarely made mistakes. He started watching audition reels of actresses reading for the lead—some of them so famous he wondered why they would even need to audition. He'd only taken a cursory glance at most of them. Until he started obsessing over one of them.

God, she was beautiful.

Fred knew that he didn't really have a chance of getting Caroline Dester on the film unless the director wanted her there. His consultation was just a sop, to keep the producers aware that Mike McGowan's name sold tickets and popcorn and to remind them that he was a celebrity himself, albeit an anonymous one. He'd learned on the first movie that stars were cast as much on their schedules as on their talent.

But still. She was something else. The sex scene in that Judd Apatow film wasn't even his favorite. He liked her best in her most recent movie. And after that mess-up at the Oscars she'd dropped out of sight. Maybe a mindless thriller was exactly what she needed next. He could still revise the manuscript some more before it had to go to Random House. He checked the word count at the bottom of the draft he was working on: 93,467. Could any more of those words be about her?

Caroline Dester came to Hopewell Cottage to be alone in the company of no one she knew, yet even here she was unquiet. Tall Rose and the big-eyed Lottie had been put out about the room, of course, as she'd known they would be. She'd heard them pointedly leaving the cottage after they'd made their discoveries. Now she'd been left with Beverly Fisher. At least he wouldn't bother her.

Caroline made the most of it. She took a shower before she'd heard any signs of Mr. Fisher's being up and about. There was nothing quite like an outdoor shower, and this one was new and had been thoughtfully installed. Then she changed into a scrap of a bikini, since she was fairly sure there were no paparazzi within shooting distance: she had paid the money-grubbing photographers more not to take photos than the papers could pay to take them.

She lay in the sun, which was still low in the sky, and contemplated her life, something she rarely took time to do. She needed to take stock. So far, everything she had done had sprung from the luck of her face. She had made no decisions herself about her destiny. It was not vain to say she was too beautiful to do anything but be a movie star; it was simply the truth. Now that she had been pilloried online she was a different kind of star, the kind who was a pariah. She couldn't ride it out like Jennifer Lawrence would have done. Even the follow-up on the late-night shows fell flat.

Now she'd give up on Oscar-bait roles and just bring in money. She'd take the role in that dumb thriller opposite whoever played the hero role this time. She'd be huge in China.

This old wicker chaise was surprisingly comfortable. She stretched her arms overhead. She wanted so much to think about something other than herself. What was going on in the world these days, anyway? Nothing much came. She was a blank. She closed her eyes, breathing in and out with the waves.

The hard crack of a hammer—*bang bang*, pause, *bang*—woke her. Where was it coming from? The roof? Was there someone up above her? She felt sick to her stomach: if it was a ploy of the press, she'd swim off this island. *Bang*, pause, *bang-a bang bang*.

It was really infuriating. The irregular crack of the hammer was bad enough, but the echo of its impact through the trees and off the rocks was really too much. She wanted to get up and yell at the hammerer to stop but steadied herself by clenching every muscle.

Bang-a bang bang, pause. Was it over? *Bang*.

"What are you doing?" she yelled over the porch railing. She cursed her voice for never having the edge she wanted it to have. Why did everything she said sound as if it were said with an invitation?

"Hammerin'," said a voice from below.

Caroline looked down. Standing there in baggy cargo shorts, a Rotary club T-shirt, and impressively large work boots was the young man who had taken Beverly and her over in the ferry the other day. Not such a teenager, in fact. He scowled at her. She smiled the smile that her directors adored but could so seldom coax out of her. On a twenty-two-year-old—from Maine, yet—it would have its ineluctable effect. It did not.

"Could I possibly ask you to stop hammering?" she said.

"You could ask," he replied.

Very funny. Caroline was a little chagrined at his response—not to the question, but to her. All the men wilted when they encountered her, especially when she blessed them with a smile. And he didn't seem gay.

She corrected her syntax. "Would you be kind enough to stop that hammering?"

"I'll stop it as soon as I'm through," said the boy. "Mr. SanSouci asked me to fix up this railing before you got here, but with you coming a day early I couldn't get to it till now."

Was this a criticism? And why wouldn't he do what she wanted him to do? Everyone did what she wanted.

Bang-a bang.

"It's done now." He put the hammer into his toolbox, shut it, and turned. "You're Ms. Dester?"

Here it comes, she thought. The autograph, the selfie together. The joke about the Oscars. You may have fixed our banister but you're not getting a shot of me in a bikini.

"I am, yes," said Caroline.

"Max," he said, introducing himself. He didn't look her in the eye. "Mr. SanSouci asked me to help you all with whatever you need. Number's tacked up over the range." And he turned and left.

She lay down on the chaise again but found no peace. The hammering had stopped, which was of course what she'd wanted, but in her head was a hammering of a different sort. Didn't he recognize her? And even if he were so far removed from *People* magazine and *EW*, wasn't she gorgeous enough to stop him in his tracks? It had never failed her before, ever. Could it be that he actually did not know who she was, or want to know, or care?

She got up and wrapped a little towel around her waist. Down in the kitchen, she found Max's name on the wall over the old electric range. The house phone only made local calls; that much she knew from Lottie's loud and unsuccessful attempt to phone her dreary family this morning. She dialed Max's number.

"Yep," he said when he picked up.

"It's Caroline Dester." She said it in the way she did for radio interviews, even as she thought, I'm being a fool.

Max said nothing.

She didn't actually know why she'd called. She looked around the kitchen. There was milk and juice in the fridge, and the few delicacies Beverly had brought, but nothing in the open cupboards, beyond some store-brand spaghetti and hot chocolate mix and popping corn.

"We'd like you to set up someone to bring us meals every day. Healthy and fresh. Could you possibly do that for us, Max?" How could he resist? "We'll pay whatever it costs."

"I can do it. Lobster all right for tonight? And corn?" It sounded like *kahn*. "I got six in the pot down here."

Caroline never ate corn and she wasn't sure whether Max had six ears or six lobsters in a pot.

"Mr. SanSouci left you some potatoes, I'm pretty sure," he continued. "Look in the larder." *Lah-dah*. "There's chard at the farmers market. Beets, too, I expect, this time of year. I'll pick some up if that's what you're askin'."

She was impressed at the breadth of his knowledge. "That's what I'm asking."

"We'll settle up when you leave," he said. "Anything else?"

"Nothing else." She paused to let him ask if she was *that* Caroline Dester. He said nothing. "Thanks." She put down the phone and remembered what her jaded old Fox publicist had said on the last press tour:

What's worse than having two hundred people yelling for your autograph?

Not having two hundred people yelling for your autograph.

Maybe she did need to get some work done after all.

CHAPTER SEVEN

*L*ottie had walked for nearly an hour, marveling at cottage after cottage. Hopewell was not even the grandest! Some of the places must have had twelve bedrooms, or twenty. There were wraparound porches, lovingly tended gardens, gingerbread molding, weathered old cedar shingles, shutters the color of the sea. And every single cottage had a thrilling view of the water. How could Robert SanSouci rent out Hopewell Cottage? Why didn't he stay there every moment of his life?

She walked up a rise and found herself on a high point that swooped down the other side to the water. Blueberry bushes spread out at her feet. Birch trees gave her shade. The water glinted as if a child had sprinkled it with gold. Three little girls, on the water's edge, jumped from rock to rock. As if on cue, a sailboat glided into view.

Ethan would love it here. Jon would love it here. She was struck with a pang. How were they? She couldn't reach them by cell or on the cottage landline. Of course, it had only been a day and a half—it seemed so much longer!—and Ethan was at his grandmom's and Jon was at work (at least she hoped he was at work), so they probably hadn't even missed her yet. Wouldn't it be wonderful, though, if they could all come here together?

The few other islanders Lottie encountered on her walk were friendly enough but they made no effort to go beyond a simple hello. There was a little post office and a tearoom, both closed. She was drawn to the sound of tennis balls being whacked on hard courts. She had watched a lot of tennis in college; she loved it, even though she didn't play. She stooped to pick some flowers to take back to the cottage, even though they had so many in the garden there. There were a lot of these little dark blue ones. Surely no one would mind if she broke off a few.

Lottie absently thought how much she wished Jon could see her now. She did not have much vanity, but she imagined that she looked her best at this moment. She could feel the late morning sun setting fire to her hair; she was happy with the flowers in her arms. She was so preoccupied with how she must have looked that she didn't hear one of the tennis players approaching her.

"Morning," he said.

"Morning," she replied.

"My sister was overenthusiastic with her annuals this year. If you'd rather cut some of them, you're welcome to them." He put out his hand. "Bill Keating."

Bill Keating was a type Lottie didn't see much in Park Slope. Tall and lean, lithe and leathery, he looked as if he spent no time indoors. He was probably twenty years older than she was, but he looked a lot healthier, despite the crinkles around his eyes (surely from squinting at the sun from the tennis court or a sailboat or a ski slope). He wore a faded baseball cap and a shirt with holes.

She took his hand and shook it. His grip was strong and certain.

"Lottie Wilkes," she said. "I'm at Hopewell Cottage."

"Guests?"

"Renters."

She expected his friendliness to wane when she told him she was a renter. Robert SanSouci's cottage book had said in not so many words that renters were on the bottom rung of the Little Lost social scale. "It's a tight-knit community," he had written. But Bill did not miss a beat.

"Do you play?" he asked.

"No, but I'm a good spectator," said Lottie. "Who's going to take the set here?"

Bill was a terrific tennis commentator. Lottie couldn't believe how much she found out about the island in about ten minutes of spectating. It was like that chapter of *The Great Gatsby* that's just names—Miss Gosnold of Great Neck and her rehabilitated sister and all that. Except here the only history was Little Lost history, and the only families were Little Lost families.

"How do you keep it all straight?" she asked. A ball flew over the fence into the tall grass.

"*Sorry, partner*," came the call from the tennis court. Lottie noticed that they all apologized for every shot, good or bad.

"The phone list is organized by island longevity," said Bill. "The first on the list was the first family here, the van Straatens, now ruled by their dreadful matriarch. We're twelfth on my mother's side and twenty-third on my father's. So not bad. Your SanSoucis are not so shabby either, though they're not the original builders. There was a lot of turnover in the twenties. Then people clung on."

"*My fault, my fault!*" Another blame-taking cry from the court.

"Those two are up here from May till October," said Bill, pointing to the handsome couple on the far side of the court. Lottie was charmed that they actually wore white to play. "The Wades. She once placed second in the Little Lost bathing suit competition, back when there was a Little Lost bathing suit competition. She's a van Straaten, originally."

"I bet she can still rock a maillot," said Lottie, pleased she knew the word.

"No, that was in. Your point!"

"Their partners are wife and wife, can you believe? A Boston marriage that turned into a legal one. She plays like a man so they're a match in mixed doubles."

"Do people like each other as much as they seem to?" Lottie asked. "Or is it show?"

"Show is as good as real after a while, don't you think?" Bill said. "It's a small island."

"Is that why everybody just walks across everyone else's property?" Her meandering walk had cut across many cottage lots this morning, yet no one had seemed to notice. "That's okay?"

"The cottages belong to their owners; the land belongs to everyone."

"This island is a *co-op*?"

"WASP communism," said Bill. "So we have to get along. Our parents were neighbors. Our grandparents were neighbors. Sometimes we marry each other. Sometimes we divorce each other. If we can't play together by this generation, we have only ourselves to blame."

Lottie considered all this. "So you've worked things out," she said.

"Most families have, even though a summer cottage tends to be a strain on the family finances. Your young Mr. SanSouci could use more family. The Ladies Association for Beautification wishes he would settle down and get married and populate that upstairs dorm room with *Kinder*, but he's not a real presence here. We have his renters instead. And not a bad bunch they turn out to be." He smiled.

"What association?" Lottie couldn't let that go by.

"The Little Lost LABs. They run the place. Beautify, socialize. Iron fist in a lace glove. They're the social committee. We're relentlessly social here."

"You should meet our cottagers," said Lottie, taking a chance. "Will you come over sometime? I make a very good old-fashioned." She had pegged him as a bourbon man.

"I'd be delighted. And you must come to the August cocktail party. It's at the Whyte Cottage. The twentieth, I think. Always the third Thursday of the month. The social calendar should be in the cottage somewhere."

"Yes, Robert left it for us."

"Bring a covered dish—recipes favored by the islanders are in the Little Lost cookbook at the library. Tons of calories. The theme is hats this year. Wear a hat."

"A hat!"

"There'll be plenty at the cottage, I'm sure. Look through all the closets! That's a renter's privilege."

"Will do."

"We dress for cocktails, so don't be surprised to see me in a jacket."

"*Out!*" The tennis players laughed, walked to the net, and shook hands, straight on, then diagonally.

"And that's a match. Want to watch another one?" he asked.

As friendly as Bill was, Lottie did not want to outstay her renter's welcome. She thought about how Caroline would exit this situation. "I won't trespass on your hospitality any further," she said, trying on a Caroline intonation. "I'll wander down another path and see what I find."

"If you head that way," he said, nodding toward a sloping path, "it will take you to the springhouse."

"That's where it is," said Lottie. "I couldn't figure it out from the map."

"The map is more fanciful than faithful," he said. "Your cottage should have a water jug somewhere."

"Yes—there's a cooler. It was filled when we got here."

"That's Max, I bet. Fill it up again before you run out. The tap water is drinkable but I try to avoid it. I still remember before we had any drinkable water. I used to cart two five-gallon jugs to the cottages for fifty cents a trip. Brutally heavy. Daylight robbery, and they knew it."

"I'd hire you if you were still doing it," said Lottie. "See you at the hat party!" She walked down the path. She'd check out the spring first and then if she could make it work, she'd top up the water cooler in the pantry. Springwater. For free.

Rose's skin burned easily, so she had to come in from her walk earlier than she'd wanted to, as she had forgotten to apply the sunscreen she had remembered to bring. The cottage was apparently empty. She could do whatever she wanted.

She unpacked for a while but there wasn't much to put into the drawers of the old painted-over mahogany dresser; a lot of her stuff was still in the car. She wasn't ready to break open her computer and she couldn't decide which of the many novels she'd brought with her she wanted to start. The sensation of not being needed by anyone was almost physical.

She looked around her little bedroom. It really was quite sweet, all white and airy and simple. And she'd slept like a rock last night. The view was . . . well, you might be able to improve on it, but you wouldn't need to. The big horse chestnut was filled with its barbed fruit. Orange daylilies tapped against the beveled glass of her window. Beyond the crest of the back lawn was the sparkling water. It wasn't the panoramic coastline view of the turret windows, but, truth be told, it suited her better.

Fred and the twins would be so happy here, she thought, especially now that Bea and Ben even had their own fairy houses. Rose was glad she had not lost her resolve to make the trip, in the early morning New York light, right before she'd gotten in the car. The twins had no clue how long a month was. She didn't either. Maybe she'd only stay two weeks. They could change so much in two weeks.

"Bye, Mommy!" She'd hugged Ben so tight that he emitted a surprised *oomph*. Then he'd hit her.

"The pediatrician's number is on the fridge," she'd said to Fred as she let Ben go and gave an even harder hug to Bea. "I love you, my sweetie pie."

"Don't go," Bea had replied, ripping Rose's heart.

"I gave my sister the number too," she continued to her husband. "And she has all my contact details." He hadn't asked which island she was going to, so she hadn't told him. "I left a signed letter of permission saying that she can take them to the hospital up in Greenwich if Ben breaks his arm or something. Not that he will." Rose hadn't wanted to think about what kinds of things might send Ben to the hospital. "You just need to get them in the car late in the afternoon after they've eaten, so hopefully they'll sleep and you won't feel like you have to entertain them the whole way up to Connecticut. The weather is much nicer today so you can take them to the tot lot right after I . . ." She'd checked her backpack: phone, credit card, some cash. "And I left a ton of food in the fridge and the freezer so you might not even need to get real groceries till I get back."

"I *am* capable," Fred had said.

"Watch me go up the stairs!" Ben had shouted. *Stay-ohs.* Should she stay and start him on speech therapy?

"Just give me one more hug." She'd kissed the top of his head fiercely. "I love you, sweetie Ben. You are a good, good boy."

"Where's my yogurt?"

"Daddy will get yogurt right now, lovie. You'll get him a YoKids, right? And Bea can have some too if she'll eat it. I think she's only eating strawberry banana this week—" She'd paused, her resolve wavering. She could run up and get the yogurt and then—

"You should go if you're going." Fred had not moved to kiss her good-bye. So she kissed him.

"I'm going, I'm going," she'd said. She headed down the stoop. "Love you guys," she'd told them all. Then she got into the driver's seat and pulled out to pick up Lottie.

Thinking about Brooklyn was not doing her any good. Rose gathered up her bag and the car keys. She went into the kitchen to check the food supplies. She took a quick scan and saw that other than the items in the fridge, there was nothing to eat but popcorn and spaghetti. She made a mental grocery list, wondered where she'd find a coffeemaker for real coffee, checked the ferry schedule, saw that she could make the next one if she hurried, and ran out the door to the dock.

CHAPTER EIGHT

*B*everly had brought the coffeemaker up to his room and set it to brew upon his usual waking time, ten thirty, but the blasted sun had risen so early he'd been up for ages and drunk the entire pot before ten.

He wrapped his cashmere dressing gown around his generous frame, more generous now that Possum had gone. It amused him that the robe—a gift from Gorsch—was made by Abercrombie & Fitch, once such a bastion of heterosexual rectitude, now advertised with gay soft porn. How times had changed. Gorsch and he could be married these days, if Gorsch had lasted. What kind of wedding would we have had? The blue-blazer "let's pass as real men" style they'd affected for so long? Or a drag queen blowout?

Beverly thought back to his countless High Teas in the Pines. No blue blazers there, God knows, even twenty years ago. Gorsch worked in the city most weekends but always provided a summer house for Beverly and Possum at the beach. Beverly didn't think too hard about what Gorsch got up to in the city, and Gorsch in turn drew a veil over what went on in the Pines. The place Gorsch rented was a shack, really, and in those days shacks were truly shacks. Back then, there was still more than enough rough trade on the beach to take the edge off. Beverly was lucky to have gotten away with so much.

He opened up his Vuitton valise and looked a bit sheepishly at the contents. Framed photos of Possum filled it to the brim. There was Possum as a kitten, Possum in L.A., Possum at the Grammys, Possum old and mean. Gorsch was in the background of almost all of them. Dear, sweet Gorsch.

Each frame was a testament to its own era: plastic and tacky in the early years; sterling at the end. Beverly picked out the first one, his favorite—he and Possum together on the terrace of the Eighty-third Street place—and put it on the painted wooden dresser on the side wall. It would take till dinner, at least, to arrange them all.

Rose spotted Lottie upstairs on the ferry when she herself jumped on. She considered not climbing the short ladder stairs to see her, but then she thought better of it. Having Lottie for company at the grocery store would not be so bad.

"I was just going over for the ride," said Lottie. "But now I can shop with you. There's a hat party on the twentieth. I said we'd bring something."

"Well, that gives us plenty of time to plan," said Rose. Lottie was the type who didn't mind being poked fun at.

"Maybe a casserole?"

That was a word Rose hadn't heard in a long time. It conjured up pictures of Campbell's soup cans and frozen vegetables. "How do you know about a hat party? Did you meet people?"

"I did!" Lottie told her about her success at the tennis courts. Rose would have found it hard to make friends as quickly. "They're not lost souls at all!"

"Maybe we can do better than a casserole." Rose thought of a summery ratatouille with lavender, if she could find it. "We don't want to let down the Hopewell Cottage side."

"Okay, but I've been told there's a whole section on casseroles in the Little Lost cookbook. It's at the library."

"There's a library?" Rose pictured a long table, a bay window, a place to write.

"It's beautiful, they say, except for the roof."

"What happened with the roof?"

"Too much rain this spring. I made other friends too," said Lottie, continuing. "The Beauchamps are here for two weeks. The Hamlins stay till October and commute to Belfast. There's an all-island work party on the fifteenth, if that's a Saturday, and a Ladies Association for Beautification picnic on Labor Day. I've never been to a Ladies Association for Beautification picnic," she said. "I wonder if we could stay another couple of days."

"Lottie, we're here for a *month*," said Rose. She still could not get her mind around that length of time. "Think of Ethan."

"Oh, Ethan will be here by then."

"What?"

"Ethan will be here by then," Lottie repeated. "And Jon, too. I can see it. Can't you?"

The ferry bumped the dock on the other side.

"I don't actually see it, Lottie. No."

"You'll have Fred here, and the twins. I see that, too."

They got off the ferry and walked over to the car, which had been washed of its mud and grime in last night's rain. The field of parked cars looked like a Subaru/Volvo dealership. Lottie deferred to Rose for the driver's seat, even though Lottie was the better driver. "Fred and the twins aren't coming here, Lottie," she said, to convince herself. She suddenly missed them so much it made her shake. The car started up right away, despite all the rain. "This is my time away from them. This is to give us all a little space. Can you read the directions, please?"

"We're going into Dorset Harbor, so it's left at the top of the hill, then second right," she told Rose, not even looking at Robert SanSouci's precise hand-drawn map, which Rose had remembered to grab from the kitchen. "I know you and I feel as if we need time away from the mess of our families, but I actually think what we need is to be together more. Bear right here."

Lottie seemed to have an unerring sense of direction.

"Straight on this road till the light. We passed through on our drive in. And I do see Fred and the twins here. They'll want to come. All of them."

"Please, Lottie. Stop saying that."

Lottie stopped talking, except for directions. Rose wanted to be angry at her, but she couldn't. The drive was just too beautiful in the daylight, and Lottie meant no harm.

They crossed the long, low causeway bridge, whose pavement hummed strangely—what was it made of?—and found themselves in Dorset Harbor, a touristy little town with the usual complement of businesses: an ice cream store; a fudge and taffy emporium; waterview restaurants; an alternative healing clinic; three T-shirt shops. But even these didn't seem too tacky: perched up on a hill above a harbor as the town was, every vista was glorious. Even the supermarket parking lot had a view.

The Dorset IGA was well stocked, and Rose felt they could all eat rather well for not too much more than she'd budgeted for food (she was used to Coop prices). Fred had told her not to be ridiculous about the money but this trip was still coming from her own account. There was a farm stand across the street, so they were able to get the zucchini and tomatoes for Rose's ratatouille, which she thought she might try tonight.

Before they left Dorset Harbor, Rose wanted to try to reach Fred and the twins. It was so hard to call them—she'd be interrupting whatever they'd be doing and reminding them that she was away. But if she didn't at least hear their voices, she'd be a wreck. Though if she called and they weren't interested in talking to Mommy—

"We need to call home," said Lottie. "I do, at least, and I'm sure you want to. Let's see, it's still only Friday, so they just got to Jon's parents' last night." She pressed the number on her cell phone. "Hard to believe we haven't even been gone two days. Service!" she cried. "Three bars!"

Then Rose saw her face light up. Ethan must have answered. Lottie prattled on and on to him, standing stock-still on one side of the parking lot so as not to compromise reception. Rose stepped a few paces away, slowly took out her phone, and dialed home. She went straight through to voice mail.

Caroline figured the cottage was 1880s, 1890s, built not long after the brownstone she was now renting in New York, with more rooms and much more light and air. Since the others seemed to be gone for the morning, Caroline decided to give herself a house tour. She would have liked to have a native guide and interpreter but that would have meant extending herself to the taciturn Max or to one of the islanders, whose tennis balls she could hear *thwoking* in the near distance. Neither of which she wanted to do.

She opened the door that led to the upstairs hallway. Thank God her room and Beverly's were so far apart—there was no insulation in this cottage, so everyone could hear everything. Hence the name, she realized suddenly. A house, no matter how palatial, is a cottage if it's only meant for three months of the year. Even the past couple of nights it had been chilly.

Caroline wandered down the dark hall, opening one door after another to take in the whole place. A bedroom, another bedroom, a sort of dorm room, another bedroom. There was a tiny sink in almost every room, a holdover from when a washing bowl and pitcher stood there instead.

Each bedroom was neat and faded and a little antiseptic. Nobody really lived here, it was clear. She went back to the dorm room. It was long and narrow and looked out onto the woods. It had surely been more than one room to start. Someone had taken down the walls to make the place a giant room for kids. Hogwarts in Maine.

Her eyes caught the markings on the plank ceiling. She couldn't figure it out. The marks were clearly footprints, and they were clearly on the ceiling. She pictured Fred Astaire doing that dance routine where he danced up and down walls. He would have had to dance in work boots to make these kinds of footprints. Hard to dance in work boots, even if you're Fred Astaire.

She looked harder at the footprints. The wide planks that made up the room's ceiling must at some point have been lying on the ground, before the house was built. A workman in 1880 stepped all over them, then used them to make the ceiling above her. Now, all this time later, the boards were still unfinished and the footprints were still there. She liked the continuity of this place. Another Max with another hammer. Maybe even the same hammer.

This dorm seemed to be a boys' room, even stripped down as it was. Striped sheets, old ticking pillows, a blue corduroy bean bag chair, three half-finished model airplanes from a time when there was such a thing as model airplanes. Carved into the wooden plank walls were a height chart and a lot of messages: "John R, 1938," "Dick + Ellie," "RMBG WAS HERE," and something else that looked like Boy Scout code. Larger nails had been banged into the walls as hooks to hang up jackets and towels. There was a door partially hidden behind a beat-up metal trunk from the seventies, probably, judging from its garish colors. She tried the door handle. Locked, of course. On the wall next to the door was an enormous map of the Harvard campus, copyright 1952, Caroline read. All the boys in this dorm room had clearly got the message: all roads from Hopewell had better lead to Cambridge.

The dorm room needed something to warm it up. She took a few cushions off the windowsill and arranged one apiece on the faded ticking pillows of each bed. It wasn't much, but it was something.

Caroline walked down the stairs, her feet echoing. The house sounded almost hollow. It must be hard to have a great sex life here, she thought. Everyone can hear everything. Though if you were into that it would be ideal.

There were two living rooms on the ground floor. On the fireplace mantel were photos of the Little Lost set in almost every decade of the past century. Little Lost tennis champions, 1947. Everyone in crisp whites. Every*one* crisp and white, in fact. Ladies Association for Beautification Society Picnic, 1972—oh, how effortlessly groovy they were. The men—so slender!—in pants that proudly clung to their crotches, with horrible facial hair; the women in long skirts or caftans, looking as close to indigenous as they knew how. Lottie would not be amiss in this group, she thought. No one obviously smoking pot but pot smoking must have gone on, even here. And then in the back row were the matrons, who must themselves have been the winners of that same tennis championship in 1947, and on the lawn the children who would be the matrons of the future.

A door, uneven on its hinges, led to the side porch. She nudged it open and stepped out. The birdcalls and nonstop chittering were even louder here. They never shut up, these animals. She had never much cared to know the difference between a pigeon and a mourning dove in the city, but here it felt like it mattered which was which. So far the mourning doves and the crows were all she could recognize. The shady path out this side door invited her to explore the island itself, but the house—the cottage—still held more interest. She wasn't ready for the island yet. Corny as she knew the thought was, the house was crying out for love.

Caroline thought about love as she went back upstairs to her own little porch. She sat down on the chaise again and closed her eyes. She imagined herself installed in this cottage, a doting tennis player mixing her a cocktail as the sun went down. Not a tennis player—he wasn't coming into focus. She was just getting a picture of who might be mixing the cocktail when her reverie was disturbed by another sound: the clump of footsteps up the outside steps to her porch. Her private porch.

"Max?" she said.

It wasn't Max. It was Rose and Lottie, peering at her from the top of the steps. She opened her eyes, and then closed them again.

"Do you need sunscreen? Because Rose brought some. That is a really tiny bathing suit. We're worried about sun damage." Caroline could feel Lottie's enormous eyes widen at the diminutive size of her bikini. And it was not her briefest.

"Then wear a hat," said Caroline.

"We thought we'd make lunch," said Rose. "Would you like to join us?"

Caroline thought that if she took long enough to reply they might go away. It was a long beat before anyone spoke.

"I think she wants to be left alone, Rose," Lottie said. "That's why she is not answering us."

Lottie had seemed the flighty one on first acquaintance, but Caroline was beginning to admire her intuition.

"Caroline came here to be alone and now we're not letting her do what she most wants to do." Caroline opened her eye just a tiny bit and saw Lottie take Rose's arm. "We've been taking care of other people for so long that we can't remember how to take care of ourselves," Lottie added. "Rose will remember, I know it. Me, too." She heard the two of them walking away, leaving her alone with the sound of the sea.

By midafternoon, Beverly had arranged his photos of Possum to his satisfaction. He had placed them just so around the unhappy-making brown box that he took with him everywhere. The room was his castle, and none of the women had been up there again to irk him. He slid his suitcase out from under the bed and removed an untidy sheaf of papers to see if he could make sense of any of it. There were so many bills overdue and yet so much money in various accounts to pay them with. If only he hadn't fired that new "manager" who'd taken over the old firm from their fusty old lawyers. It had been impulsive, but he couldn't stand the way the man's every statement sounded like a joke. And the jargon! Now it was up to Beverly to sort this out.

It was such an effort to keep up, or even to ask people to keep up for him. He vaguely remembered sending a check for some enormous amount to the heating and gas people last winter to keep them happy, but apparently that had been gone through and now more effort was required. Gorsch had been so good at money, and Beverly was so bad. Gorsch would have found them someone better to take care of their affairs by now. Beverly couldn't trust the young.

It was quite a lovely day outside. He wasn't much for the outdoors but there were some pleasant paths on this island and he thought he might as well walk down one as stare at these damnable papers. He popped a photo of Gorsch holding Possum in his pocket and went silently down his private staircase to the cottage lawn. The grass sloped down to the beach, but he had walked there yesterday and met up with Rose and Lottie gathering shards that they called sea glass, and he did not much want to see them again.

He set forth on the boardwalk. Not easy for a man of seventy-eight, he thought, but I still move well enough.

He noticed a flash of something moving in the ferns alongside the path. An animal, certainly. Too loud and big for one of those myriad brown squirrels that make so much noise all morning. Of course, he could tell nothing about the color. What if it was a cat? thought Beverly. A cat in distress?

Beverly supposed he should follow.

The boardwalk took him away from the cottages and then dissolved into a little dirt path through the soft moss under the enormous trees. It was green and quiet, and the creature had disappeared, which suited Beverly fine. He had resisted pedigreed kittens proffered by neighbors, strays in Village side streets, ASPCA giveaways in Union Square. A mangy cat from Maine, if it was a cat, would have no hold over him.

Then the cat cried.

I'll just make sure it's not injured, he thought. If I can even find it.

It was much cooler here under the trees. The moss was spongy underfoot and the trees—spruce, he thought—provided shade. He was glad he had worn his walking shoes, particularly in this spot, where twigs and even branches lay in a messy pile on the ground.

Why so many here? he thought. He was never much interested in flora and fauna but this island had so much of both that it was hard not to notice. Especially as there was nothing else going on here.

Beverly leaned against the big tree and tried to catch his breath. He didn't want to sit down in this big muddle of twigs and leaves; the moss beyond was too damp. He thought he'd head back to the cottage once he'd had a bit of a breather.

He heard a loud birdcall above him. *Sweet sweet sweeet* in an upward arc. Not an urban cry. He looked up into the branches of the tree and saw that at its top there was a huge unruly mess of a nest. *Sweet sweet sweeeet sweeeet,* came the cry again. So plaintive. So raw.

Wouldn't Gorsch love to hear this bird's song? he thought. Gorsch would make it into a song. And he'd sing it to me.

Beverly allowed the tree to support him as his knees gave way.

CHAPTER NINE

*I*t was at dinnertime when the whole thing started to unravel. Lottie had spent the afternoon exploring the island. She wasn't quite brave enough to order tea at the teahouse, which seemed such a local place, but she took the winding boardwalks into the woodsier parts at the top of the island, and got a sense of the shady cottages hidden there. She happily allowed herself to double back a couple of times when the path she thought would lead back to Hopewell took her farther from shore. But you can never really get lost on an island, she thought. Little Lost or not.

The sun, the tramping around, and the salt air had built up Lottie's appetite, so she was ravenous by dinnertime. She had collected enough blackberries and blueberries on her walk for dessert. And she'd love to make a cocktail for anyone who asked. She wasn't great in the kitchen but she really could mix a drink. She had bought ginger and Hendrick's Gin at the IGA—so convenient to have liquor in the grocery store!—and if she started infusing tonight there'd be delicious ginger tonics for them all by tomorrow.

The kitchen was empty when she got back.

"Rose?" she called. "Caroline? Beverly?"

There was a rap on the screen door to the kitchen. "Anybody home?" came a voice.

Lottie went over to the door and saw Max the ferry driver. "Max the ferry driver," she said.

"Delivering your lobsters," he said. She was tempted to ask him to say "lobsters" over and over but stopped herself. "And the corn." The way he said "corn" was even better.

"Oh, we're having lobsters and corn?"

"Guess so."

Caroline must have arranged this. "Thanks, Max," Lottie said. Then, much as she didn't want to, she asked, "How much do we owe you?"

"The lady of the house said she'd settle up before you leave. That's fine with me," he said.

Lottie hesitated. Rose and she had bought so much this morning at the grocery store and Rose was going to make ratatouille for dinner. Lottie hated to nickel-and-dime about food, but how much would this kind of service set them back? With the car and the gas and the liquor and the food they'd already bought, her stock certificate proceeds were burning up.

"Oh, that's fine, then," she said—bravely, she thought. "Thanks."

Max set a basket of corn on the floor and a brown bag on the table. Then he was out the door.

The bag moved.

"Oh, shit, they're alive," said Lottie.

She heard Caroline's light tread on the stairs.

"Has the food arrived? I'm starved," said Caroline.

"Me too," said Lottie. "It'll be a little while, though—we have to cook all these things. I wonder who's going to turn out to be the cook among us."

"God, not me," said Caroline. "I'm hopeless in the kitchen. It will have to be you or Rose, I think. You have children, so you must cook."

"Yes, I do cook but I'm better at Annie's mac and chicken tenders than I am at lobster. Corn I can do. And drinks. Would you like a drink?"

"Ketel One on the rocks if you have it," said Caroline. "With a twist. I'll be up on the porch when you have it ready."

Lottie liked people who knew how to order a drink. She had bought Grey Goose, not Ketel One, though. She bet Caroline would taste the difference.

Caroline couldn't help being the way she was, Lottie decided. She'd been brought up with servants, probably, or at least a nanny, and now that she was famous she'd had to keep her distance from ordinary people like Lottie. And Lottie was happy to get a drink order. There were a great number of glasses to choose from—jam jars, cut-glass goblets, tumblers, and old-fashioned glasses with the island's insignia imprinted on them (five giant spruce trees in a circle). She couldn't even reach whatever glasses were on the top shelf. She picked up one of the Little Lost glasses and thoughtfully placed ice cubes in it. She really did miss tending bar. It was the job that put her through college after she didn't make the cut at the pole-dancing audition. "Too short," the manager had said. "But nice tits. Can you mix a drink?"

Vodka on the rocks with a twist wasn't too hard to make, and Lottie had gone to the trouble of lugging back a bag of ice (frozen from the inside out), so the ice cubes were pure. The lemon was fresh, and the vodka pour was generous. She found a little linen cocktail napkin in the old breakfront and brought it with the drink up to Caroline's porch.

Caroline seemed startled to see her, as if she had forgotten all about her drink request. "Thank you, Lottie," she said, genuinely.

"You're welcome." She saw Caroline hesitate, as if she realized good manners called for her to invite Lottie to join her. But Lottie did not want to be asked out of good manners, so she turned and headed down the stairs. "We'll call you for dinner," she said. "I'm not exactly sure when it will be."

She was about to head downstairs to the kitchen when she thought instead she might pop in on Beverly. Would he want a cocktail? Would he join them for dinner?

She knocked lightly on the door. There was a sound within that sounded like someone trying not to make a sound within. "Beverly, will you join us for dinner?" she asked through the door. "Would you like a cocktail? I'm good at cocktails."

Still no answer.

"I'll be downstairs if you need anything," Lottie said. She paused again, waited for an answer, and when none came, she headed back down toward the kitchen.

"Have you got the water on yet?" It was Beverly's voice, through the wall. "Unless you're grilling them."

He was talking about the lobsters. She did not have the water on yet and how would you grill a lobster? Beverly must have heard the lobster discussion from up in his ivory tower. Everyone can hear everything in this place, she reminded herself. "Water's just going on now," she said. "We'll eat in an hour or so."

"Please see that we do," said Beverly. Lottie was very pleased that Rose could not hear him.

Down in the kitchen, the bag was still squirming. Lottie felt certain she should put it in the refrigerator but she did not much want to touch it. She could at least husk the corn, and start that water boiling. She wasn't sure about lobsters. The only cookbook in sight was *A Little Lost in the Kitchen* and there was no boiled lobster recipe in it—everyone just knew instinctively how to boil a lobster if they had a cottage here, Lottie realized. And there was no way to get online to check. She looked in the cupboards for a pot big enough to hold the writhing creatures. Nothing in the kitchen, but in the little pantry next door there was an enormous double boiler–style pot. It had jaunty red lobsters painted on the sides! She lifted the lid and investigated. There were holes on the bottom of the top pot—aha! "You steam lobsters," she said aloud, and she liked the way she sounded.

She took the pot into the kitchen, filled it with water, and set it on the stove. The tap water didn't look so great for boiling corn, so she used the springwater for that. Someone would have to get more soon.

All this water would take a while to boil. She fixed herself a drink—just a gin and tonic, neat, like the English (using cold tonic and squeezing in a whole lime made all the difference)—and got to work husking the corn.

As she peeled the fragrant, watery green outer leaves from the translucent white corn, she thought about Ethan. He loved corn. He was a typewriter corn eater, like his dad; she was a roller. She wished Ethan were here with her, exhausting her on exploring expeditions around the island, maybe even exhausting himself. She wished Jon liked their son better. He loved him, of course, he'd run into a burning building to save his life, but he didn't really like Ethan to be around. He didn't much like Lottie to be around either. She wondered if he was having an affair with that new lawyer at work. Carla. Carla probably looked just like her (Jon was true to type) but a younger version, and surely she had never had children. Jon didn't realize how many times he said her name aloud at home.

The lobster pot was boiling, sooner than she'd thought it would. The corn water was almost ready too. Now what? The corn would only take a few minutes, but the lobster, she had no idea. There was nothing for it but to call for help. They needed to work on this together.

At that moment, the screen door banged, and Rose walked into the kitchen, flushed from her walk.

"I found some basil and chives in the flowerpots by the dock and there was lavender planted right outside the window at the boathouse. I don't think I have time to do the ratatouille tonight but I thought I'd make up a salad for dinner and then we can call our companions." Lottie could tell she wanted to make a fresh start with Beverly and Caroline. Soon, however, she would notice the pots boiling on the stove.

"What's in the pots?" asked Rose.

"Caroline had an idea that we should have our food delivered," said Lottie tentatively. "So now we'll have fresh groceries every day."

"That sounds like a great idea, but did they even ask us about it?" Lottie shook her head. "What if we don't want Max's food? What if he brings hot dogs?"

"Tonight he brought lobsters."

"Still." Rose went to the base of the stairs and called up. "Caroline! Beverly! Do you have a second?"

Not a sound.

"Eventually someone will come down here and we'll talk about it then. In the meantime, I'll start the salad. There are beautiful gardens here! People really put time into them." She started running water. "I hope this is okay for washing vegetables."

"It's supposed to be. I'm using it for the lobster water."

"If Caroline ordered the food, Caroline might cook the food, don't you think? I know she's used to servants."

Beverly walked into the kitchen. "I don't know if you two realize how your voices carry in this house. The walls are not insulated, you know."

Lottie saw that Rose was not going to rise to Beverly's bait. Instead she got busy tearing lettuce and washing it splashily under the brown water coming out of the tap.

"You've spoiled my enjoyment of the sunset." Beverly took a shallow bowl from the cupboard, filled it with water, and walked out of the kitchen. "Why don't you use a spinner?" he said as he left.

"I'm sure there's no such thing as a salad spinner in this house," called Rose.

"Where is he going with that?" asked Lottie.

"Who knows?" said Rose. They heard a screen door slam. "Was that the front porch or the back?"

"Back, I think."

"Have you even looked?" called Beverly. He came back into the kitchen, got his bearings, reached to open a cupboard to the left of the sink, and pulled out an aged salad spinner. "This will do," he said. "Fresh greens can be so gritty; do wash them well."

Lottie noticed Rose's shoulders getting closer and closer to her ears. She desperately wanted to pour oil on the troubled waters of the kitchen but was not exactly sure how. Maybe if she got started on the lobsters ...

She approached the writhing bag. "I'll do the lobsters," she said. "Do you just dump them in as is or—"

"You most certainly do not just dump them in as is," said Beverly. Rose practically bashed into him as she took the carrots from the fridge. "And Rose, no need to peel those as long as you wash them well, even in this water."

"Thanks, Beverly. I have actually prepared a carrot in my life."

He lifted the lid on the great lobster pot. "There's not enough water here. It will boil away before the poor creatures are dead. Add some more, please, and where's the top of the pot?"

Lottie pointed. "There?"

"That's the lid, not the top."

She wordlessly handed him the top of the pot.

"You steam lobsters," she said.

"*I* steam lobsters, apparently," said Beverly.

"None for me," said Rose. "I'll just have the salad."

"Don't be ridiculous," said Beverly.

"Shall I help?" asked Caroline, gliding down the stairs. "No one's picked the wildflowers for the table. Lovely drink, Lottie."

Beverly expertly located a pair of scissors in the overcrowded kitchen drawer and wielded them in the direction of the lobsters.

"You're not going to cut them up?" asked Lottie, both fascinated and horrified.

"I'm going to cut off the rubber bands," said Beverly. "You don't want to steam the rubber bands as part of your food," he told her, sounding incredulous that she had not thought of that already. He pried off the rubber bands with the rusted dull scissors. The lobsters were lively, flipping their tails, stretching their claws. "These look like they came out of a trap this morning."

Lottie looked away. As Beverly dropped the poor struggling creatures in the pot, she thought she heard them trying to claw their way out. "Do lobsters feel pain?"

"Lobsters feel nothing." Beverly adjusted the heat. "Electric," he said, and sniffed.

"I'd rather like a drink of water," said Caroline. "Do we drink this brown stuff?"

"There's water in the cooler in the pantry, Caroline," said Lottie.

"Which Lottie replenished from the spring earlier," said Rose.

"Thank you kindly," said Caroline. "Oh, but this is almost gone," she said, trying the cooler and finding nothing but a drop of water from the spring. "Did someone use it all?"

"I believe Lottie used it to boil the water for you for the lobsters that no one asked anyone else about," said Rose. Lottie wondered if she'd realized her small dig was lost in her syntax. "Why don't you get us some more?"

"Oh, I'm happy enough with the vodka for the moment," said Caroline. "Was it Grey Goose, Lottie?"

"Excellent tasting skills," said Lottie.

"Also, I don't think I should take the privilege of fetching the springwater from you. I know how much you enjoy the spring."

Caroline must have spied Lottie down at the springhouse earlier that day: she had done a small interpretive dance after she drew the water. She had wanted to feel like a wood nymph, and it had worked.

Rose was snipping chives with vigor. "All ready," she said after she'd tossed them into the salad. "I guess we'll have a feast tonight."

Beverly tasted Rose's carefully made vinaigrette. "It could use a bit of a kick," he said. "No need for a dressing to be anemic."

Caroline tasted it too. "Umm, yes. More salt, at least."

"I'll set the table, shall I?" asked Lottie. "Caroline, flowers would be lovely."

"Did you get any wine on your peregrinations?" asked Caroline. "A glass of white would be delicious just now, don't you think?"

"There's a bottle in the fridge," said Rose. "If you'd like to open it."

"*Where* in the fridge?" Caroline asked.

"Oh, for God's sake," said Rose.

Caroline leaned into the refrigerator, her flawless profile silhouetted by the light. "Oh," she said. "Chardonnay." And she closed the refrigerator door.

"It's *French* chardonnay," said Rose, taking it out herself.

"Still," said Caroline, pregnantly. "I'll have that last drop of water. Lottie, will you go down to the spring again tomorrow?"

"I love the spring."

Rose's attempt to open the bottle of French chardonnay ended when the elaborate corkscrew broke the cork.

"You'll need to tell me when the lobsters are done," said Beverly. "They'll want to be thoroughly red, but of course I'm color-blind."

CHAPTER TEN

*D*inner did not get much better for the entire first week. Caroline would have skipped it entirely, but she was ravenous every evening and there was nowhere else to eat on Little Lost. And now she'd have to face yet another one. Tonight would be especially bad, she thought, as it had rained the entire morning and it was still raining now, in the early afternoon. Added to that, they had missed the fabled market boat on Monday—a floating farmers market!— as Lottie had misread Robert's handwriting and mistaken his European-style 1 for a 7, insisting it came on Monday nights and not Monday afternoons. That put everyone in a bad mood.

She'd gone through all the books on her iPad and couldn't download any more. Plus, like an idiot, she'd forgotten her charger, and apparently she'd have to drive to Bangor to get another or wait four days for FedEx, which only delivered to the island sporadically.

Acting like a regular person was not that much fun.

There were plenty of books to read in the cottage, but none of them really engaged her. No juicy Victorian novels. Either they were hoary old volumes like *Flower Stories for Little Minds* or they were leftover paperbacks from the seventies—*Trinity*, or a biography of Betty Grable.

The sound of the rain on the roof was hypnotizing, and Caroline was almost ready to close her eyes for a nap up in her turret room when she noticed something else about the boards in the ceiling. There was a rectangular outline cut through the wood. It could be a patch in the ceiling, or it could be another way to the third floor—a secret way for the most enterprising of the boys. As she studied it carefully, she thought it looked like a trapdoor with one of those folding staircases. There was no rope pull, but no lock, either. She decided to investigate.

Caroline got up from her bed and made an inspection. If she climbed up on the chair right below it she could pull the door down. She stepped up, teetering a bit.

Even with the added height she wasn't quite tall enough to reach, so she grabbed a couple of thick volumes from the bookshelf. With the *Armed Forces Hymnal* under one foot and *The Thorn Birds* under the other, she could just get a grip on the unfinished wood. It was hard to do without a pull of some kind. She imagined there was a tool that would hook into the gap between the door and the ceiling, but she had no such tool. She had only her nails and her curiosity. They worked. She pulled down the door.

Caroline was half-expecting a cascade of dust, but the door was well oiled, and it and its hidden stairs came down neatly. She realized that perhaps the reason there was no rope pull was not that the attic was old and unused, but rather because its owner did not want anyone going up there.

There are such things as locks, even in Maine, Caroline thought, and started up the steps.

The rain was much louder here, almost deafening, really. It could have been oppressive if it didn't sound so comforting. Caroline craned her neck and looked around the room in the dim light.

She didn't know what she was expecting, but not this. It wasn't really an attic at all—it was an entire third floor, very open and surprisingly airy and light. She took in the overstuffed sofa with its faded chintz, the pale braided rug, the starched white curtains, the ancient leather trunks promising antique treasure. And so many guitars and stringed instruments hanging on the walls. Whose room was this? Hers now. Separate from all the others and made to fit her perfectly.

She felt not like the madwoman in the attic but like Goldilocks. This was just right.

It only took about three days for Rose's sleep schedule to change utterly. No sooner had the sun's rays finally left the sky and the stars shone their brilliant pinpricks of light than Rose sought her soft eiderdown and fell into a deep sleep. She still felt bad about the first night, with the lobsters. Now that she was waking with the dawn the house was finding its own rhythm, and everything started to melt away.

Lottie woke early too. They got into the habit of picking up Beverly's shopping list, which perfectly complemented Max's fresh produce and fish, and taking it into town as the little IGA opened its doors. Only once had they left the car keys in the cottage and found themselves in the parking lot on the other side with no way to get into town. "A rookie mistake," said one of the islanders, though he said it with good humor. "I'll be your ride, if you like." Rose was beginning to accept, if not rely on, the kindness of the strangers here.

Generally, they were back on the eleven o'clock ferry, in time to spend the late morning picking out sea glass on Sea Glass Beach, which was what the islanders in fact called it, before the tide came in. That left them free to watch a bit of Little Lost tennis in the afternoon—Lottie had introduced Rose to her island friends—and then to get ready for dinner in the evening. Then another glorious sunset and the day would have flown by. Considering they did next to nothing all day, the first week went quickly. Even so, it took Rose that long to register that she was truly away.

Before they did their shopping in the mornings, loading the groceries in canvas bags to make boarding the ferry easier, they took themselves to the West Dorset Public Library. It was a sweet little structure that looked like a humble wooden Greek temple, but it had sadly been "improved" inside and lost most of its architectural character. Still, the librarians were friendly and the Internet was strongest here, even out under the portico, where they sat before the library opened at eight thirty. Lottie was on the brick steps, absorbed in texting on her phone, when the librarian came by and unlocked the doors. Rose wasn't much of a texter, so she waited till she could use the one free terminal to check her e-mail. There was no message from Fred.

She considered. No news was good news, supposedly. It meant the twins were fine. It meant there was nothing to worry about. It meant Fred wasn't interested in how she was.

Should she write him? Would it make it worse to say, "I'm away from you and I love it here"? Could she say, "Wish you were here," and mean it?

She wondered what Lottie would say about the idea of asking Fred to come to Maine. Even just for a weekend. Actually, she didn't have to wonder. She knew.

"He wants to be with you, Rose," Lottie replied when she broached the subject. "Why would he not? You're beautiful—"

Rose shook her head.

"No, you are beautiful. This whole state suits you. Probably in Park Slope you look kind of tough and severe because you have to keep your guard up. But here you can let your guard down."

Lottie's compliments were always hard to take.

"I look better too. Jon will like that."

"Jon?"

"I'm going to ask him up. Oh but wait, I forgot to tell him about his shirts."

She texted quickly, talking as she typed.

"I feel so different here. It doesn't seem right that I have all this and he doesn't have any of it. I think he'll come. He'll come for Caroline Dester, but he'll stay for me."

Rose glanced at her screen again, in case anything had come in from Fred.

"I told him the ferry schedules," said Lottie. "This is what his mother wanted for us, anyway." Lottie had gone into painstaking detail on the trip up about who would be watching Ethan and when. Her mother-in-law was her staunchest ally, apparently. "She wanted us to be alone. Her husband had a wandering eye too."

Rose wished Fred's mother were so wise.

She stared a long time at her Gmail. Maybe she had missed something. There were lots of messages from the poetry e-mail lists she was on, and a few from her sister asking questions about the twins and what her nanny needed to know for when they arrived. Not a word from her husband.

"We've got to get back, Rose," Lottie said. "We'll miss the ferry."

Rose pressed Refresh one more time, just to make sure she missed nothing.

A boldface message appeared: **From Robert SanSouci.**

She leaned in closer to read it.

Hope you are in fine fettle & enjoying Little Lost. I will be in nearby Brooklin for a visit with a friend on August 19 & would like to come across on the last ferry to pay a visit and pick up one of my instruments there if it is not too inconvenient for you, Lottie, et al. Horseshoe Beach is lovely & not so easy to find without a native guide & interpreter. I would like you to see it.

Regards,
Robert.

What to make of this?

"Rose, come on."

"I'm coming, Lottie."

She hesitated, and was lost. Did she write him back and say come, come? Did she bar him from his own house? Should she consult with the others?

"Rose—the ferry!"

Her hands hovered over the keyboard.

Come, she wrote. It was all she had time to say.

CHAPTER ELEVEN

*J*on opened the bathroom door to the heavy heat of August in New York. The bedroom air conditioner was jacked up too high: but it was the only room in the house that was cool. His feet stuck to the bathroom tiles. He was already starting to sweat. He turned the shower on, let the water run cool, and got in. The lukewarm stream sluiced down his scalp. At least he had a full head of hair. Women liked his hair.

The phone rang but Jon couldn't bring himself to get out of the shower to answer it. Probably one of the Happy Circle moms. They were constantly calling and they were all sexless, like Lottie was now. The moms left messages about who had an ear infection, whose babysitter hadn't come in on time, what party was where. How was he supposed to keep all this straight? Even with Ethan gone to his parents—thank God they'd come through for once—Jon was still hearing from the moms way too much. The one he wanted to hear from was Carla.

He turned up the water hotter and reached for the soap.

Clearly it would be a mistake to get involved with a firm associate. But Christ, was she firm. Ha!

Carla had tits that she didn't mind leaving mostly exposed. They'd be nice and heavy, a real handful. And a trim little ass. She wore short skirts all spring and favored jeans on dress-down Fridays that showed a thin slice of skin when she sat down. Sometimes she wore those summery dresses that would cling. He liked to think about what she'd look like with nothing on. He thought he pretty much knew.

But it was Lottie's name he called out when he came.

Jon wrung out the washcloth and shut off the water.

The icy blast of the air conditioner hit him as he stepped back into the bedroom. At least without Lottie here he could keep it as cold as he wanted. He went to get a shirt from the drawer and found he was on his last one. Jesus, Lottie. She knew he'd need shirts for the whole time she was gone.

The phone buzzed. It was her.

hi sweetie— shirts being delivered later today. Ethan sounds like he's having a great time w ur folks. caroline dester says hello. did you open the pics? i think you should come here this weekend. love you, Lx

The only thing that registered in her note was the name Caroline Dester. Caroline Dester was in Maine with *Lottie*? *The* Caroline Dester?

Jon wrapped the towel around his waist tightly and started a text. Then he thought he'd better phone. He pressed her speed dial but of course he couldn't get through. This whole week it had been impossible to reach her. She must be e-mailing from the coffee shop on the mainland. Why couldn't he get through?

The phone swooshed again.

PS: I think Beverly Fisher could use a good lawyer. Lx

"Lottie, what are you talking about?" he said aloud. He didn't know who the hell Beverly Fisher was but Caroline Dester was worth a fortune. The Desters were surely represented by some ancient white-shoe firm, but there could be some billing for a scrappy IP attorney like him if he had an in. What was Lottie doing hobnobbing with Desters? Wasn't she sharing the house with that other mom from Ethan's school?

Jon pressed Lottie's speed dial again. Where the hell was she? And now he was getting late for work. It was another rotten day in August and the last thing he wanted to do was have to walk fast and sweat through his jacket. Carla sweated, but in a good way.

The landline rang.

"Lottie?" But it was his mother. He couldn't believe he hadn't checked before he picked up.

"Jon, dear." He could tell from the sound of her voice that something wasn't right.

"What's the matter? Is Ethan okay?" His heart raced.

"No, Ethan's fine," she said. Jon let out his breath. "But we need you to take him back home this weekend. Your stepfather has a summer flu and I can't take care of them both. I'm sorry, Jonnie. I called Lottie so she could break it to you but I couldn't get through to her."

"Can't you have him sleep over at Mrs. what's-her-name next door and watch him during the day?"

His mother didn't respond, as she tended not to when Jon turned into the eleven-year-old version of himself. Which happened every time he spoke with her.

He sighed extravagantly. "Okay, Mom, I'll take him for the weekend. But I can't deal with him next week, too." His stepdad was probably not that sick. "Somebody in this family has to work every day and right now that person seems to be me." God, I am a spoiled brat, he thought. "Are you going to bring him down?"

"No, Jon, I am not going to bring him down. You're going to come here, pick up your son, and take care of him. Come up tonight after work and then the two of you can leave in the morning. I'm sorry for Ethan but I can't take care of both of them. Call in sick."

"People don't get sick at law firms, Mother," Jon said. "I haven't taken a sick day since I got there."

"All the more reason to now," she said. Her tone was irksome but reasonable. "They won't fire you for being sick."

"Ha." Little did she know. Partners were fired for sneezing too much. And the goddamn Acela cost a fortune.

"I'll pay for the train fare, Jon. I know money is tight. Here's Ethan."

"Hey, bud," said Jon. All he heard was Ethan's breathing. "Buddy?"

"Daddy?" said Ethan.

"Yes, little buddy?"

"Can you come get me?"

God*damn* his mother.

"Okay, guy. Daddy will come get you."

He'd have to call in sick. He hoped no one would move into his office—such as it was—while he was gone. He'd take his mom's car and drive up to Maine like Lottie said he should for the weekend. Leave Ethan there for the week or even the month. And then he'd head back to the office to see that narrow slice of skin again.

The next morning, after a dreamless night of uninterrupted sleep, Rose did not feel the urge to go into town, either to get groceries or to find a signal. Now that they'd stayed more than a week on Little Lost, having days at a stretch without getting in a car and going to the mainland was much more appealing than not. Nor did she want to knock on the door of another cottager to use his landline, especially since now she awoke with the sun. Fred used to kiss her hands and call her Rosie-fingered Dawn.

Hopewell was on the west side of Little Lost Island, so they did not get a direct view of the sunrise from anywhere at the cottage. That was a small price to pay for the sunsets they saw, looking at another cluster of islands off in the distance (Mount Desert? Deer Isle? Rose wasn't sure). Even so, the ambient light of dawn, and the stillness of the earth as it awakened, was enough to get Rose out of bed, into something resembling clothing, and out of the cottage to greet the day.

The coffee situation was still not settled but Lottie had found one of those drip cones for pour-overs and made a filter out of a paper towel, so Rose did the same, as they kept failing to add coffee filters to their shopping list. She'd do it now if she could find a pen.

It was cold down here. Rose wrapped herself in a blanket from the couch. She'd had no idea she should pack flannel pajamas and wool socks for an August vacation. While she waited for the coffee to filter down she stared absently at her favorite Hopewell mug, a coffee-stained seventies KEEP ON TRUCKIN' model that was just the right size and had an excellent handle. She had found it the first morning in the cupboard, where it sat next to a piece of ancient spatterware and an insulated cup that spelled out something in semaphore.

Rose added milk to her coffee, then grabbed a dark green fleece from the line of hooks next to the front staircase and quietly opened the screen door to the front porch. The deck was slick with dew and the old wicker chairs were damp. She found a dryish towel on the railing and used it as a cushion.

The wind came up and breathed in the rich molecules of the atmosphere on the island. The air was wet and cool and gray. Anywhere else you'd call this damp, but *damp* was such an insalubrious word. Better to call it sea tinged, redolent, complicated. Healthy, too. And fresh.

She liked to read early in the morning. Now that her life was such a mess she went back to the old books, the words that were a comfort to her. *Persuasion* never let her down.

She was undisturbed on the porch for an hour. Then she heard Lottie's soft tread down the hall toward the bathroom. She wasn't ready for Lottie yet, so she put the book down, patted the front cover, which was curling from the humidity, and headed toward the beach.

She was still surprised by how different the little beach looked at low tide versus high tide. Low tide exposed a wide swath of tiny rocks and weird-looking seaweed. It looked to her as if the tide was on its way in now. She walked down to the water's edge. This same water had seemed so treacherous when they had first arrived: black, cold, wet, hostile. She wasn't sorry that they had flooded the engine; the ferry was their rescue boat that night. She wondered about laconic Max as she let the water run up against her ankles. It was cold now; how frigid it had seemed that dark night.

She wasn't frigid—not at all, in fact—even though she and Fred didn't have sex as much as they did in the old days. It used to be they couldn't keep their hands off each other. They had no money, back when they were both in grad school, but the few times a check arrived from a generous aunt or an unexpected prize, they spent it on travel. They couldn't go far, of course, but the Greyhound got them out of the city and into deep country within two hours. If they left early enough and got off where they could camp, it was that much cheaper, so that's what they did.

Rose wasn't much of a camper before she met Fred. Her family was indoorsy: two bookish sisters and a much older brother whom

Rose rarely saw then or now. Fred always liked her to go first on the trails, though she would have been happier following him. "That's no fun," he would say. "This way I get to follow that great ass of yours. Very motivating."

She grinned.

In those days Fred had had a fantasy of pushing her down on the moss and having his way with her in the forest—his words, of course. That was half the reason they went camping at all. Rose wouldn't let him do it right away; that was too predictable, and anyway half the fun was to work themselves into a lather as they hiked. He'd never know when she'd come across the right bed of moss (it wasn't the most comfortable place for sex, to be honest). And she'd never know when she'd feel like being taken. Plus, both of them were aware that they could be spotted by other hikers. One time she knew they had been but she had not let on. She felt a thrum through her body at the memory of it.

Fred wasn't here, though.

She thought about Robert SanSouci. Did he really have a thing for her?

She was beginning to get the impression he was fantasizing about the cottage as matchmaker. He wants someone to stay at Hopewell, fall in love with it, come back to New York, fall in love with him, marry him, open him up, adore his lute playing, and live happily ever after.

"Fat chance of that," Rose said to the cormorant spreading its wings on a rock. Cormorants have no oil in their feathers, a fact that popped into her brain from nowhere she could locate. They look like little pterodactyls. Rose thought about the twins in their preverbal stage. They squawked back then. Like pterodactyls.

I'm a married woman with two children. She didn't have to wait for the familiar pang as she thought the words. Pangs, really. Two pangs came: one for happy little Bea and a fierce one for her darling misjudged Ben. And then another one. For Fred.

Rose crouched over to pick up a bit of greenish sea glass. Lottie had gotten carried away yesterday and come home with a bucketful of bits and pieces in all different colors, many of which looked like Heineken bottles only recently rendered unto the sea. Rose was more discerning. Her eyes adjusted to the details of the tiny rocks that covered the sand of the beach. Each stone was different. Why are we all so entranced by snowflakes? It's stones that should blow our socks off. She wiggled her bare toes.

She felt a few pieces of sea glass in her pocket. The fleece she had pulled on before coming down to the beach now felt like the plastic bottle it once was. It didn't smell great either. The sun had burned off the haze and it was already warm. To say the island's weather was changeable was an understatement by any standard. In her small bedroom under the shadow of the back of the cottage, it was cool. On the sunporch it was predictably cozy. On the path up and over the top of the island it was chilly, and here on the point it had gone from rainy and cool to bright and hot. Very hot. At least in a fleece. She would have peeled it off if she had anything more than a holey tank top on underneath it.

She peeled off the fleece. Not everything is a metaphor, she thought.

The pull of the water was much greater once she had stripped down. The sun was brazen—suddenly, real August heat, the first she'd felt here. Rose didn't know too much about seas and tides, but even she could tell there was a big difference between low tide and high. It took her just a couple of paces or more to reach the water's edge. Her feet came into contact with much alien flora and surely some fauna. Deadly slippery green slime, sharp-edged rocks glittering with something that begins with an *M*, the name of which eluded her. A bird that sounded like a car alarm called out. Branch-long fronds of seaweed with stems as thick as a garden hose sometimes blocked her way. By the time she waded ankle-deep into the soft waves and belatedly registered their icy cold with a shock, she realized she was freezing.

On an island I live within the weather; I do not battle it.

It was a good thought, and it made Rose happy as she picked her way—more nimbly now—back to her fleece. It was there as she'd left it, only she wasn't cold anymore. She climbed up a bank of imposing boulders. How old can these be? she thought. What a history in their past. Each one had its own pattern of stripes or cast of glittering sparkles (she must look it up; Fred would know it). Some were smooth as a baby's behind—giant versions of her sweet twins' bottoms, when they were tiny—and who cared if her metaphors were mixed? No one, not a soul, was in sight. Rose was sweating now from the sun and the exertion and she knew she had to get into the shade or she'd be slathering on the aloe.

But first.

She wanted to lie down on the rocks but there was not a single one that could accommodate her without her having to drape herself at a terribly awkward angle. Instead she sat down on one warm stone and rested her back against another. The tank top was suddenly ridiculous, so she slipped it off. The shorts will stay on, she thought; it's more respectable to be topless than to be nude as a renter on a Maine island. Or is it vice versa?

It made her smile that she was even thinking about this. She lazily moved her head from side to side and still saw no one. A loon called out its crazy cry. What a loon, she thought. The waves lapped at the shore not far below. The buoy bell tolled far in the distance. The earth breathed, and so did Rose.

And not five minutes later, when a lobster boat loudly putt-putted into her consciousness and she opened her eyes to see the lobstermen barely fifty feet away, calling and waving, she waved back.

Maybe she *would* call Fred.

CHAPTER TWELVE

*B*everly could not believe his ears. He was unhappy enough being with these two provoking women, and the silent Dester as well, but if the women were inviting men—overbearing, dreary boyfriends with no manners, he was sure—it was a different proposition altogether. Women, however shrill, at least made soft cooing noises when they heard about Possum (and even more when they heard about Gorsch). It was what he needed, what he deserved right now. Men would be stupid and obtuse. They'd make him feel foolish for putting out fresh water every day, hoping that the cat he'd heard near the osprey nest would stop by. Not that he wanted another cat. It was far too soon for that. But everyone deserves fresh water. Except these boyfriends.

The more he thought about it the more he was certain that nothing had been said in the e-mails about men invading the place; if there had been he would have declined to come.

"What is his name, Lottie?" asked Beverly abruptly.

She turned to him with a slight surprise. Beverly realized it was the first time he had addressed her directly. "Jon," she said. "Jon Mellish."

"Mellish?"

"Yes."

"A friend?"

"In a way."

"A boyfriend, then."

"Not at all. A relative."

"A blood relative?"

"Not blood. A husband."

God, this woman was exasperating. "A husband." Suggesting one of many. What a way to talk. Always that faux-naive twist to everything. Or was she genuinely a naif? Why couldn't she say "my husband"? The straights took so much for granted.

Besides, Beverly had assumed Rose and Lottie were not married at all. That they were two more of those careerist women who couldn't attract a man. There had been an absence of mention of husbands in the e-mails, which would not be natural if such persons did, after all, exist. And if a husband was not a relative, who was? Gorsch had died after same-sex marriage became legal but before he and Beverly had gotten around to being legally wed. Of course, he'd often called himself the unofficial Mrs. Samuel Gorsch, a joke that Gorsch, to his credit, never ceased to be amused by—to cherish, even. What if they had made it legal? What a grand time Possum would have had at the wedding. Beverly felt his eyes burn. A relative; not blood, she'd said? What did she know?

Beverly was not going to have the place overrun by people with whom he had no acquaintance. "This is unheard of," he said. "To invite guests to a summer cottage." Even as the words came out of his mouth he knew they were ridiculous.

"That's ridiculous," said Caroline, radiant from something she'd been up to that afternoon. He'd heard footsteps on the floor above him and large objects being moved around while he was napping. Doubtless she'd had a tryst with a tennis-playing islander or that handsome young Max, the caretaker. At least she was fairly discreet about it. No doubt Lottie and this Mellish would bang on the walls all night and there'd be no peace.

"It's only for the weekend," said Rose. "He'll have to leave on the Sunday late-afternoon ferry. Or Monday morning, latest. And we don't even know he's coming for sure."

"You see," said Lottie, leaning across toward Caroline, "we arranged, didn't we, in New York that if any of us wanted to we could each invite one guest. So now I'm doing it."

"I don't remember that," said Beverly, his eyes on his plate. The chowder could have stood some fresh parsley but of course the women had forgotten to pick it, as he'd asked, from the pots on the dock.

"Oh yes, we did—didn't we, Rose?"

"Yes—I remember," said Caroline. "Only it seemed so incredible that we'd ever want to. The whole idea was to get away from our friends."

"And our husbands."

"And family affection," said Caroline.

"Or lack of family affection," said Rose. Her voice was quiet, but not too quiet for his failing ears to hear.

"Here's the thing," said Caroline. "Jon Mellish might be coming up. The place is big. I've actually found a room I'd rather stay in, on the third floor, so I'll go up there and then Lottie can have the turret room, which is what she wanted in the first place."

Rose flushed even deeper.

"Oh, but Caroline, it's Rose who'd like that room. It's rose-colored, like Rose herself. And don't say you wouldn't know, Beverly, because you're color-blind; we already know you wouldn't know. But even you can see the roses in those prints on the walls, regardless of what color they are." Beverly noticed that Caroline was still enjoying Lottie's bluntness. "If you've really found a room you'd like better, then by all means move in. But I love my little nook downstairs, and I think Jon will love it too, once he realizes that he's meant to be here. Rose, you take the turret. That will be the perfect place for you and Fred when he comes up."

"When Fred comes up?" said Rose. "Fred is not coming up."

"Not yet, but he will. Fred is Rose's beloved husband," Lottie explained. "He looks like a young Franz Kafka, according to Rose."

"Hot," said Caroline. It did not go over well.

"And Beverly, you'll be away from us all in the other tower, which should make you perfectly happy."

"What will make me perfectly happy," said Beverly, "is having a friend of my own come up to the cottage. In fact, I've already mentioned the idea to Kenneth Lumley, an acquaintance of long duration." Of course, he had done nothing of the kind. "He will be my guest. And I will choose his room."

Beverly had not spoken with Kenneth Lumley since Gorsch's memorial, and even then they'd only exchanged a few words. Before that, it had been years since they'd met. He couldn't even have said where Kenneth lived these days. Or *if* Kenneth lived these days. But he'd be damned if these women could have friends come up and he not a soul.

"Wow, it's a friends contest," said Caroline. "I'm sure I could scare up a few *thousand* people who'd like to spend the weekend here. Not a husband, though." Her voice, always thrilling, had just the right note of sadness for that little speech, Beverly thought. She should have won that Oscar.

"So Hopewell is to be invaded by no less than three, and no more than a few thousand guests," said Lottie. "I'm glad it is such a large place. There should be room for all."

The Milky Way had never been a big part of Caroline's consciousness, but here on the island it stirred up the sky. She had never seen quite so many stars before, and so close, and so bright. She lay on the fainting couch in her third-floor room and was astonished at the stars' presence through the window. It made her want to see them outside.

It was only a little after eight thirty and it felt like midnight. She crept downstairs; she didn't want to wake the others. She took a dark green fleece from one of the pegs by the front door and pulled it over her head as she went outside into the sharp air. The night smelled like pine; the fleece smelled like an old friend. She looked up. The stars were dizzying. She hadn't brought a flashlight, so she had to be careful picking her way down the cottage lawn to a place where she could get a view unobstructed by trees. She wanted to lie down on the grass but it was already too wet with dew. The moon had gone down, or at least Caroline couldn't see it anymore. If she walked to a slightly higher vantage point, she might be able to see better.

The fleece had a flashlight in its pocket; its light was dim, but it led her through the path she thought would take her to an expanse of lawn outside one of the island's shared buildings. She followed it, trying and failing to pick out any constellation other than the Big Dipper, which actually did look like a gigantic ladle in the sky.

She was not alone on the upward path. Other flashlights were shining ahead of her, following the same path. As she approached the lawn she was looking for, the pitch-blackness was diminished by a blaze of lights in the public building—the assembly room. She wondered what was going on inside. Home-movie night? A bridge game?

Not even two weeks into her stay and Caroline realized there were a lot of island activities that Hopewell Cottage, filled as it was with renters, was not privy to.

Whatever the activity was, it was loud.

She opened the dark green screen door, which creaked; the noise in the building stopped abruptly.

She took in the room. This one looked as if it could have been a one-room schoolhouse, with a raised platform stage at one end and wooden chairs in a neat row along the walls. Pendant lights hung down from the crossbeams, and tiny Christmas lights wound around the rafters. She wondered if they had dances there. They should, she thought.

"We're allowed to be in here till nine thirty!" said a boy. Caroline guessed he was nine or ten years old. "We can play in the assembly room even when no one's watching us as long as we don't break anything."

"We broke something!" said a little girl, much younger. "We broke something!"

"Quiet, Paige! You didn't have to tell," said the boy.

Caroline did not care whether the children had broken something, but the girl, Paige, red-faced and querulous, looked like she was about to collapse if she didn't confess. "What did you break? Maybe I can fix it."

"We broke a chair. James bashed it," said another boy. He spoke in a whisper.

"Shut up, Wills. It just kind of broke on its own," said James. The ringleader, clearly.

Caroline was not much good at fixing things, but an adult presence in the room took the anxiety out of the kids, or seemed to.

"We had a fight about the island show," said one of the kids. "So

James broke it. The show is supposed to be next *week*! We're trying to do it and nobody wants to do it right."

"We want to do it right; we just don't want to do *Sarah*'s dumb play," said James. "We want to do a *good* show, with pirates."

"We'll get in trouble if there's no island play. All the kids do it every year. We can't break the tradition. My grampy will kill me if we do."

Paige started to cry.

Caroline considered for a minute. They wanted to put on a play; she knew how to put on plays. "Usually a grown-up is in charge but Kitty used to do it with us every year and now she's too sad so she won't do it anymore."

Someone's depressed? On Little Lost Island? At least they're not *all* fit and healthy, Caroline thought. "Why is Kitty sad?"

"Max is bad!" said a kid named Reece.

"He broke her heart," said Paige.

Max, a heartbreaker. She would not have expected it.

"Could you do the play with us? You're a grown-up. We don't know who you are, though," said another of the girls.

"I'm Caroline."

"My name is Jessie. And this is Georgia, and Garrison, and Tucker. And this is Wills. He's supposed to be in bed but my mom says she needed a break so we have to be home by nine thirty. James has a watch."

James showed off his watch. A Timex, not a Rolex.

"Please?" said Wills, in a very tiny voice.

"Okay," she said, "but I'm not acting. Because what I really want to do is direct." She knew no one would get the joke.

"We're doing *Peter Pan*!" said James. "And I'm Captain Hook!"

"*Frozen!*" said all the girls at once.

"Don't fight!" said Wills. He put his fingers in his ears.

No wonder that poor Kitty isn't directing this year, Caroline thought.

"We have to have princesses."

"I hate princesses. Princesses are stupid."

"Peter Pan is stupid."

The argument was going nowhere.

"*You* have to decide," said James, looking right at her.

"No," said Caroline. "*You* guys have to decide. You decide, and I'll make everything work."

There was silence for a moment. Then Wills shouted out, "*Frozen Peter Pan!*" and an owl hooted.

"Whoa," said Jessie.

They all looked at Caroline.

"All in favor say aye-aye!" she said.

They were all in favor. "Aye-aye!"

CHAPTER THIRTEEN

*R*ose was only a little envious as she watched Lottie spend all Friday morning getting ready for Jon and Ethan. They loaded up on egg noodles, strawberry yogurt, string cheese, apple juice boxes, and hot dogs for Ethan; Maker's Mark, chips and salsa, and a great-looking peach pie for Jon. It was hot and muggy on the mainland, and there wasn't enough time to stop at the library and call home. Besides, it would have been hard to talk to her family knowing that they weren't coming, while Jon and Ethan were.

The ride over to Little Lost cooled them off, just in time for the long, uphill, wheelbarrow-pushing path to Hopewell.

"I'm going to lose weight on this vacation," Lottie said. "And get new muscles."

Everything was working out for Lottie, just as she had said it would. It would be nice if *all* Lottie's predictions came true.

"Where is he going to sleep, Lottie?" Rose asked as they unloaded the groceries. She noticed there were fresh wildflowers on the table. "Caroline's been up, I see. Are you going to put him in that dorm room? It's kind of big for one kid."

"I know," said Lottie. "Ethan could never sleep there alone. But there's a little room adjoining mine. I didn't even know it was there till I was poking around yesterday. It's either supposed to be a really big closet or a really tiny bedroom. But it has a window. I'll show you."

Rose peeked into the sweet, small room adjoining Lottie's. "This house is Castle Gormenghast," she said.

"What's that?" Lottie asked.

"A gigantic place. In a book," Rose said. One of Fred's old favorites.

"Maybe you can help me bring down a mattress from the dorm room?" Lottie asked.

Rose and Lottie found one that they could easily get downstairs. The room was just the right size for it. The tiny window opened easily, to their surprise; a night-light there worked when they plugged it in, and behind an old velvet curtain there was a supply of quilts and pillows.

"Ethan might actually sleep here," said Lottie. "Which would make Jon happy."

"I'm sure," said Rose.

Lottie smiled. "We had a ton of fun together before we got married. We still have fun a lot of the time. He's a good guy when he lets himself be."

"I'm sure we'll all love him," Rose said, even though she wasn't sure at all, and she was wary of having the balance of the cottage change with a new arrival.

Lottie grinned at her. "He's really a sweetheart under all the bluff. Beverly won't want much to do with him at first—that I know—and Jon will be totally blown away by Caroline when he first meets her. I hope he doesn't show off too much."

Yikes. "Maybe I'll go upstairs and round up some books for Ethan. I haven't gotten myself to the library yet. I keep taking the wrong path and ending up at the post office."

Rose went back upstairs. She imagined the twins in the dorm room, having a blast with Ethan. Unlikely, she thought. She'd spend all her time making sure Ben didn't alienate the other kids and, more to the point, the other parents, and he'd be awful to Bea and then Fred would say she was too involved with them both and the whole charm of the island would be spoiled. Nice.

She went over to the bookshelf and found a pile of Dr. Seuss books that she imagined Ethan would like. When she got downstairs the alcove had aired out, and between the books and the little nest of a bed and the light streaming in from the window, it looked like a cozy spot.

"Am I crazy to think he'll sleep in his own bed here?" asked Lottie.

"I think he will," said Rose. "I see it."

The car trip from Providence to Little Lost took forever, even though Jon had started as early as he could. Ethan was a trouper in the car: the iPad was a big help there, and a long nap got him through as far as Bucksport. He was pretty whiny on the last stretch, but he perked up on the ferry. Lottie met them on the dock. Ethan flung himself into her arms as Jon lugged the bags up to the house. Jon was hot and tired from the ride. He'd had no idea it was going to be such a long walk up from the dock. If the place weren't so pretty, he'd really be steamed.

"Race you, Daddy!"

"I can't race with all your stuff."

"You can run to the end of the boardwalk, Ethie. Then stop at the top, okay?"

"Do you seriously get water from a spring? Why isn't anybody bottling it? Lost Island Water!"

"Little Lost Island."

"Way better name than Poland Spring." This island could be

monetized in a second. He spotted the sign for Hopewell and Grundys. "How much farther?"

"Not a whole lot. It's still uphill, though. Hold my hand, Ethan. It's rocky here."

A few steps farther and Hopewell Cottage came into view. He could not believe Lottie was calling this giant place a cottage! This mom friend of Lottie's must be loaded. "Is this Rose Arbuthnot's place? Or Caroline Dester's?" Jon asked.

"Neither," said Lottie.

"What do you mean, neither? If I could get even a piece of the Caroline Dester business I'd rake in the billing," he said. "When do I meet her?"

"When she's here, Jon. Everyone wants a piece of her. Rose and I said we wouldn't be gawpers. You won't be a gawper, will you? Maybe give it a day before you talk to her about it."

"I'm only here till Sunday night so I'll strike whenever the iron is hot. And I feel it heating up," Jon said. "Are we upstairs?"

"No, down here."

"What's heating up?" asked Ethan.

"The sun," said Lottie. "Here's where Mommy and Daddy sleep."

"I don't want to go to bed!"

"It is *so* not bedtime!" Lottie said. "I won't even show you your room till later, how about that?" She turned to Jon. "I'll take him to the rocks over by the Grundy cottage. That's where I saw the crabs, Ethie!"

"I could crush a crab!" said Ethan.

"I picked up some Shipyard ale for you, Jonnie. You can grab that and take a shower outside. Or if you want a freezing swim just follow the path out the back door." She was always good about figuring out what he needed, and what he needed right now was to unwind from the drive so he'd be ready for the movie star.

"Crabs! Crabs! Crabs! Crabs!"

"We're going, Ethie. You can meet the others later, Jon. I'm not sure where they are. You'll find the kitchen. Oh, and you can see France from upstairs!"

Lottie was always a little hazy on geography.

He checked his e-mail. Nothing since 3:36 P.M. There really was no service here. Luckily on a summer Friday not a lot was getting done, even at his billing-hungry firm. He'd have to go into town first thing tomorrow to see what he'd missed. He kind of hoped Carla would hold off on sending any more flirty texts till he headed back on Monday. She'd been fairly free with them while Lottie was away. They were both playing it pretty safe still—no isolated body parts—but he didn't want Lottie picking up his phone and seeing a selfie of Carla posing with his briefs (a law firm joke that never got old).

The cottage seemed to be empty. He wasn't surprised. It was a gorgeous afternoon. Every window he looked out from had a view and here on the porch the landscape kind of blew your mind. The sun, low in the sky, lit up the water: sparkling, clear, calm. It almost looked warm—could that be possible, in Maine? Jon remembered from grade school that some parts of the coast were warmed by currents from the Gulf of Mexico (thanks, Miss McCabe), but was this one of those spots?

He grabbed a little towel from the washbasin in one of the bedrooms. I won't go in the whole way.

He clomped down the stairs and pulled off his shoes and socks. He left them messily on the back porch—I'm on vacation!—then charged down toward the path. The stones were tough on his feet, unused as they were to being out of socks and shoes. When had he started wearing socks so much? The stones were bigger and warmer as he approached the sea, but the water looked a little more intimidating. And cold. Now it looked *cold*.

He put his feet in. It was really, *really* cold. But shit, it might feel good to go in after that drive. Wash off four hundred miles and unread e-mails and unpaid credit cards and the hours he had yet to bill this quarter right here in this bay or whatever it was.

He stripped off his shirt. He'd been eating lean, just in case anything did happen with Carla. His chest was pale but if he tensed up there was a pretty creditable six-pack for all to admire. The sun felt so great on his back. He could go in wearing his boxers. He took off his jeans and laid them on a rock. Or he could go in without his boxers.

Nobody was around.

He stripped down to nothing and felt fantastic. Ha! This little towel barely covers my dick, he thought, and laughed. It was possible to laugh at himself here in Maine. He wrapped it around his waist—Lottie always liked that effect; she said he had swimmer's shoulders, and she was right—and walked out a long way to the water's edge. Clearly low tide. Jon hadn't thought about tides since he was a kid.

He dropped the towel on a rock, ran through the shoals, and dived in.

"*Jesus Christ!*"

A small wave lapped at him.

"*Fuck!* It is fucking *cold!*"

He was puffing like a whale, making terrible noises. But Jesus, it was like ice. Why would anyone swim here?

"Whoo!" He ducked his head under and threw it back. Cold cold cold! But God he felt good. He splashed his arms and puffed some more. He was a sea monster in the icy water. He was a kraken. "Release the kraken!" he roared, and splashed some more. "*Release* the *kraken!*"

As Jon ducked his head in and out of the water again, he noticed someone on the shore. Not Lottie and not Ethan. A man. A man in a blazer?

The man in the blazer was sitting on Jon's jeans and shirt on the rock. He looked very comfortable. Jon had been in for two minutes and his teeth were starting to chatter. Then the blazer man spotted Jon's towel at the edge of the water. He headed deliberately toward it. "Hey!" Jon called out when he picked it up. "Hey—that's my towel!"

Either his voice didn't carry or Blazer did not care. Blazer did not let go of the towel.

"That's my *towel!*" Jon cried out with a note of alarm, which sounded babyish, even to him. He was freezing now but he kept treading water. He wanted to get out and he wanted his towel. How long till hypothermia set in? Would he die here? Would he be a dead kraken?

"Yo!" Jesus, will he ever go?

The man folded the towel neatly, put it over his arm, and placed it and the rest of Jon's clothes far from the water. Nice of him, but who gives a shit if my towel's a little wet? Blazer man turned to head back to the path and Jon started stomping out of the water. I don't give a flying fuck if the old codger sees me. It'll be the thrill of his life, I bet, even if my balls are the size of chickpeas right now.

When the water was at his knees and the towel was only twenty paces away, a figure stood up from the rocks that jutted around the corner of the cove where Jon had been swimming—or rather, splashing. Holy Christ, had she been there the whole time?

"You must be Lottie's husband, Jon," she said in that voice of hers. It was Caroline Dester. She had a full frontal view. "Beverly!" she called to the man in the blazer. "Come back and meet our new houseguest."

Jesus. Caroline Dester was ten feet away and he was standing there with his dick hanging out. The sun was warm on his back but he was so chilled he shook.

"Oh, that must be yours," said the man—Beverly?—and he

pointed to the towel, still some distance from Jon up the rocky beach. "I folded it for you."

"Thank you," said Jon. There was nothing for it now and he decided what the hell. "Jon Mellish," he said, and boldly extended his hand to Beverly. Caroline was approaching him, getting more stunning with every step. "Lottie Wilkes is my wife. And you are?"

"I am Beverly Fisher. I've taken the house for August with your wife and the others. It's a pleasure to meet you." He turned to Caroline as she approached, smiling broadly. "This is the lovely Caroline Dester."

"Ms. Dester. Delighted to meet you," said Jon. Water is dripping off my dick, and I'm shaking hands with a movie star. Shit. Fuck.

"My pleasure," said Caroline. Christ, she was cool. Eye contact only. Meanwhile, God only knows where Beverly Fisher's eyes were looking. "Lottie has said so many wonderful things about you." She had? "I understand that when you're not standing naked on beaches, you're an accomplished attorney."

If Jon hadn't been so ruddy from the swim, she would have seen him blush. Good old Lottie. "Would you excuse me while I get my towel?" he asked.

Neither of them made a move, but Beverly said, "Of course."

Of course, my ass, thought Jon as he turned up toward the house. Well, I'll give you the full show. At least I've been working out.

He took the twenty paces nice and slowly. At last he reached the towel and wrapped it around his waist. Not that it even made a difference now.

"Hope to see more of you soon!" called Caroline.

As Jon walked deliberately back to the cottage, he heard Beverly speaking to Caroline. "It has been quite some time since I've seen a naked man in the flesh." Great. Where has he seen them? "Jon Mellish is a strapping fellow, no doubt about it. No wonder Lottie married him."

Damn right, thought Jon.

Once he'd whipped into the outdoor shower at the back of the cottage and blasted himself with hot water, he was surprised at what he felt. He didn't blame Lottie; that was the oddest thing.

"Ha!" he yelled aloud. Caroline Dester just saw me naked and I was supposed to make such a good impression on her. She must think I am a moron, but I don't even care.

The Dr. Bronner's peppermint soap tingled on his scalp.

Yes, Lottie could have warned him that Caroline and Old Blazer prowled the little rocky beach in front of the house. She could have kept guard and then introduced him to Caroline when the time was absolutely right so Caroline would have (a) wanted to screw him and (b) snapped him up to be part of her legal team. But Lottie had done neither.

If Caroline wanted to add him to her legal team, she still could. Clothed or unclothed.

He laughed and rinsed the last of the gritty sand off his toes. He had been at this "cottage" for less than an hour and he already felt like a million dollars. "I feel like a billion dollars," he said to Lottie as he bounded into their little room downstairs. She was reaching up to a high shelf above the little daybed for a fleece for Ethan and a little skin showed. He grabbed her around the waist and gave her a tight and provocative hug from behind. She fit herself into his embrace.

Lottie turned around. He kissed her mouth and she kissed him back.

"I missed you," he said into her hair.

CHAPTER FOURTEEN

*T*he sound of buzz saws started at eight a.m. on Saturday, their second Saturday at Hopewell. Rose was sitting at the ancient table in the kitchen, reading a *Down East* magazine from July 2006. She and Lottie had decided last night they wouldn't go into the Harbor to get groceries: the Harbor on the weekends was strictly for tourists. She had planned a morning of looking out on the water and an afternoon reading the early childhood books she'd lugged here with her. She hadn't even cracked one open yet. But now this noise.

"What is going on?" said Caroline. She rarely emerged before ten o'clock. The saw was making her tense; Rose could see it in her face. Even so, every expression she had was an adorable expression, Rose thought. Even when she looked upset she looked adorably upset. Seeing her do anything was like watching a scene in a movie.

Caroline was an awfully good actress in the one film Rose had seen her in. The long, meandering one that people thought was improvised but was actually tightly scripted. She'd be good as the female sidekick in the movie of Fred's new book. She'd class up the act. "I don't know. I hope it stops soon, though." Another saw started up. "It's eight o'clock in the morning. On a Saturday."

"*Et in Arcadia ego*," said Caroline.

"Nicely put," said Rose.

"It was my one line in that Woody Allen movie when I was a kid."

"That was you?"

"That was me."

"Woody Allen always picks Oscar winners. Diane Keaton. Cate Blanchett." As soon as she said the words, she wanted the earth to swallow her.

"Thanks," said Caroline. Her long eyelashes lowered.

"Oh God, I'm so sorry." Very bad gaffe, Rose! Save it somehow. "You were robbed." She must have heard that a million times before. Say something honest. "It must have been excruciating. I can't even imagine."

"No, you can't," Caroline said. She was being honest too.

"I haven't seen you in everything but you always light up the screen when you're on. And you've been doing it a really long time."

"A really long time." Caroline looked in the fridge, took out nothing. "That Woody Allen was my fifth movie. Or maybe the seventh? I can't remember. We'd have to IMDb it."

"Everything's online now." There'll be no ephemera when this generation fades away, Rose thought. Historians will be so much the poorer. The saws roared again. "That noise is horrendous."

"Why are they cutting down trees, anyway?" Caroline asked. "The trees make the place. I love how you can barely see the cottages, even when they're next door to each other. I could spend a lifetime up here. Away." A noisy, bright orange vehicle clattered past the kitchen window. Even Beverly could have identified the color. "What is this about? We're supposed to be on a tranquil Maine island and suddenly we're in a construction site."

Lottie wandered sleepily onto the porch. She was wearing the Oxford cloth shirt Jon had driven up in. Swamped by the shirt, she looked even more like a child than usual. She had Robert's cottage guide in her hands. "It's the work party. That's what all the noise is. 'Do not be alarmed by the noise and activity that will begin early in the morning on the second Saturday in August.' That is so Robert," she said. "I haven't even met him and I know that is so Robert. 'It is the annual all-island work party. You need not join in, though you will be welcome. The tasks are generally divided by gender—'"

"Very Little Lost Island," said Rose.

The violent whines of the chain saws sounded again. "I hope they're only taking down the dead ones," said Caroline.

"Islanders?"

"Trees."

"Jon would love to traipse around clearing brush," said Lottie. "Super manly. I don't think he has anything like work boots, though."

"There are work boots in the hall, where the jackets are," said Caroline. "What do the women do?"

Lottie continued: "'. . . with the men clearing brush, and scraping and painting the railings of the dock, the boardwalks, et al. The women minister to the public spaces: the assembly room, the library, the teahouse.' He wrote in a newer note, though, in pencil: 'This has changed in recent years.'"

"Thank God," said Rose.

"Has anyone even seen the assembly room?" Lottie asked.

"It's where the kids play at night," Caroline said. "Up at the top of the island."

"I might go over to the library," said Rose. "I'll volunteer there and see if they'll take me, a humble renter. I think it's on the east side, over by the tearoom, so maybe this awful chain saw noise will not reach that far."

"I may go too." Caroline's voice dropped half an octave. "If it's all right with you."

"I'd love it," said Rose. She actually would.

"I'll keep Beverly away from the painters on the dock," said Lottie. "Or who knows what colors he'd choose."

"He's a good soul," said Caroline. "Even if he is color-blind."

They heard heavy footsteps in the hall. Lottie grinned. "Jon. He clomps."

"It's sort of okay to have another man here," said Caroline. Rose was still adjusting. The cottage was big, but the four of them had just learned how to get along. Now with Lottie's husband there Rose felt less ownership. It made her miss Fred more than she already did.

"Plus Ethan!" Lottie said. "He slept through the night last night. All night. In his own bed. He was still asleep when I woke up."

Rose's heart hurt. Lottie gave her a hug. "Don't say it, Lottie," said Rose. "I know you see them here."

"What is up with all this noise?" Jon walked into the kitchen already dressed in shorts and a T-shirt, but looking as sleepy as Lottie. They clearly did not get much rest last night. "Good morning."

"Buzz saws," said Rose.

"Sounds more like chain saws," said Jon.

"It's the all-island work party. You can tramp around in the woods clearing brush."

"Not my idea of vacation. Is there any coffee?" Jon asked.

Lottie explained the Beverly situation with the coffeepot. "So we're doing pour overs. Or drinking instant."

"I'm not drinking instant," said Jon. "We've got to be able to find a decent coffeemaker. We could go to the mainland today, Lottie, and buy a coffeemaker and do Maine things."

The chain saws stopped but there was a new sound. Less revving. More steady. Loud.

"Is that a helicopter?" Caroline asked. She looked pale.

"No, that's just the chain saws," said Jon. "When they're not sawing they sound like helicopters."

"I wouldn't mind escaping the work party," said Lottie. "I'm feeling more Wilkes-Mellishy than islandy today. If we drive over to West Dorset we can play minigolf and get soft ice cream and avoid the crowd in the Harbor. I can't believe Ethan is sleeping through all this." She looked over at Jon, gathered her hair up into a wild loose bun, and shook it out again.

"Let's go check up on him," said Jon. Good for Lottie. Good for them both.

"I can't stay here," said Caroline. "Rose, let's go."

"Could you hold on for a moment while I brush my teeth?" she asked.

"I think so. I'll leave a note for Beverly."

Rose used the little sink in her bathroom. These are the taps that everyone wants in Brooklyn, she thought. They looked so jolly, like jacks: COLD and WARM, they read. No false promises.

Rose went back out to the porch and found Caroline already at the foot of the stairs.

"Can we take this path?" she asked. "There's no boardwalk but I think it goes to the top of the island and then down to the other side."

Caroline was right—there was a little path in the woods that Rose hadn't noticed. It took them through a heavily wooded stretch of the island. As they walked farther from the cottage, the noise diminished. Caroline's shoulders looked less tense. She's so young, really, Rose thought. Yet she's done so much, accomplished so much. She must work incredibly hard.

A mourning dove sang its soft song. Once. Twice. "You must work incredibly hard," Rose said.

"I do. I work incredibly hard."

"Since you were a baby."

"Since I was a baby."

"Did you like it?"

A grasshopper bounded across the path. Rose had no idea they could jump such a distance. I've got to show Ben one of those guys, she thought. We could rent another cottage some year if Robert won't have us back next year. I wonder what Lottie sees about next summer.

"I don't remember the early stuff." Caroline's voice was freighted with emotion, always. Rose didn't know when to trust it and when not. Now seemed like a time to trust it.

"The *National Velvet* remake was the first thing I really recall. I liked my trailer. I shared it with my mother. She was the one who kept getting the roles for me."

"Did you want them?"

Caroline didn't say anything for a while. The walk was steeply uphill here, so maybe she didn't want Rose to see that it was an effort. Or maybe she just didn't want to talk.

"You don't read very deep on the websites, do you?"

"I don't read them much at all," said Rose.

"The eminent Dester family is congenitally weak, like the House of Usher. I did that as an HBO special, in case you're wondering. Every once in a while, we fall."

"I thought you were all rock solid. Except . . ." Rose recalled hearing stories of a Dester uncle. Embezzlement? Bigamy?

"Darling Dad basically snorted a fortune up his nose in the eighties. So my job was to build it up again. I had the face for it. Mother kept all the accounts. Even so, beloved Pa ran through it fast. That's why we moved around so much when I was little. Everywhere we went, we kept up appearances till we couldn't anymore. Wait—is that Beverly's cat?"

Rose stopped to listen to what sounded like a baby crying. "Beverly has a cat?"

"He's putting water and scraps out on the porch every night for a cat he thinks he heard. Not here, though; down on the point."

"I think that may be a seagull," said Rose. "Not a cat. Or a baby. He's an odd one, Beverly. I was so afraid of him the first week."

"Poor Beverly! He's just a teddy bear."

They were at the very top of the island now. Rose thought she had exhausted all the views on Little Lost but this was another stunner.

"Just when you think the whole place couldn't get any more picturesque," said Caroline. "What's going on with the stones here?"

There was a small tower of stones at the summit of the hill. The base was made of larger stones, and the pile got progressively narrower and more precarious as it got higher.

"I think that must be a cairn," said Rose.

"A cairn is what, exactly?"

"It's a pile of stones that people put together. To mark something significant. This is the highest point on the island and the cairn makes it higher."

"This island is the high point of my year," said Caroline. "It's been a bad year, as you so delicately pointed out this morning."

"I'm sorry—"

"I'm joking. Sort of. Do you make a wish with your cairn stone?"

Rose hadn't heard of making a wish with a stone. "Why not?" she said.

She watched as Caroline picked up a small flat smooth stone. She rubbed it once, steadied it on the top of the pile, and closed her eyes.

When she opened them again, she smiled. "I wish I wish my wish comes true," she said. Then she turned down another path and waved to Rose as she left. "I'll head this way now," she said. "See you at supper."

You'll get your Oscar yet, Rose thought.

She consulted her map and found her way down to the library. There was a whole cluster of cottages on this side of the island she hadn't seen yet. These were the ones Lottie found that first day and couldn't find again, even with her keen sense of direction.

The path hugged the shore for a while and then led into an open field. A few more fairy houses dotted the path. The fairies were probably at a work party of their own. In the distance she could see a building that looked less like a cottage and more like a public building. LITTLE LOST LIBRARY, read the sign, without irony. She climbed the wide steps and stood under the portico for a few moments. This was not like the library in the Harbor, she could tell already. It was built of stone, not wood. And she was quite sure that when she went inside she'd find that no one had changed a pebble since the ribbon was cut in 1887, the date that was carved on the cornerstone.

The day was beautiful, so Rose imagined that most of the work party would be working out of doors. She was right: a sign on the front door read, AT WORK PARTY. COME BACK LATER.

She pushed open the door. There was a pile of waterlogged books on a long narrow table that had been covered with a blue tarp. FOR SORTING, read the sign. So Rose began.

CHAPTER FIFTEEN

*I*n the days that followed her discovery of the third floor, Caroline had been through three trunks and was delighted today to find a fourth. The island seemed more quiet than ever after the commotion of the work party. Sunday really had been a day of rest, though in the afternoon, she had met up with the kids again at the assembly room. *Frozen Peter Pan* was pretty much a shambles, but the kids were having a good time, and she was too.

Today's big activity was the market boat, which she was determined not to miss this week. There were a couple of hours before she'd have to head to the dock to see what it was all about. But for now, since there was a cool breeze and the third floor was calling, she was up there again.

All the instruments must be Robert SanSouci's. She'd thought that when she first went up there and knew it now, from what Rose had told her about him. A lutenist. Who knew there even was such a profession? She wondered why he didn't need all these guitars in New York. They must be his extras.

She assessed the guitars, chose one, and lifted it down from the wall. She strummed the strings: very out of tune. And it was the lute she really wanted to play.

It was quite a strange instrument. It didn't fit right in her hands. She wasn't sure how to hold it, even. The strings were strangely quiet, but loud enough for this still room. Things were quieter back then, she guessed.

She felt a little bad playing the lute. It felt too intimate. She put it back on the wall as carefully as she could. The trunks of clothing, the furniture, the rugs—she felt entitled to disturbing them. They needed it! But the lute—that was not her domain.

The garments she had already exhumed, most of them too thin and threadbare to wear, were exquisite in their making. The pin tucks were exacting; the pleats were just so; the tiny wasp waists were taken in perfectly. She planned to try them on. She wanted to be who-ever it was these clothes had belonged to.

The fourth trunk was rusted and hard to open. Caroline thought about the last time she had packed a suitcase. She'd thrown together her clothes for Maine, and now that she was here she found herself wearing about 10 percent of what she'd brought. Her suitcases had rollers and were made of material developed no doubt by someone at NASA. They were ugly: zippers and handles and made to fit in the overhead bins of commercial airlines. And even on private flights she kept her cosmetics in containers of no more than three fluid ounces. Force of habit.

These trunks were made of wood and leather. Thick, hardy leather, probably from a kind of cow they don't even have anymore. A yak, or a buffalo, maybe. Each of the trunks had brass buckles and hasps and locks. This woman, the owner of these trunks, she knew how to travel in style. The initials on the three trunks were IOM, but on the fourth they were IOS.

"Imogen Olivia Monroe?" Caroline mused. She tried on a hat with a narrow brim. "Isabelle Oona Merryweather?" A small navy wool cape came out next. Caroline fitted it onto her shoulders, freckled now from two weeks in the sun.

"And then she got married," she said. "Isadora Osgood Saunderson." Probably her lady's maid packed for her back then, though maybe the young and lissome Isadora did it herself. Caroline liked to think she did.

Isadora Osgood Saunderson was not a movie star. She was not in the spotlight. She had her white linen dresses and a cottage in Maine. And she had Mr. Saunderson, the man she had married. The man she loved?

It was a little after twelve forty-five, and this market boat was apparently not to be missed, so she grabbed what cash she had and headed down to the dock. She wore her sun hat and sunglasses in case anyone was filming, although by now it seemed like an unnecessary precaution.

As she arrived on the wharf she saw a two-masted boat being tied up at the dock by a couple of teenagers in pale yellow shirts that read FAIRWEATHER FARM. On this side of the island, the breeze had disappeared. The sun was hot and there was little shade on the dock, but a number of islanders were clustered next to the boat, talking and snapping up the blueberries, the late summer squash, and most popular, the baked goods that the floating farmers market so prettily offered for sale. Max was bringing salmon tonight, and Beverly planned to put it under the broiler with a sesame ginger marinade. Caroline thought a strawberry-rhubarb pie would be the perfect complement; there was one left. She went to pick it up when an older, statuesque woman seemed deliberately to get to it first.

"Strawberry-rhubarb is a tradition in my family," she said to

Caroline. Then she turned to a knot of women on the dock and spoke in a stage whisper. "People with new money will take over these islands if we're not careful. You would think the bylaws would have something in them about who exactly gets to rent here."

Thanks, lady, Caroline thought.

"You're in the minority, Kay," said another of the women. She sighed. "We've talked this one through at the Annual Meeting a number of times."

The other woman was silent for a moment. She looked over the tomatoes on the boat, found them wanting. "Ferry was late again this morning," she said to the others on the dock, turning her back on Caroline. "We should give island teenagers island jobs. Not these people from town."

The kind-looking farmer who ran the market boat gave Caroline a supportive smile through his unkempt beard. "Kay van Straaten. She's a mean old biddy," he said. "You're a movie star."

"You're right," she said.

"That explains it," he said.

"Explains what?"

"She doesn't like rich people. Or people who didn't get rich the way she did."

"She doesn't like most people, from the sound of it."

"That was about Max, the kid who drives the ferry. Kay doesn't like him. Or really, she doesn't like that her granddaughter likes him."

"You know a lot," said Caroline.

"The market boat gets all the gossip," he said, and smiled again.

Caroline looked over the lush produce and the delicious-smelling baked goods. There were some sticky buns and some biscotti, but she didn't see any more pies. "Pies all gone?" she asked.

"Kay got the last one."

"See you next week," she said. "Save a strawberry-rhubarb for me."

Caroline walked past the knot of older women on the dock and the old bat continued to hold forth. "I hope it chokes you," she said in a voice that no one except possibly Kay van Straaten could hear.

Jon woke late. There was no one next to him, and the smell of coffee was strong in the clear cool Maine morning air. Lottie must be making breakfast. He was glad he'd found them a new coffeemaker. They needed him here. He sat up in the crisp sheets and got up to check on Ethan in the little room adjoining theirs. Asleep. Sound asleep. Incredible.

It was Tuesday morning and he had told the office he had pneumonia and he'd be out all week. They sent a get well e-card and told him as long as he was back for the client meeting on Friday and covered his e-mails and called in for the daily scrum, he'd be fine.

Somebody's already taken my chair, I bet.

He couldn't leave Maine yet. He and Lottie were having a ball and the minute Ethan hit the island he got on some primeval sleeping schedule and slept through the fucking night. With fucking being the operative word.

He'd known Lottie would be happy to see him, but he hadn't anticipated how happy he was to see her. They'd had a blast in bed last night. He'd wanted to devour her and she'd let him. "I'm a greedy girl," she'd said. Jesus. It made it even hotter that they had to be so quiet, with everyone just a few thin planks away. And this morning before dawn he wanted her again and again and she wanted him. He'd missed it so much he almost thought he would break her in two.

Ethan slept through it all. A miracle.

Now Lottie was making him breakfast. Could he take her as she bent over the stove? What if Caroline Dester was there, watching?

Whoa. If he hadn't had such a good time this morning he'd run with that idea. Instead he reminded himself that Caroline Dester needed an IP attorney, not an invitation to a threesome.

Ethan wandered in sleepily from his little room next door. Jon loved how much their son looked like him, especially when he was rubbing his eyes like that. Jon was a sex-machine kraken who loved his kid and had made friends with a movie star who knew how he looked with his clothes off.

Maybe he'd skip checking his e-mails in the Harbor today. Screw real life. "That's why they call it vacation, dude!" he said to Ethan and they both laughed hard. "Lottie! Heat up the griddle!" he called. "We're making pancakes."

"Oh, hello," said Rose. "I didn't know whether you were open or closed."

Big as the cottage was, when it rained that afternoon, Rose felt restless. Lottie, Jon, and Ethan were playing bombardment chess, a game involving bombing chess pieces with other chess pieces, which she knew Ben would have enjoyed. Caroline was making a project of rearranging the furniture in the formal sitting room. When Rose had questioned whether Robert, who was scheduled to arrive soon, would want his furniture changed around, Caroline said, "This room is crying out for help and if he doesn't see it, he needs to," and that was that. Beverly had installed himself in the kitchen, and they all knew by now not to disturb him there.

So Rose took a slicker off the peg in the hall by the stairs, pulled on a pair of short rubber boots, and headed for the door. Lottie took a break from bombarding to see her off.

"It's a nice rain," she said.

Rose nodded. "I'll be back by suppertime," she said. "I wouldn't miss a Beverly meal." He was grilling swordfish tonight if the rain abated.

"Tell us if you discover anything new," said Lottie.

"Maybe there's a Walmart here and we haven't seen it yet," said Jon.

"Or Chuck E. Cheese's!" said Ethan. "There could be Chuck E. Cheese's and we could go."

"I'll let you know if I find a Chuck E. Cheese's, Ethan," said Rose. She kissed him on the head and thought of Bea and Ben. Please let them be okay.

The path from the back door led toward the north end of the island. It was true, they hadn't done much exploring there. The rain was not hard and not cold. It felt like another manifestation of the water that was all around them. She walked for some time and found herself again at the library. All roads lead here, she thought.

She had expected an elderly lady behind the desk. Or an older man, hard of hearing and peeved at being intruded upon. She saw instead a strapping redheaded teenage girl with earphones on. She hadn't heard Rose come in but then looked up, startled, as Rose walked up to the desk. "Oh, I'm sorry! I'm not supposed to wear earphones in the library. My mom will kill me. Can I help you?"

"No, I'm fine, thank you. Can I just browse a bit?'

"You can browse all you want and you can also borrow anything that's not in the reference collection. If you can tell what the reference collection is." She looked around dolefully. "We had a flood here right before the island opened up for the summer. The roof leaked half of May and the place got pretty wrecked. They were going to close the library all summer and do a big revamp in the fall but people wanted it open, but now nobody comes. It even smells bad! And the Young LABs are supposed to do the cleanup but everybody's putting it off."

"The young labs?"

"The Young Ladies Association for Beautification. It's a dumb name, especially now because there are guys in it. We're the next generation of Little Losters and we're supposed to take responsibility for our shared community." She was using a lot of air quotes, but there wasn't an edge to them. "But, um, try getting everybody here on the same weekend and then when they're here try getting them to weed through mildewed books. Hashtag I don't think so."

Rose smiled. Not everyone here on Little Lost was impervious to the outside world.

"I can help," she said. "I actually did some sorting during the work party last Saturday. I don't think we've met. I'm Rose Arbuthnot." She extended her hand. The girl shook, with a good, firm grip. They all had old-fashioned manners here.

"I'm Meredith Whyte. We could use some help, to tell you the truth. But the Young LABs are supposed to be doing the cleanup. I don't mean to guilt you into it."

"You're not guilting me into it."

Meredith checked her phone again. "I can't believe the island actually voted against Wi-Fi even in the library. I mean, come on. Actually, I can believe it. At least my phone gets a few bars at our cottage. My friends are coming over on the three o'clock ferry. This rain will make them crazy."

"It's almost three o'clock now," Rose said. There was an old mantel clock on top of the library fireplace.

"I'm supposed to be here till four. Committee rules."

"I'm sure no one will mind if you go." Rose hadn't the slightest idea whether anyone would mind or not, but with the rain still coming down, no one was leaving her cottage except a few grim souls in bright slickers who were wheeling carts down to the dock to greet the ferry before the weather got any worse. "If anyone comes in, I'll say you'll be right back. Or something."

"If anyone comes in I'm in deep doo-doo with the Old LABs. But I'll risk it."

"Do I need to lock up when I leave?"

"Oh no. The door doesn't lock. I mean, if you want to go through that pile over there and see if there are any books worth saving, you can do that, but you totally don't have to. Don't actually throw anything away. They hate it when you throw anything away on this island."

Meredith came out from behind the library desk. Like everyone here, she looked as if she had been born with a tennis racket in her hand: lots of muscle, no apparent body self-consciousness, ponytail.

"Okay, I am out of here. You don't really need to cover for me. I'll square it with the head of the LABs."

"Who's the head of the LABs?"

"My mom." Meredith grinned.

"You don't have a jacket?" The girl had on short tennis shorts and a T-shirt. No slicker, no sweatshirt. "You'll be drenched."

"I'll dry out." Meredith's attention was distracted by a figure in the rain coming toward the building.

"Jesus. It's that little shit, Max Cranmer. Excuse my Anglo-Saxon."

As the figure got closer Rose recognized their own Max from the cottage.

"Max? Who does the repairs? He seems like such a low-key guy."

Meredith was gathering her things quickly now. "So low-key that he forgot to tell his girlfriend he didn't want to see her anymore."

Was this girl Max's ex? They didn't look like a perfect match. "It wasn't me, if that's what you're thinking. It's Kitty van Straaten. She's a wreck." Meredith swung on her backpack. "I have to go. Don't do anything crazy with the books. This island is so fucking small sometimes. Sorry."

She sprinted past Rose, the screen door slamming behind her.

Rose watched from the arched window as Meredith trotted through the meadow, back to the path to the ferry dock. The rain was coming down very hard now, and Rose heard the unmistakable drip of a leak in the roof. She looked up. The ceiling rafters had clearly been recently patched, and they looked watertight, but there was that drip.

She followed the sound. There was a small puddle at the far end of the building. The ceiling fan seemed to be the culprit. The area rug had been rolled away already, so this was not the first time there had been a leak in that spot. She looked around for a bucket, and found nothing till she went into the minuscule bathroom off the back of the building. It smelled none too fresh in this driving rain, and Rose remembered some talk on the ferry about the unpleasantness of having to deal with septic fields at the end of the summer. The benefits of renting, she thought.

She snagged the wastepaper basket from the bathroom, which was a repurposed five-gallon spackling drum, and placed it under the leak. That would do.

The library was hers now.

Her eyes scanned for the poetry section. Did they even have one? It was a little hard to tell how the place was organized. There were some current best sellers with their splashy covers and discount stickers, which looked as if they had been bought in bulk. All three of Fred's books were among them. Of course. She turned them facedown. Aside from that attempt at restoring the collection, there was very little that wasn't damaged, or at least wasn't in danger of being more damaged than it already was.

The screen door clattered again. "Meredith?" Rose said.

"Nope."

It was Max, drenched to the skin.

A small frisson of desire ran through Rose. She was surprised by it. He is fifteen years younger than you, cougar. And he just dumped his girlfriend.

Max was interested in the ceiling fan, not in Rose. "Any leaks?"

"Just one that I can see," she said. "Over in the back. I'll show you."

He took a look. "That bucket will do for now," he said. "We'll get the crew on it tomorrow if it's dry enough. You doing okay in Hopewell?"

"We're doing fine. Thank you for bringing in the food. It's been fantastic."

"No problem," he said.

"We have more people up there now. My friend Lottie's husband is there. And their little boy, Ethan. He's three."

Max said nothing. Rose was incredibly curious about the breakup but obviously couldn't ask for details. She wished Lottie were here. Lottie was so good at asking infuriating questions that were impossible not to answer. "I just met a young woman in here," she began. She didn't really know where she would go with this. "And—"

He got out his drill and fired it up. There would be no conversation today.

"I think that'll hold it for now," Max said. He picked up his tools and headed out. "And in case Meredith was talking to you, Kitty was the one who dumped me."

CHAPTER SIXTEEN

"*L*et's take Ethan on an adventure," Jon said. "Want to do that, buddy? Want to go on an adventure with Mommy and Daddy?"

Of course Ethan was all for it. Poor guy hadn't had both Mommy and Daddy pay attention to him in a long time.

"The cottage owner has a boat," said Lottie. "A little Whaler. We could go on a boat ride. We could get a lobster roll for lunch. What do you think of that, Ethan? A boat ride? And Daddy will let you steer with him. You can help steer the boat!"

Driving made Jon think of the long road up here, which made him think of the long drive back, which made him think of the office and his e-mail. He heaved a sigh. There was so much shit he had to do that he wasn't doing.

"You're thinking of the crap you have to do for work, I bet," said Lottie. She always was weirdly intuitive. Jon had almost forgotten. "If you need to go into the Harbor to the library it's okay. It's really fine. Ethie and I will read books for a while."

But the thought of hearing clients whine on the phone or

explaining to the partners how he would increase revenue to meet the revised forecasts made him feel sick. Jon didn't want to do any of that.

Lottie reached for a jacket for Ethan and Jon grabbed her just the same way.

"I still have pneumonia," he said. "Even a lawyer is allowed to be sick every once in a while. Just ask my mom." Lottie's tits pressed up against his chest. "Still love that," he said. "Let's go on that boat ride."

She kissed him. "Pick out one of those life vests in the hall for Ethan," she said, and he heard it as a request, not a demand. Maine was working on him. "I think the boat keys are here, with the blue float." She picked a battered keychain from a nail by the door. "Robert left gas in it—"

"Robert?" asked Jon. He tried to keep the tiny edge out of his voice but he wasn't sure he had succeeded. If Lottie was horny because she'd been fucking someone else up here, or even thinking about fucking someone else, he would—

"Robert owns the cottage. Robert SanSouci. I haven't met him. Only Rose has. He seems to have a crush on her."

Lottie swept a mess of stuff into a boat bag: sunscreen and a water bottle and a couple of blueberry corn muffins. "Beverly made these yesterday. He's a sweetheart, even if he acts mean all the time."

The bag continued to expand under her hand. Jon ran through what he would be feeling at home in Park Slope, where everything was such a production. Were the right snacks packed in Ethan's stroller? Did they have backup juice and wipes and a fresh shirt? Was the rain gear stashed in the bag? Would a run to Trader Joe's upset his naptime? And Ethan squirming and whining the whole time.

Here, it was so different. So easy. They needed a life vest for him on the boat: there was one of every size hanging from pegs in the hallway. He might get hungry: he'd eat the muffin. No juice boxes? Try water.

"Come on, Daddy!" said Ethan.

"You bet, buddy," said Jon. "It will be good in the boat." Lottie slipped her hand into one of his and he took Ethan's in the other. "Let's go really fast."

They took off down the path that led to the dock. Lottie already seemed to know everybody on the island. "Not everybody," she said. "But there are a lot of families here. And no one is talking about what schools their kids go to. Or if they are, I don't recognize them."

"If we lived here, we'd send Ethan to public school," said Jon.

"If we lived here, we'd have to be filthy rich or have a family that had been smart enough to buy a place in nineteen twenty," said Lottie.

But as Jon looked around, he started to try to think of a way. "We could live here if Caroline Dester needed a new legal team."

Lottie nodded in that knowing way that could sometimes annoy him at home but that simply looked like wisdom here. "Caroline could need you, I'm sure," she said, "but I wonder if that would be up your alley—Hollywood and all."

"Who doesn't want Hollywood for an alley?" said Jon, but he'd seen other attorneys handle celebrity clients, and he was pretty certain he wasn't cut out to cater to a star. "I think she liked the look of me, though." He grinned.

"Who wouldn't like the look of you?" said Lottie, and she grabbed his waist and gave him a smooch.

"Mommy! You have to love me," Ethan said.

"You're right, I have to love you. Group kiss!" said Lottie. Goofy as it was, Jon didn't mind a group hug and kiss in the woods of an island in Maine. He even managed to grab Lottie's ass while he was at it.

151

"Oh, I didn't mean to disturb you." Rose's soft voice cut through their group huddle. She deserved to have somebody up here to grab her ass. Jon would do it but he didn't go for the tall, strong, blond types so much. "You're not disturbing us. Want to come on our boat ride?" It was so unlike him to invite a virtual stranger to a family outing. Mostly because he never went on family outings.

"It's so gorgeous out but I'm sure you want to go on your own—"

"We need you, Rose," Lottie said. "You're the one who almost got the engine running that night we came over. I'm bad with boats."

"You're not bad, Mom," said Ethan.

"Come on, Rose," said Jon. "Let's explore the place by water. We want you to come."

That seemed to do it. Ethan raced Lottie down to the dock. Jon and Rose followed behind.

"Look at those big boys," said Ethan.

He was pointing to two perfectly toned, perfectly golden, sun-kissed teenagers. They had the kind of body Jon didn't have—long and lean, their skin the same color as their hair. Everything honey blond, that's how Lottie would describe them. Jon watched to see if she was paying attention to them but her eyes were on Ethan as he tottered down the ramp to their Whaler.

These kids are up here all summer, Jon thought. Lucky bastards.

The boys had the grace of dancers, the way they stepped from the surety of land to the uncertainty of water. In one gesture, they untied their boat, ripped the cord, glided out of the haul off, impatiently kept the throttle rationed till they were out of the no-wake zone, and were gone.

My little Brooklyn boy will never be so good with boats, Jon thought. He was glad he'd had all those summers of boat time at camp in New Hampshire growing up. He might not have the natural grace of a sixteen-year-old anymore, but he could get an outboard motor started with a couple of pulls. He hoped.

The boat was tied with an elegant knot—they hadn't used it since Max retrieved it from the mainland the day after they arrived. There was a sounding map in a plastic case under the bench, which was handy. Jon knew enough about these waters to know that so many rocks meant a lot of shoals. And nobody wants to run aground in another man's boat. Especially in front of wife and child.

"Get in, guys," said Ethan, who could not step into the boat without help. Jon lifted him from Lottie's arms to his own. "Sit next to me, little guy," he said. "You can steer once I get her started up."

Rose stepped into the boat with surprising aptitude.

Everything smelled of hot fiberglass and gasoline, the way boats do before they're out on the water. "Let's just go and then decide where we're going," said Jon.

"Good idea, Daddy!" said Ethan, which pierced his heart. Here goes nothing, Jon thought. He pumped the gas line, pulled out the choke, ripped the cord once, twice—and the motor caught.

"Cast us off, Lottie!" he said, triumphant.

Ethan yelled over the engine noise. "Go fast, Daddy!"

"Let me clear the dock, buddy," said Jon, as he surprised himself by handily reversing out of the slip into the bay. "Then we'll let 'er rip!"

"Sexist pig!" said Lottie, but she didn't mean it. The Whaler had a 9.9-horsepower engine, so with the four of them it didn't pick up much speed. It was enough for Ethan, though. He was thrilled.

"Want to see what's on that little rock out there?" said Jon. He figured if he kept within the channel markers and bounded himself by the lobster buoys he wouldn't have a problem with rocks. "If a lobster boat can get in there, I can get in there, right, Ethan?"

"Right, Daddy!" Jon had forgotten how much fun it could be to spend time with his son. Who wouldn't want an echo to agree with your every word?

He hadn't been on the water like this in years, but he'd always thought he'd be a good boat captain. Okay, so they were in a twelve-foot Whaler, but he felt the call of the open ocean.

"Where are we going?" yelled Rose over the motor.

"Seals!" cried Ethan, pointing to a swell in the water.

"Take pictures, Lottie!" said Jon. "Everybody looks good on a boat."

"I didn't bring the phone!"

"No phone!" said Jon. "Insane. I'm glad there's a chart in this boat. I think it's this way to Dorset Harbor."

"We can go in and get some fresh caramel popcorn if we time it right," Rose said.

"Yikes, no-wake zone." Jon slowed the boat down fast. They were going through a narrow channel. The cottages they could see from the boat were just as generous as the ones on Little Lost.

"What's that?" cried Ethan.

"Look at that thing!" said Lottie.

Ethan, the smarty, had spotted an incongruous yet somehow perfect addition to the salty channel.

"Daddy, it's a bouncer! It's a bouncer on the water!"

For some reason, the enormous floating trampoline anchored in the channel seemed to make everything more real. "I'm going bouncing!" cried Ethan. There were three kids jumping on the thing and then off the thing, into the water.

"We'll have to ask them first," said Lottie.

Ethan was already screaming his heart out. "Can I bounce too? Can I bounce?"

The kids must have realized the Whaler was heading straight toward them because the bouncing stopped and there was a pointed lull.

"They're big kids," said Lottie, once they got closer and realized that these were twelve-, thirteen-, maybe fourteen-year-olds.

"They might not want to play with a little kid like me," said Ethan, understanding at once.

"Well, they might worry that you'd get hurt," said Rose.

"I won't get hurt!"

"Let's ask them." Jon was damned if these little twerps wouldn't let Ethan have one bounce on their trampoline. "I'm sure they could be persuaded." Why had he only brought credit cards, no cash? He put the motor into neutral as they came up alongside the tramp. The teenagers took in the three pale New Yorkers and a kid who was jumping out of his skin with excitement. They might turn them down just for fun.

"Oh my gosh! We wanted a kid!"

"Can we bounce him? We wanted a kid to bounce!"

The teenagers were *nice.*

There was a new kind of happy on Ethan's face—an elation mixed with just the smallest bit of fear—that Jon had never seen before. He looked at Lottie to see if she was catching it and she was. She beamed at him. "I love you," she mouthed.

"Be careful," said Rose.

"We're good with kids," said the chief girl. She looked competent, like a babysitter. "I'm Mackenzie. I babysit all the time."

"I can tell," said Lottie. "How did you get out here?"

"We swam," said the kids in unison.

"We swim from the dock to the float," said the chief boy. He was wearing a baseball hat featuring an unusually cute puffin. "And then we get up on the tramp."

"And then we bounce."

"And sometimes we bounce *into* the water."

"That's gotta be cold," Jon said.

"It's *freezing*!"

"You ready, dude? What's your name?"

"I'm ready! Let's go!"

"He's Ethan," said Jon.

"I'm Jamie. Come on, Ethan!"

Ethan was ready to burst. He climbed on the trampoline.

"This is how we do it with little kids."

There would not have been a chance in hell of Jon letting strange kids take his child even onto a swing in any playground at home. They basically didn't hire a teenage babysitter without Googling her parents and checking their apartment value on Zillow. He wasn't naive enough to think that everybody in Maine was a saint (though maybe they were) but right here, right now, Mackenzie and Jamie and the other kid were Ethan's heroes, and his, and Lottie's, and maybe even Rose's. He was helpless in the presence of Ethan's terrified, brilliant, uncontainable laugh.

"More more more!" Ethan said and the kids complied until their teeth were chattering and they'd all started feeling the cool afternoon air. "I think we better stop now, buddy," said the other girl, Hannah. She was the most athletic of the lot. "Give Jamie his hat back."

"Mine!" said Ethan.

"Ethan, sweetie, not yours," Lottie said gently.

"You want to keep that hat?" asked Jamie.

"Yes!" said Ethan. "I want to!"

"Ethan," Jon said, but without too much conviction, "that's Jamie's hat."

"He said I could keep it."

"I said he could keep it," said Jamie. "It looks good on you, dude. It's my dad's, anyway."

These kids were as sure-footed on water as they were on land. Maybe even more. They handed Ethan into the boat without the slightest hesitation. "Come back again, you guys," said Hannah. "We like bouncing you."

"If you need a babysitter, you can call me," said Mackenzie. "We're on Big Lost in the cottage book. The Hills."

"Maybe the grown-ups will get wet next time," said Jamie. "Bring your suits."

Lottie looked at them earnestly. "You are champs," she said. "Thank you so much."

"You betcha!" They all said it at once.

Then they sprinted across the tramp, flipped into the frigid water, and splashed noisily away.

Jon watched them swim with the big, extravagant movements of teenagers. He pulled the cord and started up the engine. "Everybody ready?"

"Ready!" called Ethan.

"Let me put some more sunscreen on you so we don't get called in by Maine Children's Services."

"I think Maine Children's Services have more to do than monitor sunscreen protection," said Rose.

"Well I wish they didn't," said Lottie. "Everyone should live like this forever. Hold still for one second, Ethan."

He twisted away and as Lottie grabbed for him Jon sharply rounded a channel marker.

"My hat! Mommy! My hat!"

Ethan's cap was in the water and had already raced twenty feet away in the wake of the boat. Jon jerked the boat around to circle it.

"Daddy, not so fast!" Ethan cried, suddenly tired and worn out and oversunned from their day on the water. He wailed, "Home, Daddy! Home!" even as he tried to climb over Lottie to get in the water.

Jon wasn't sure what the message was from Ethan, but Lottie's eyes seemed to be saying home was more important than hat, which had already bobbed out of sight.

"We're going home, Ethie," said Jon. "I'll get you home right now."

"No, Daddy! No! No!" He was practically climbing out of the boat now.

"Get hold of him!" cried Jon.

"My hat will drown!"

"Ethie, we'll find another one."

"Stop it, stop it!" He was exhausted, spent, overexcited, hysterical. And he could slip out of Lottie's grasp if she didn't hold on tight. "Don't let it drown!"

"There it is!" cried Rose.

And she dove into the water.

Jon cut the engine. "Where is she? Can she swim?"

"She's there!" cried Lottie. "It's too cold in that water for a regular human being to swim. Oh, Ethan! She got it! She has your hat!"

Ethan's screaming stopped immediately. He looked over the side of the boat. "You got it, Rosie!" he called. "You got my hat!"

Rose had to be too far to hear their cheers, but they kept them up till she pulled herself alongside the Whaler. It was a lot harder to get her in the boat than it had been for her to jump out, and the fact that she was fully dressed didn't help. But Jon hauled her up. Lottie swathed her in the one dry towel they had left.

"Rose," she said, "you were magnificent!"

Rose emerged from under the beach towel.

"You betcha," she said.

CHAPTER SEVENTEEN

*O*f the twelve hat boxes in the third-floor attic, only nine contained hats, and only four of those hats were actually wearable. And only two of them were flattering. Caroline tried them each on more than once. If they were truly going to the island hat party that afternoon, she definitely needed a great hat. The lighting in the attic was not ideal. She knew she looked dazzling in full sunlight, a great advantage of being young. Or youngish, at least in movie years. She propped up a couple of mirrors and angled them so she could see herself front and back.

The navy straw broadbrim set off her pale skin, as she had known it would, even without her stylist here. She piled her hair at the nape of her neck to make an even bigger deal of her cheekbones. She looked like Faye Dunaway in some period drama—had she ever been in a period drama? (Oh, yes, she was campily resplendent in *The Three Musketeers*.) But angularity and good bone structure wasn't what she was going for. All the women here were angular with good bones. Most of them could pass for lesbians in the city—no makeup, except a slash of frosted pink across the lips; hair cut short (so easy); clothes that might kindly be described as comfortable. Their idea of a hat was a tennis visor, she was sure.

This navy straw floating creation, worthy of Cecil Beaton—when would Isadora, the lady of the house, have worn it? Before she adopted that new monogram in marriage, or afterward? Caroline considered herself again. The hat was coquettish, and it felt à la mode, even now, a century or more after it was first made. In the mirror the flirty angle of the brim and the lift of the long ostrich feather gave her mystery and presence. The perfect hat for attracting a suitor. And Caroline was sure that Isadora had had no shortage of suitors.

Caroline considered another of the Little Lost group photos she had found. This one was from much earlier than the one downstairs. It sat on a small painted-wood side table all on its own. There were two young bucks in flannels and shirtsleeves who looked as if they might covet an Isadora. They'd snatch her up and take her to Boston and squelch her, and then they'd run off and have affairs with the newest sylphlike blond girl on the tennis courts as Isadora thickened with childbearing and age. Caroline shuddered. That's not going to happen to me.

In the back row of the photo, squinting into the sun, was some-one more Isadora's type. He was bookish, nearsighted, and unfash-ionably bearded—his beard was longer and more straggly than the others'. Unlike the other young men, he had not removed his jacket, which even Beverly would be able to identify, as it was white. They were all pretty much in white.

Caroline looked at his blurred features for a long time. What kind of hat would pique this young man's interest? Oh, he'd love the look of her in the ascot-worthy straw, but if she wore it he'd leave her to the young bucks. He wouldn't have the nerve to compete.

She took the Cecil Beaton hat off.

The hat in the last box was a straw cloche, the very definition of the word *humble*. Most women would look dumpy in this. Lottie would certainly look dumpy in this. This was the roast chicken of hats: Worn badly, it was ordinary, tasteless, and tough to swallow. Worn properly, it was perfection. Caroline gingerly lifted it from the brittle tissue and put it on.

She could really roast a chicken.

By the time she got down to the sunporch, the others had gone. "We couldn't find you so we went ahead. Meet you at the Whyte cottage." Lottie had left a note in her fat, girlish hand.

"They're gone at last," said Beverly as he padded silently into the room. Though hatless, he was dressed for the event, and he wasn't wearing the brown tie. "Of course no one asked me if I wanted to attend."

"I thought they asked you last night," said Caroline, "and you said, 'By no means,' if memory serves." She loved using "if memory serves" with Beverly.

"Did I?" he asked. "I don't recall."

"You did." She smiled her most genuine smile for him. "But the sign said all are welcome, so that means you too. There's a straw boater up there that I think would go with your blazer. Shall I bring it down?"

Beverly sighed heavily. "I suppose so. Of course I won't know whether it matches this shirt—ecru, is it?"

"Pink."

He blanched. "I'll change," he said suddenly. "I'm color-blind, as I may have said."

"You have. And don't change. You look terrific."

"Then if there is such a thing as a boater that can be worn with a pink shirt, please bring it down."

"And we can go together?"

"Of course."

Caroline turned to head up the stairs to her aerie.

"That cloche becomes you, by the way."

As they walked down the sylvan path—the first and possibly only time Caroline's mind had ever sprung that word on her—Caroline was pleased that Beverly did not press her about what she was doing on the third floor. Instead, they looked together at the Little Lost map, which had been drawn in 1922 and evidently had not changed to this day, and found the way to the Whyte cottage. Beverly had trouble when the boardwalk to the cottage changed to a dirt path. But once he had his footing he became unusually chatty.

"The great unwashed of Little Lost Island don't seem to recognize a goddess in their midst," he said. "Do you suppose they've never seen you in a film?"

"They saw me disgrace myself at the Oscars," said Caroline. "And they don't like a bad sport."

"Were you a bad sport at the Oscars? I haven't watched it since they snubbed Gorsch for Best Song."

Good old Beverly. "Maybe it was that time in Montauk with the SUV. They've decided they don't trust me around any summer colony."

"That wasn't you, was it?" asked Beverly, and Caroline smiled.

"No, it wasn't me."

"Maybe they are afraid of their island being discovered."

"But I love it here." She surprised herself with that declaration.

"The hat party will reveal all," said Beverly. They had arrived at the Whyte cottage. It was not quite as grand as their own. This one was painted white, with dark green shutters and green trim. It may have been older than their place—it was clapboard, and looked more like a farmhouse than a summer cottage.

"Oh, look at the windows," said Caroline. She loved old, irregular glass—glass made by hand, not by a machine set to Olde. The window boxes bloomed with petunias, and something that smelled like honeysuckle grew up the sidewall. An oak tree loomed over the roof. There was a refrigerator on the back porch that anywhere else would look tacky, but here looked sensible. Beverly took his time climbing the few steps. This island was not easy terrain for a seventy-eight-year-old New Yorker. "Be careful of those shoes," she said. There were at least seven pairs of sun-bleached Keds and Tretorns on the side of the porch, and a full complement of gardening clogs. "They're all eccentric in their own way, aren't they?" she observed.

"The islanders or the cottages?" asked Beverly.

"Both, I suppose."

All at once, Lottie appeared hazily through the screen door. "I thought I heard the Caroline voice," she said. "Come on in! They have mushroom melts!"

Despite the current trend of Kobe beef sliders and lobster mac and cheese in shot glasses, English muffins slathered in butter with canned mushrooms and Velveeta had not made an appearance in Caroline's hors d'oeuvres circuit. They were fantastic.

"I suppose we'd better do this," said Beverly. "We're here."

"That hat is gorgeous on you," said Lottie. "Where did you find it? Oh, this is Bill Keating—I met him playing tennis. Say hello to Caroline, Bill."

"Hello, Bill," said Caroline in the voice she knew from her accounting firm was worth a fortune.

The affable Bill looked startled, and then shot out his hand. "Nice to meet you but I was just getting a drink for the matriarch. I'll be back in a bit."

"Super," Caroline said, but she was sure he would not return.

Her eyes scanned the room. The hats were impressive. There were indeed a few matrons in their tennis visors, but most people there had made an effort. The hats all fit the faces pretty well. A lot of women don't know how to wear hats in the modern era, Caroline thought, but these women seemed to have the knack. Probably because their hats all came from similar attics and were originally made for similar gene pools.

She looked around for Rose. She was deep in conversation with one of the island matriarchs, a very old, very wrinkled lady with brilliantly clear eyes and a permanent smile. Rose was nodding, intent on the conversation. She towered over the tiny woman. Caroline ventured over but Rose did not notice her, and she was loath to interrupt, so she became absorbed instead in her surroundings. There was a Whyte family crest over the mantelpiece, a relic of the fifties, probably. The white Whytes of Whyte.

But Caroline supposed these people couldn't help being WASPs any more than she could. She was to the manor born and they were to the cottage born. She reached for a deviled egg on the weighty Victorian table and made up some pedigrees for the guests before her.

"You're very smiley," said Jon. "I hope you're not still thinking of that episode on the beach."

"I wasn't," said Caroline. She somehow felt as if Jon were an old pal, since she had seen the precise size of his penis (average, though of course she would exaggerate its size if asked; all women were actresses in that regard). "Lottie's making friends over there," she said. They both noticed Lottie standing alongside a fireplace mantel made from what looked like beach stones. "She's very lovely up here, isn't she?" Caroline remarked.

"She is," said Jon. He smiled at Caroline. "And Ethan is easier to take up here. Even when he almost throws himself out of a moving boat, like he did yesterday."

"I take it you rescued him?"

"Rose rescued his hat, which meant no one needed to rescue Ethan. Now he's at this party and he's fine with playing with the big kids outside." Caroline looked where Jon was gesturing. Her young thespians were playing Wiffle ball and making dandelion chains. They had another rehearsal on Saturday morning, though right now she didn't much feel like extending herself for their island parents.

"Little Lost Island is working its magic, I guess." She tried not to sound too down.

"But not on you," he said quickly. "Where are the hordes that should be surrounding you? Lottie says she heard there was another big movie star or a movie mogul or someone trying to buy up a whole island community somewhere south of here. I bet that's why they're all shunning you."

Caroline blinked as she said, "I *did* come here to be away."

"It's still weird how they don't flock around. I'd flock around you if I didn't have Lottie." He said it in such a friendly way that it didn't sound creepy.

"They don't like people who make spectacles of themselves here." She took off the cloche and shook out her hair, in as far from a stagey way as was possible with that gesture. "Would you be a dear and get me a Ketel One with a twist, Jon? I'll see if Beverly needs taking care of."

Caroline need not have worried about Beverly. He was talking with two earnest young men, who weren't in the least WASPy. One had a sleek, polished Eurasian look; the other was surely Indian. They were handsome and well dressed and were entranced by Beverly.

"They're called the Gay Blades," said Lottie, coming up behind Caroline suddenly and diving into her thoughts as she tended to do. "A cappella. They sing Gorsch's songs at college. They were about to bust out that 'Blue Willow' song for him here but he wouldn't let them. None of them can believe that there's someone here who knew him."

"Knew him intimately," said Jon. He had arrived, plastic cup with vodka in hand. "No Ketel One. They're not great believers in brand-name alcohol at this cottage." He kissed Lottie on the lips. "You look gorgeous in that hat," he said.

"I'll have to take it off when we go back—it's raining," said Lottie. "The weather never stays still here. Ethan's coming in. I guess the game broke up. How was the game, lovey?"

"I won and I got new friends," said Ethan. He looked vastly pleased with himself. "This is my lucky hat."

"You are our lucky kid," said Jon.

Caroline did not want to be around such happiness, even if they did not mean to exclude her. She would have spoken to Rose, looking ethereal in the garland of flowers she'd made for a hat, but she was still intent on the elderly woman with the bright eyes and Caroline did not have the heart to wade in.

"I'll duck home, I think," she said. "The hat party has not been a success for me."

With the twins at their aunt's and his manuscript begging for yet another twist and possibly a new location (Lake Toba?), Fred was more than happy to leave the apartment. It had taken some doing, but he was on his way to his film producers' office for a casting consultation. He felt rather sheepish, as the casting decisions were supposed to be based on videos. Holly had to go to such lengths to make this happen. She was a good agent.

He had chosen his outfit the night before—something he never did, but he wanted to strike the right note, since he was posing as his agent's assistant and Holly would be at the meeting as Mike McGowan's agent. It was a thin ruse, but he had to get in front of Caroline Dester somehow. He needed to know if he'd be as obsessed with her in the flesh as he was with her on his laptop. Holly figured there was an ulterior motive for his tagging along incognito—"Are you going to reveal yourself at last?" she joked—but she didn't pry. Danny Lowenstein generally liked to please authors and their agents (he had literary pretensions), and the meet and greet was confirmed. "You could just say you're Mike McGowan," Holly had told him. "They're not going to recognize you as Fred Arbuthnot from the MacArthur website, that's for sure. I'd make you get a new photo if you actually wanted to be known. You look like a young Franz Kafka in your genius picture, and not in a good way." Holly always knew how to cut to the chase, also not in a good way.

He gave himself a last glance in the mirror, decided to ditch the tie. Writers are supposed to be the worst-dressed people in the room, he remembered someone—Charlie Kaufman?—saying. Maybe I'll wear the tie after all.

The office wasn't as glamorous as he'd thought it would be, and he'd thought it wouldn't be glamorous. The Lowenstein Company clearly believed the framed lobby-sized movie posters were impressive enough. And they were: all the big blockbusters and a whole bunch of Oscars had been conjured out of this office. His movie almost paled in comparison with the rest of them. But it had been

Danny Lowenstein's baby, and he knew how to make a cash-cow franchise. *The Pentagon Conscription* was a clear moneymaker in the U.S. and had brought in a lot of gravy overseas, so Fred congratulated himself on deserving his place on the wall. He allowed himself to stare at his poster—he felt suddenly legitimized in this context— with "Based on the novel by Mike McGowan" in the same point size as the screenwriter's credit, per his contract.

A soignée assistant, doubtless unpaid, smiled mechanically as Holly and he took the three or four footsteps to the reception desk. "We're here for the Mike McGowan meeting," Holly said.

"The meet and greet," the assistant replied. "You must be Holly Stampler. And you are . . . ?"

"This is my assistant, Fred Rose," said Holly. It was the alias they had decided on; it sounded wistful now.

"Please wait here. Can I get you some water?"

"Please," said Holly. She had warned Fred to say nothing.

"Cold or room temperature?"

"Either," Holly said.

Two ostentatiously humble glasses of tepid water were produced in an instant.

"I love when they pitch to *us*," she said to Fred and clinked glasses with him. She was the type of agent who hovered over every deal, saying whatever everyone wanted to hear and then agreeing to nothing until she got every single thing she wanted. Fred had made Holly rich, and she him. He had barely put his glass to his lips when the assistant said, "Follow me, please."

They wound down a narrow corridor festooned with more posters, to a nondescript windowless conference room. "Danny will be with you in a few moments," said the assistant. Fred named her Montana in his head. Four or even six years in the liberal arts and now poor Montana was a dogsbody to a reputed bully and ingenue fucker. He wondered idly where the economy would be when Bea and Ben were her age.

It was a lot more than a few moments.

Holly was texting, so Fred picked up *The Hollywood Reporter* and started to read the self-aggrandizing ads that proliferated even now, in the dead of August. He loosened and tightened his tie.

"Should I keep the tie?" he asked, stupidly.

"You are very needy today," Holly said without looking up.

Had she guessed his obsession with Caroline Dester? If she had, she was refusing to acknowledge it. His plan was not quite clear, but he was scripting it in his head. Caroline walks in; something pulls her gaze to his undeniably manly presence, which cuts through the pretense of Hollywood to the intellectual superiority of the literary world and all it carries with it. Their eyes lock. The meeting proceeds, with Holly and Danny bluffing their way through it while he and Caroline screw with their eyes. She suddenly excuses herself, giving him the glance that unmistakably means I want you to fuck my brains out. He follows her twitching ass into a beige office with a large couch made for the purpose, and before they even get to the couch, he does exactly that.

"Holly!"

Danny Lowenstein's gravelly voice crushed the fantasy to pieces. Holly rose to shake his hand but Fred did not dare rise. He hoped his failure to stand would be taken as deferential—as Holly's assistant I am too inconsequential to be acknowledged, was his message. It seemed to work. He was unnoticed, as was Danny's assistant, who had shrunk into a corner when Danny came in.

Danny and Holly's exchange of pleasantries was actually a

pissing match: his movies versus her books that spawned his movies. Fred barely registered. Would Caroline follow through the door Danny had come in? Or from the door behind him? Was she usually this late? (Their meeting, scheduled for four thirty, was already running forty-five minutes behind and it hadn't actually begun yet.) How late could he be to call the twins if she wanted him more than once?

Jesus, Fred. Get a grip. Listen up.

"Mike sends his regards," said Holly. "He loves you. He loves the movies. He can't wait to see what you do with the next one. And he's so pleased that you were able to get Caroline Dester set up for this." She glanced ever so swiftly in Fred's direction. Oh, she knows, he thought. "Will she be joining us soon?"

"I love Caroline but Caroline's out of town," said Danny. "I set up this meet and greet with you and she skips out."

Fred caught his breath. What a stupid fool I am. Of course she is not going to show up for the author's agent. Much less for the author. The walls felt more windowless than they already were. Let me get out of here. What a schoolboy.

"It's August, Holly. No one's working except you and me."

"Oh, that is too bad," she said, "when we came down here especially. Mike said specifically I should meet her face-to-face so he could feel comfortable with her in the part."

"Mike will feel comfortable when he cashes the checks," said Danny, "if Caroline is attached."

"She did have that unfortunate moment at—"

Danny cut her off. "You know she's good for the franchise; she'll kill this part. It'll stretch her." He grinned.

Fred imagined Danny with a bleeding, broken nose.

Holly proffered the autographed "commemorative" edition of the new book that Fred had signed for Caroline. It was one of the hundred clothbound boxed copies Random House had had printed for collectors—an easy way for the publisher to make more cash in the age of e-books, and nice for movie stars.

"This was our leave-behind," Holly said with her don't-deny-me smile. "It's for Caroline."

"I'll make sure she gets it," said Danny. "Nice to see you, Holly."

The assistant rose to accept the book from Holly. She'd be pretty if she didn't look so scared, Fred thought. A young, scared Liv Tyler.

"Oh, I don't want to burden you with that. We'll send it to her," Holly said. "If you let us know where she is."

"All we know is she's on an island somewhere," Danny said. "We can't reach her."

Fred was defeated and humiliated. He signaled to Holly. "Your drinks date is next," he said in a quiet assistant voice. Montana gave a tiny smile of solidarity.

"Mike asked me to put this into Caroline's hands today," said Holly. "I'll fly it to Tenerife if I have to."

"If I could tell you where she went, I would," said Danny. "I'd do anything to get Mike's blessing on this casting decision; you know that. But I really don't know where she is. She texted me her coordinates before she left. My assistant is supposed to keep all my texts but she's an idiot and she deleted it." Montana blinked twice. The kid must be new, Fred thought with sympathy. "Too bad, Holly. It was great to see you. I'll let you get to your cocktails. Anyone I know?" He gave Holly the requisite air kiss. "The kid will take you to the elevator," he said and left the room. "If she hadn't screwed up, we could have helped," he said with utmost fake sincerity, and closed the door.

Holly and Fred wound through the long corridor back to the tiny entryway to the elevator. That's when Montana, bless her heart, spoke up. "I didn't screw up," she said, with something of a pout. "Here it is."

Fred's pulse raced. "Oh, well *done*," said Holly. "Fred, take it down, will you?"

Montana showed him her screen. Not only was Caroline's cell number in evidence; she had given Danny Lowenstein her precise location. Fred thought he could memorize the address of anywhere Caroline might be, but he couldn't memorize this.

44.333640° N, 68.049994° W

He took a snapshot with his own phone. The elevator door closed.

"*She'll* never work in this town again," said Holly. Fred, staring at his phone, did not reply. "Careful what you wish for, Fred Rose," she added. Fred barely heard her.

Holly's car was waiting but Fred elected to take the subway so he could search the jumble of numbers as he walked. He stood on the sidewalk outside Tribeca Grill and willed his hands to stop trembling. "If she's not in Maui, I'm going," he said. And she wasn't in Maui, that much he knew from the 44th parallel. "Come on, come on," he said as his phone churned. "Shit."

He must have entered the numbers wrong. Google was not showing an island. Would he have to wait till he got home to figure this out? He couldn't.

He took a deep breath, got himself onto the Google Earth site: much more accurate. He found it at once.

Little Lost Island, Maine.

Jesus Christ, she's on an island in the same state as Rose, he thought. Why can't I catch a break?

He Googled "number of islands in Maine" and the second site gave him his answer. God bless mainethingstodo.com, he thought.

Maine's coast is sheltered by as many as 4613 islands.

That was enough. He looked up from his screen and thought of having his way with Caroline on the soft moss of the forest floor as she begged him for more. He was going up there, if he had to row the whole way. He sighed a deep sigh. Maine is a very big state. Forty-six hundred thirteen is a lot of islands.

He whistled as he took the subway steps two at a time and planned his trip. "What are the chances?" he thought.

CHAPTER EIGHTEEN

*C*aroline was now getting pissed at Little Lost Island and its Little Lost denizens. What was wrong with them? She shouldn't be that much of a pariah. Especially in Maine.

She pulled off her stupid cloche and threw it into the woods. Let the raccoons get it, she thought. It'll look better on them than it does on me, anyway.

She passed a couple of women in large straw hats who smiled at her and said, "Evening." Caroline did not reply. Everyone was having fun here except her. It was time to go.

She pulled out her phone and started texting her pilot. He could be here in two hours. But the texts did not send. Which meant there was no phone signal. Why is there never any fucking signal on this fucking island?

She would drive home in the Mini.

Caroline couldn't remember the ferry schedule and she thought she might already have missed the last one. She was almost tempted to row across in somebody's boat but she didn't much want blisters or the humiliation of getting halfway over and collapsing of exhaustion and having to be pulled the rest of the way by some grinning motor-boater. Who would sell his story to *Hello!*

She remembered that the schedule was tacked on the bulletin board at the island post office, which was pretty nearby, wasn't it? She turned off the main boardwalk onto a side path through the woods. The post office was right in front of her.

The sight of the low building, with its spindly columns and wide porch, its sweet wooden sign with the island's zip code and its altogether hopeful aspect, cheered Caroline slightly. This is the post office that Isadora must have gone to when she was roaming the island in her long white pin-tucked linen dresses, Caroline thought. She mailed letters to the handsome buck her parents wanted her to marry and hid among them postcards to the young, earnest, bespectacled scholar she actually loved. Caroline had heard about the current postmaster from Lottie—he was an elderly former waterskiing champion who took the job very seriously and couldn't hear very well. He took an outboard to the mainland every day to pick up the mail and sort it into the heavy brass boxes with tiny windows, one for each cottage. Maybe he was a descendant of the first postmaster on Little Lost, the one who must have brought Isadora her mail. She would come down here early every morning to see if her scholar had written her again, hiding his elegant penmanship from her parents. Only the postmaster knew what was going on between them.

"Jesus," said Caroline. Where is my mind going? It's turning into mush on this island. The post office was closed for the day but the building was open. Nobody locked anything here. She checked the schedule on the wall. If she ran down to the dock she could get on the five-thirty. She'd drive to Boston and take a shuttle if they were still running. She'd be home by midnight if luck was with her.

She ran down toward the dock.

On the *Eleventh Hour* Max had already started the engine; she could hear it from the boardwalk path. She knew he would pull out if she wasn't on board at the stroke of the half hour, so she turned on the speed. One thing about movies: they keep you in good shape. She was barely out of breath as Max untied the boat. She walked calmly on and went upstairs to the upper level. Barely anyone was going over to the mainland on such a gorgeous evening. Why would they?

Caroline looked down at the shimmering water as the boat turned toward the shore. The lobster buoys were like confetti on the surface of the water. Max could pilot a boat, that's for sure. They skimmed over the channel to the landing.

This was kind of a foolish thing to do, now that she thought about it. She'd have to send someone to pack up her stuff. She didn't even have her license in the clutch she had brought to the hat party—a clutch that she had taken from the third floor of Hopewell, in fact. At least she had some cash in the pocket of her linen sundress, surely enough to get home by car. Just don't get into any accidents on 95, Caroline. Not the press you want right now.

A waterbird made a sudden dive into the water as they passed. Caroline still didn't know its name. She did know that she wouldn't learn it in New York.

The one she felt worst about leaving was Beverly. Naked Jon was pretty funny too, and Lottie, so annoyingly jolly. And she believed she and thoughtful Rose might have been friends.

Too bad.

The ferry pulled in to the dock on Big Lost. Max tied up. Caroline alighted from the boat. "Thank you," she said. She wanted to tell him that she was leaving and not coming back. She wanted to give him another chance. To give them all another chance.

"See you," he said.

Crushed, Caroline tried to get a signal again before she got in the car. There was nothing. She opened the door to the oven that was the Mini and started on the long road back to New York.

The city would be dead. No one is there in August. She could go out to the Hamptons to that richer-than-thou scenario, but after this it did not appeal. She could take the plane somewhere else, somewhere where no one knew her and she could figure out who she was meant to be. That was exactly what she had wanted to do on Little Lost. I am a little lost soul, she thought, aware she was full of self-pity. Wherever I go, there I am.

The road back to Route 1 followed the bend of the river into town. Caroline hadn't even known exactly what an estuary was till she got here and Rose explained. "It's a salt river we're on, not the ocean itself. A river with tides, a river that runs into the sea."

Rose could make anything sound like a poem. Their river was called the Dorset. Everything around here had an English name if it didn't have an Indian name. Penobscot, again courtesy of Rose.

Would it be easier to get the others out of the cottage than for her to leave? If she were all alone, no one to intrude, no one to say she was beautiful or luminous and no one to imply she was not, possibly then this exquisite place would be bearable.

Her phone dinged. She was back on the grid.

She was right in front of the Dorset library. She would text her mother and say she'd be out in the wretched Hamptons tonight and to leave the alarm off.

Before she could swipe open her phone, she saw what had come in when it dinged.

It's Mike McGowan. . . .

Who's Mike McGowan? she thought as she slid open the phone and scrolled.

The writer of the movie you're considering. One of the movies.

A screenwriter was texting her on her private phone? Where the fuck had he gotten the number? And the gall?

Caroline did not respond. Her phone dinged again.

Mike McGowan. I wrote The Benghazi Contraction. The book.

Oh, this was the author of the book. The secret genius. Why was he texting her?

How did you get my number?

Danny Lowenstein's office.

I'll kill him. **Why are you texting me?**

I want to see you. I need to see you.

Ah, this kind of message she recognized.

Give me one reason you need to see me. Half a beat. Was he hesitating?

Mon triste coeur bave à la poupe. :)

Ha! Texting in French! He's done his homework, I'll give him that. What does it mean, though—my sad heart dribbles on the poop deck? She knew it was a quote from something but she couldn't remember what. Caroline thought back to the short time she was at Brown. French lit was going to be her concentration till she took that eighteenth-century English novel class with that teacher she loved so much. Professor Phelan. Tweedy, bearded, though not pipe smoking, he was her vision of a college professor come to life. They read *Clarissa*, with which she struggled, *The Monk* for a laugh, and *Tom Jones*, which she adored. After Phelan, she was going to change her concentration to English, but she dropped out when she got the call for the Oliver Stone movie (which ended up not getting made).

Which was why her French was rustier than the publicists said it was.

Where are you?

I'm in New York but I could be there tonight.

Do not come tonight.

A gawper. Back away. Although, on reflection, a little admiration from a genius would not go amiss here. She was not going to regret toying with Mike McGowan.

Don't come unless you're prepared to tell me who you are. Who you REALLY are.

There was a pause then. Caroline had been told by asshole Danny Lowenstein how carefully the Mike McGowan myth was preserved.

To learn who was behind the name would be a coup, like finding out that Dan Brown was really Philip Roth.

She tapped the screen away to text her mother. Mike McGowan came back strong.

I can tell you in person.

He was persistent.

Not till I say so.

Please say so.

This guy had it bad. She looked up from her screen and smiled at a couple of little girls who were heading into the library. It was their late night tonight.

We'll see.

Caroline followed the girls inside. They peeled off toward the children's room, a festive-looking place that she'd go into another time. She went instead over to the fiction shelves. Patterson, O'Brian, O'Connor, McMurtry, McGowan. *The Pentagon Conscription* was there, but not the newest one. Or the one with a part for her, of course. He was still writing that one.

She looked back at her phone. No message from Mike McGowan, which was good; any more after her last would have been too much.

She went to the desk, where a tattooed librarian looked over chic glasses, waiting for her to make an overture. If you want something, ask for it, was the message in Dorset.

"Good evening." She used her most embracing voice. That good evening implied not only do I respect and truly understand librarians, but I also like your eyewear choice, which she actually did. The librarian smiled. "I was hoping to get a book by Mike McGowan."

"Oh, he's very popular," she replied. "We have a waiting list for his newest."

Caroline's face fell. She knew how to do bravely overcoming disappointment.

"It's not long. Three or four more weeks. I would order more copies if we had the budget." The librarian was almost too Yankee to glance in the direction of the Capital Improvement Fund donation can.

"Oh, I had so wanted to read it today," Caroline said. She didn't even realize she had used her own, genuine voice. Maybe the librarian recognized her. Maybe she just thought Caroline was an unusually needy book patron. But she reached under the counter and rooted out her bag, another chic little number, vintage alligator.

"Here, take mine," the librarian said. "I'm a blogger. The publishers give me advance copies for free. Mind you, give it back to the library's secondhand book sale, though." She withheld it until Caroline gave her assent.

"I will. How kind you are." She made a mental note to make a generous donation to the Dorset Harbor Library fund.

"Not at all," said the librarian. *A-tall.* "It's not very good."

"I'm sure you're right," said Caroline. "Thank you."

She studied the flashy jacket as she left the room. She ran her index finger over the raised letters of the author's name. MIKE MCGOWAN.

A genius? A gawper? A conquest? A diversion?

True love?

She took out her phone.

Little lost island, maine. She could still get out of this. **But not till I say so.**

An immediate swoosh back.

Please say so.

The Blue Moon

CHAPTER NINETEEN

*T*here was no excuse, really, for Robert to visit Little Lost. He had never, ever disturbed a tenant before. He'd waited for an invitation from his various renters for lo these many years but had not received one. This year he needed to make a visit, invited or not. He didn't want to spoil the magic of the house by arriving unannounced, but at the same time he had a sense that the island wasn't working its magic for this year's guests. For Rose, actually. Just for Rose.

It was enough, mostly, to have peace at his own place as well as time and money to play his music. But she needed magic, and frankly so did he.

Don't be pathetic, Robert.

The pursuit of love had driven people to schemes far more mad than driving up to Maine on a lovely August morning. He actually enjoyed bombing up through Massachusetts and the corner of New Hampshire and over the Piscataqua River Bridge to Maine. Even though it was a summer Friday, he hadn't encountered much traffic. He'd gotten in the car just a little after six thirty a.m. and it was only eleven thirty when he stopped for a stretch at the welcome post at the start of the Maine Turnpike. He'd do as he'd said he would when he wrote to Rose: visit a guitar maker he was friends with in Brooklin for a few days. Then if his ardor was still pricked, he'd go up to Little Lost.

The engine ticked as he turned off the ignition. He opened the door and took his first deep breath of Maine air. Sharp and thin and fresh, even in the dead of August, it woke up his body every time. He stretched his legs out of the car and made use of the facilities. He didn't spend long at the place, but took note of the pleasant-faced retiree behind the information counter and nodded as a longtime visitor to a real Mainer. He knew his place.

Robert indulged himself in a long reverie on the next leg of the journey. He imagined showing Rose the whole island, walking the periphery at low tide. He'd will a seal into view as they gazed out over the water at sunset. He'd look at her in the light of every room in the house. And he'd take her up to the third floor, the part of the cottage that was truly his home.

The traffic still wasn't bad, so when he got to Brunswick he decided to go up Route 1 instead of pounding up 95. He was only going to Brooklin tonight, not all the way to Little Lost. He thought about what it would be like to introduce Rose to the other islanders. They always liked couples more than single people there. Especially single people who hadn't grown up on the island.

Red's Eats traffic held up everything outside Wiscasset, as usual. He didn't mind, though. It was a pretty day, and the water, when he could see it, gleamed. If things with Rose didn't work out, maybe he would rent out in July next year and save August for himself. You really can't beat August in Maine.

The traffic was at a standstill, so he checked his phone as inconspicuously as he could while he still had a signal. He'd take a break before Brooklin at the Farnsworth Art Museum. Perfect idea. He could go see some Andrew Wyeths. He'd visit the paintings of Rose before he saw Rose herself. If they had any there. He couldn't remember.

He typed in "Wyeth Helga Maine Farnsworth Museum" and was surprised to see they didn't have Helga paintings in their collection. But among the search results appeared one from the Colby College Museum of Art:

Currently on View:

Andrew Wyeth: Helga on Paper.

He just caught the turn for 27 North. Waterville was practically on the way.

Over the next few days after the hat party, Lottie made more friends on the tennis courts and was the first to be invited to tea in the Little Lost Tearoom. "It's like being in a village in eighteen eighty-two," she said, "but with teeth whitening."

"I don't even think they whiten their teeth here," Jon said. "They're just born with those genes. And then they're out in the sun all the time getting tan, so no wonder their teeth look so white. Lots of wrinkles, though. Unlike you." He squeezed her from behind again.

"*My* mom!" cried Ethan.

"Mine, too!" said Jon.

"Mommy is not your mommy," said Ethan. "Mommy is my mommy."

"Who's *my* mommy?" asked Jon.

"Grandma?" Ethan answered.

"Yes, Grandma! Let's call her, Ethie," Jon said. He really should phone in to see how his stepdad was doing. "Want to take the fast ferry into town with Dad? That way you can have some time to yourself, Lottie. You've earned it. And I," he said, picking Ethan up and lifting him overhead, "can call in to the office to see what happened at the meeting this morning, if they remember who I am." It had been a full week since he gave them the fake pneumonia excuse and now he was going to miss the client meeting. Time was hard to calculate here.

"Wait!" said Lottie. "I'll come with you." She gathered up her bag and sunglasses. "I hope in a way they don't remember who you are, Jonnie. We could all move up here and become glassblowers in town and sell Christmas ornaments to summer tourists."

"Dream on," said Jon. He took Ethan's hands and swung him down the porch stairs. The screen door banged as they left.

Lottie, Jon, and Ethan were a happy, goofy unit: the three of them with their dark hair and big eyes and loud voices. Now that Caroline had recommitted to Hopewell Cottage, she took more of an interest in them as a family. She would never have been friends with them in real life, but here, she was.

She watched them go. She'd heard enough of the conversations from her upstairs porch to know that Jon did not much like his job. She'd love to just give him and Lottie a year's salary, but he wouldn't take it. (Lottie might.)

"They're not a bad bunch," Beverly called up to her. He was below her, knee-deep among the ferns.

"Beverly," she said. "You have emerged from your lair."

"It's such a beautiful day. I wanted to take a walk but then I saw this."

Caroline couldn't see what he was referring to. He was standing in a patch of weeds.

"This garden needs seeing to. Come help."

If anyone was going to summon Caroline, it would have to be Beverly. She took her own large-brimmed hat from a peg on the wall and descended the stairs to the garden. Or what Beverly called the garden.

"This is not what I would call a garden," she said.

"Have you ever had a garden?"

"No. We never stayed in one place long enough."

"It's what I call a garden. See? Here's a peony trying to hang on. And on that other patch, you can see a trellis." She could just make out a wire frame among the overgrown ferns. "That was a vegetable garden. There must have been tomatoes once upon a time." She liked that he said *tomahtoes* so unself-consciously. "We should turn that bed for next year. And pull out the weeds in this one. Trim back the *Rosa rugosa*, too. Those roots will be a bear to pull up; they spread everywhere. I hope you are strong."

Caroline was not at all sure what he was talking about. The only thing she recognized was the black-eyed Susans, which Wills had written into their *Frozen Peter Pan*, which reminded her that she needed to do something about costumes for their play next Wednesday. She was actually glad she'd caught a ride back to Hopewell from the library that night.

"If anyone took the time to come in the spring they could plant some nice flowers here. Look, these lupines have reseeded. Catnip would grow like a weed here. Of course it practically is a weed."

"Beverly, how do you know so much about everything?"

"I know very little about anything," he said. "I did not enjoy the privilege of a university education."

"You cook, though, so beautifully, and you know about flower gardening."

"And vegetable gardening. And herbs, actually. We could set up a modest kitchen garden while we're still here. Since none of you is particularly good at remembering to bring me herbs from the dock."

"Did your father teach you all this?"

Beverly rubbed the bridge of his nose and bent down to pull up some weeds. "If you don't mind too much, perhaps you could help me. An herb garden is simple enough that we might achieve it in the time we have left here."

"Which ones are the weeds?"

He sighed and pointed. "Start here," he said, "in the flower bed. In the vegetable patch we should dig everything up. Then you could call that young lunk, Max, to work the soil. There must be compost on this island somewhere. Then we can plant herbs for right now and bed the rest down for the winter. I imagine there's more nitrate in the kelp on the beach than in horse manure."

"Come on, Beverly. Were you a landscape gardener? Did you run a large household in England?"

He kept pulling up plants. Weeds. "If it's not too much trouble—"

Caroline resumed pulling. If I pull he'll talk.

"Get them by the roots, Caroline, if you please."

She let the only sound be the ripping up of plants for a while. She was careful to take only what Beverly pointed at, and to get them by the roots. It was satisfying work.

"If you must know," he said, "I went to the garden when I was a boy to get out of the *way* of my father. He did not like that I was a 'different' little boy. He didn't mind, either, that my brothers pushed me around. They were younger than I was, but he considered them manlier."

Caroline kept silent.

"We had a staff. It was more common back then. Bridey was the cook and Joe Meade was our gardener. They were married. Irish. Her face was a map of Clare, she used to say."

"Vivid," said Caroline.

Beverly sat on a stone wall that Caroline had not noticed before.

"Theirs was a mixed marriage. I didn't understand it till later, but he was from the North, and Protestant, and she was deeply Catholic. Both sets of parents were against it. So they understood something about being not quite up to expectations."

Caroline nodded and kept weeding.

"My mother had to back my father so Bridey took care of me. She cooked and I chopped. Joe gardened and I weeded. After a while I picked up quite a few things."

"You certainly come in handy around this house, Beverly. This cottage."

"It's quite pleasant here," he said. "Even now with Lottie's Jon here. And the boy."

"Ethan."

"He's afraid of me, I think, which is just as well."

"They're not doing awfully well, Lottie and Jon," said Caroline.

"I think they're doing quite well," said Beverly, "from the tousled way she emerges in the morning. Quite well indeed."

"They seem to be happy, but Jon seems awfully weighed down by his job." She wanted to sell it, but not too hard.

"He's a lawyer, is he?"

"I think he is, yes."

"If he doesn't like his job, he should be happy that he doesn't have to attend to the kinds of things Gorsch expected me to attend to. Papers, letters, *e-mails*."

"That is right up his alley," said Caroline.

"If it's up his alley, he should do something about it."

"Sounds like a fine idea," said Caroline.

Saturday morning, Beverly opened the suitcase he had been dreading looking at the entire time he was there. Two and a half weeks already. He had barely settled in, but it must be dealt with. The conversation with Caroline had stirred him up.

Gorsch had left an ironclad will that gave Beverly very little to do. The instructions were clear: Frank E. Campbell and then a benefit at Weill Recital Hall. Done. The old lawyer took care of everything, and his last official act was to move all the accounts to Beverly's name. So many death certificates. The one thing Gorsch had asked him to do— *one* thing, in all the years—was to act as musical executor when he was gone. And Beverly had agreed. Anything to stop Gorsch talking about death. Yes, I will be your musical executor even though I have barely a musical note in my body, said Beverly, stroking Possum, and so now he had a job. He'd never really had a job in his life.

This suitcase was his job. Letters from ASCAP. Letters from high schools and community theater companies. And God knows how many e-mails. Those he could not even look at. He despised the computer.

This Maine cottage was to be his refuge, if not his strength. He would apply himself to all these needy people and decide who could sing what, and how they could sing it. The new lawyer had told him more than once that he'd do anything he could to help him. "Just give me some avails and we'll set something up." But what were avails?

He wanted to be kind to all these people who were so needy, and who loved Gorsch's music so much. Goddammit, he missed Possum.

A cup of coffee would help him get started, but dammit if Lottie had not taken the coffeemaker out of his room, where it by rights should have stayed. She was enforcing community and he wanted none of it. Beverly was paying his fair share for this place and if he wanted a coffeemaker for himself, he should have it. Now he would have to go downstairs and talk to people before he'd had his own cup of coffee in his own room. He was quite sure it was deliberate on the girl's part. She was forcing them to be a group of people who actually spoke to one another before breakfast. Well, he'd show her.

Beverly pulled on his bathrobe, a gift from Gorsch ("It's raspberry, not brown"), and slipped on a pair of striped espadrilles that he'd bought for next to nothing when they traveled to Sanary-sur-Mer to taste the bouillabaisse. (Gorsch had been a good millionaire: he'd had no trouble spending his money once he got used to having it.) They were shot to hell but he could never replace them. He trundled downstairs. The knees, the knees.

Someone had already been in the kitchen, as the pot of coffee was minus a generous cup. He opened the cupboard door to locate his favorite mug, HARVARD 1955, the year he might have graduated from the august institution had he had a different father, and not been a pervert.

How many of those Harvard crimson lads were having fumbling, sweaty encounters with each other in the boathouse on the Charles? Beverly thought. A lot. If I had only known.

"Good morning, Beverly!" chirped Lottie as she came in through the pantry to the kitchen. He still had not got the lay of the land on this floor. Every day seemed to uncover a new room.

If he were not such a slow mover he would have had time to stop Jon and her from pouring coffee into their own mugs as they bounded into the kitchen, clearly delighted with themselves for having had some sort of sexual encounter before breakfast. Their little one must be a sound sleeper. Jon was pouring himself all but the dregs of the pot when he saw Beverly's empty mug.

"Coffee?" he asked.

"There's none left."

"I'll make you a new pot." He went over to the tap to rinse out the carafe and started to fill it.

"Not with that water. I'll need springwater for my own coffee. The tap water is barely potable."

Lottie came over and gave him a kiss on the cheek. He only flinched a little bit.

"Isn't it a beautiful day, Beverly? *Potable*'s a good word. Where did you come up with that?"

"It's in common usage," he said. He knew it wasn't these days, but Gorsch and he had had many discussions about potability when Gorsch traveled, especially in Mexico. "I wouldn't touch my lips to that water."

"Lottie's been getting the water from the spring, haven't you, Lottie?" said Jon with a prideful grin. "Let me get it now, though. It's awfully heavy to carry."

"Have you been down there yet, Beverly?" asked Lottie. "To the springhouse?"

"No, and I don't intend to go."

"Why don't you and Jon go together?" she said, as if she did not understand English. "I'll stay here for when Ethan wakes up. He sleeps like a baby here."

"Better than a baby." Jon flashed her a lascivious grin. It did not go unnoticed by anyone. "Come on, Beverly. You take my coffee, and I'll have the next pot, but we'll both go down to the spring together. Then I have to go into town again. Even fake pneumonia only lasts so long."

Jon handed him his own mug, MBNA AMERICA BANK, and Beverly took it.

"I hope they believe you," said Lottie, "about the pneumonia."

"I made it sound like I was about to croak." He coughed, for effect. "I'm well enough to get springwater, though. Come give it a try, Beverly."

There was something rather charming about Jon, and he did have those very tight buttocks, so Beverly found himself saying yes before he could think better of it.

Lottie gave her husband a lot of fairly lengthy instructions about how to pump the water and the least cumbersome way to carry the cooler and not to forget to fill up the primer jug, and Jon took them all with admirable patience. He fetched the cooler that stood in the pantry and motioned for Beverly to follow him out the back door.

"I'm not going in a bathrobe," said Beverly.

"I'll wait," said Jon.

Beverly took his time changing, but Jon was true to his word.

Beverly was not so steady on his feet anymore, but the path to the spring was easy, the way well worn. "Tell me about Possum," said Jon. The walk went quickly after that. Beverly heard himself talking about all the years they had been together. Which led to all the years he and Gorsch had been together. Which led to the suitcase full of letters. Jon was an admirable listener.

The ground near the springhouse was a lot spongier than the rest of the path, and as they approached the low roof that covered the pipes, things got muddy. Beverly was not fond of mud. "I've walked enough," he said. "You go from here. I'll watch. Mind you, don't soak yourself, or you'll have to strip off again." He heard Gorsch's snappy voice in his head—"You should be so lucky"—and he smiled.

Jon was manly, but he was clearly confounded by something as old-fashioned as a water pump. Beverly knew just how to work one—there had been such a mechanism on his own grandmother's farm in deepest New Jersey, a place that at the time was as undeveloped as this. Jon had clearly not listened to his wife because he started pumping vigorously and no water was manifest. The hand pump was noisy and clattering, rusted in places, surely built in the gay nineties. It was older, even, than Beverly. And it would function if Jon knew how to do it.

Jon turned to him and smiled warily. "I'll get this going in a second," he said and redoubled his efforts. Beverly might have reminded him that he needed to prime the pump first, as Lottie had actually told him, but he enjoyed the working of Jon's muscles in his remarkably thin T-shirt, and so withheld comment until Jon stopped again.

"There's got to be something wrong with it," he said. "I'll find someone to fix it. Robert should be told." Jon was clearly not used to being unable to achieve what he wanted. Beverly thought again of Lottie and how cheerful she looked this morning.

"Have you heard the expression 'prime the pump,' Jon?" he said. "It's used crudely in some circles, but it does have a specific meaning."

Jon looked at him blankly.

"Do as your wife said, man. Pour some water from that jug on the left—"

"The blue one?"

"I wouldn't know, as I'm color-blind," Beverly said, patiently, he thought. "Either one. I'm sure they're both left there for the same reason."

Jon inspected two jugs, both of which looked a dull gray to Beverly. "That's right," he called as Jon gestured to him with a full jug of water. "Then pour water from that jug into the pump"—Jon started pouring—"*while* pumping. I'm sure a strapping man like you can do it."

And indeed he could. A few more pumps of the handle and the

water gurgled loudly, bubbled up from the fecund earth, and splashed with shocking abandon onto Jon, who was standing in the way. He moved out of range quickly.

"No nudity—this is a kids' island, now!" he said to Beverly with a grin.

As the beautifully clear water cascaded into Jon's coolers, Beverly smiled to himself. The water made Jon a little boy. The striving lawyer was washed away, not to put too fine a point on it.

"Could you take a look at the business with the music while we're here?" asked Beverly before he could think better of it. "Gorsch's music?" His voice caught in his throat but Jon could not have been aware.

"Sure. I'd be happy to." He ran his hand through his hair. He was wavering. What could he be thinking about?

"Oh, money," said Beverly. "Are you thinking about money?"

Jon grinned. "Not your money. I had been thinking about how to bottle this water and sell it in Brooklyn. But now that doesn't seem like such a cool idea. Want to taste this, Beverly? You won't believe how cold it is."

He filled one of the gray jugs with fresh water and brought it over to Beverly. "Try it," he said. "Cup your hands."

Beverly did as he was told. Jon poured the water into his hands and he recoiled just a bit from the shock of it.

"It's so good," said Jon.

His wrists were almost numb from the cold as he lifted the water to his mouth. This was water you could taste—tangy, iron water that pierced his right eye with cold.

CHAPTER TWENTY

*L*ottie reflected on her August sojourn. This was already their third Saturday at Hopewell. So far it had been shockingly marvelous. In fact, she was afraid that she would tempt the gods if she enumerated all the things that had gone right on Little Lost Island. Jon and she had had a ton of sex, for one; here she was, doing laundry. She actually loved doing laundry on the island. The washer and dryer were not in a dingy basement as they were in her apartment building in Brooklyn. There were no quarters to scrimp together. She didn't have to wait to get into a machine.

No, here the laundry room had a view of the trees and the path down to the springhouse. She could just dump her laundry in a pile near the washer and do it at her leisure. She even picked up Beverly's laundry and did his, as she was quite certain that he was not a laundry doer himself and he would be embarrassed to admit it. I am Dobby the house elf, she thought, but liberated.

The cottage had a long, squeaky clothesline on a pulley that seemed to have been installed before Lottie was born but still worked if you applied a little elbow grease. She pulled the sheets out of the washer and put them in the garish plastic basket so she could hang them on the line.

She knew even as she was romanticizing the hanging out of sheets that she was romanticizing the hanging out of sheets. But it was hard not to. Clothespins were just not a big part of life in Park Slope. And they were such a clever invention. There was a basket of them in the laundry room and then another bag of them out by the line. She debated the merits of the two kinds of clothespins that she encountered: the very old-fashioned kind with the button cap and a split up the middle—no metal, no spring, just wood. She liked them the best. They didn't always hold the clothes so well, though. But they were so smooth and kindly. They were kind clothespins.

The other variety, more modern, vintage rather than antique— those she knew about already. They were good for small things, especially. She liked to hang her bras from the line. Now that she was having sex again she thought they looked saucy instead of forlorn.

The sheets were the best. They were big and clumsy to get situated on the clothesline, but once she had them set up properly, they billowed in the wind and bleached in the sunshine like sails. And when they were dry and back on the bed, they smelled like the outdoors.

Today's was a sheet load. Two and a half weeks here and a lot of the visions she saw when she arrived had already come through. Jon was here, and Ethan, so her most important predictions had come to pass for herself, which was nice for her but not so nice for everyone else. Rose had blossomed like the rose she was, and Lottie was rooting for Fred and was still very sure that Rose would invite him up, maybe even today.

She tugged on the line again. Beverly seemed to have a crush on Jon, or at least he was flirting with him just the tiniest bit. That was good for both of them. There was nothing Jon liked more than atten-tion, and he got it from Beverly and then gave it back in return. The mess of letters and e-mail printouts in the suitcase had been reduced to neat piles, and only two of those piles comprised really tough chal-lenges. Beverly promised to answer one of them a day with Jon's help, and they had made a good start. It gave Beverly an excuse to talk about Gorsch. He really needed to talk about Gorsch, Lottie thought.

She pulled another sheet from the basket and tossed it over the clothesline. She straightened it out and pinned it to the sheet before it, taking care to economize on pins, even though there were hun-dreds of them.

"I think Jon has actually been fired," she said aloud. He hadn't been able to get on the firm's network yesterday, either on his phone or at the library terminal. If we were home I would be a wreck, and he would be out of his mind. "I'm glad we're here."

She gave the line another tug and listened to the impossibly loud chatter of the brown squirrels in the high pine trees—no, spruce (she was learning)—overhead. Squirrels were just not this noisy in Pros-pect Park. It was like they were a whole different breed here. In fact, they were.

They'd have to leave this place eventually. Real life would rush in. She wondered what they would do to pay the mortgage. And tuition bills. Bartending was good money; a start.

The fitted bottom sheets were a pain to hang up and a worse pain to fold. Lottie usually just rolled them up into a ball and stuffed them in the tiny linen closet at home. She'd had a German boyfriend once who insisted that fitted sheets were an abomination, and would not lie down in a bed that had one on it. He had been sleeping with his former girlfriend the entire time they were together, so she went out and bought herself two deep-pocketed fitted sheets the minute she'd booted him out of her tiny Alphabet City apartment. But he was prob-ably right about fitted sheets.

All these sheets reminded her of ex-boyfriends. Only one of them was good at doing laundry—he had, in fact, taught Lottie how to iron shirts: sleeves first, then collar, and then the reward of the body of the shirt. That was before Jon and his neat white boxes from the dry cleaner. He wouldn't have to wear those shirts if he'd been fired. They could just hole up here and gather mussels and huckleberries (she knew the difference now between them and blueberries) and eat off the land.

Of course, the house wasn't heated. Or insulated. It would be bit-ter here in the wintertime. Romantic, but bitter. Plus, they didn't own the cottage. A small wrinkle.

Lottie shook out the last sheet from the clothes basket. Rose had seemed romantic yet angry when she got to this place, but now she just seemed romantic. Romantic without an object of her affection. Lottie had no doubt that Robert SanSouci was coming here because he had an interest in Rose. He wanted Rose, married or not. But did he really want Rose, or just someone to take care of? All men want that. All people want that.

I am a philosopher here. Dobby the house-elf philosopher.

Caroline was only too happy that Beverly had by now taken over the kitchen almost entirely. His meals were simple, delicious, and effort-lessly prepared. All day yesterday he was simmering lobster shells on the back burner and that night they had a lobster bisque that she would never forget. Beverly in the kitchen was different from Beverly everywhere else in the house. A dictator, yes, but no moping here.

"If you're not going to help at all, and I'd rather you didn't," Bev-erly said on Saturday evening, "then you might at least set the table."

Just as Caroline's voice could never be anything but honey, Beverly's manner was never anything but peremptory. It was just the six of them, again. Caroline was still dangling the author on the thread of her texts; she'd found a place, in a corner of her third floor, where she could get a little bit of service. She wondered if she should tell the others she'd be having someone come up. Her own summer visitor.

The sunsets took their time here; even now at seven thirty it felt like daylight would never end. The low, sharply angled sunlight streamed through the western windows into the kitchen.

"Shall we eat in the dining room tonight, Beverly?" asked Caroline. It would make a change from the old spindle-legged table in the kitchen.

"Dinner will be on the table at eight o'clock," he said, "and I don't care what table as long as everyone is seated and everyone is appreciative." They'd had a little trouble with getting Lottie seated.

"Then I think we shall migrate to the dining room," said Caroline. She was already picturing herself there with Mike McGowan. She wanted him to love the cottage as much as she did.

She had been to town twice to text him before she found the hot spot. He was clever and ardent and he said he was writing a part just for her. She liked the idea of a writer. She hadn't had one before.

They had barely been in the dining room at all. It was musty. If this were my place, I'd take down those curtains for a start, Caroline thought. There were two walls of windows, one looking south, the other east. Very wise to have the dining room out of the fierce light of the setting sun. She liked this old architect more and more.

She reached for a chair so she could get the curtains off their rails. They were clearly additions from the sixties—brown and orange wide-weave affairs with overlarge flowers on jungle-like stalks. The chair didn't budge. A further pull determined that it wasn't stuck to the floor—it was just inordinately heavy. There wasn't a stick of furniture here that was flimsy or made to be worn out. They built for generations when they made things back then.

She dragged the chair to the first window and lifted off the curtain rail. Much better. As she stood there looking out from on high she could see the mountains off in the distance. If the trees were not in leaf you could see so much more. "How would it be to be here in the winter?" she called to Beverly.

"Very cold," he said. "There's not a shred of insulation in this house, if you'll recall."

Of course that was true. Still, as Caroline dragged the chair from one window to another, she thought of fires in the fireplace and a dusting of snow on the ground. "It would be pretty, though," she said. "We could have tons of people. They could sleep in that big Hogwarts room and pretend they're kids."

"If you wanted them to freeze to death," said Beverly. "Where did Rose put the garlic?"

Caroline didn't answer. Now that the curtains were down and sequestered in the sideboard, the room was much more alive. It needed air, though.

She tried to get the windows open, but only two of them would move at all, and not without a struggle. It took all her strength and a lot of maneuvering. "*Fuck*, this is hard," she said. "Why doesn't anyone take care of this place?" The window opened with a shriek.

"Caroline, what on earth are you doing?" asked Beverly. He came in from the kitchen with half a peach in his hand. "Isn't that best left to young Max? This is dripping. And peach juice stains." He disappeared back into the kitchen.

"I'm getting some air in here," Caroline called. She followed him in. "What are you making tonight, Beverly? You are a talented old

205

fellow." She gave him a kiss on the cheek. He brushed it off. They all liked to give him kisses on the cheek to see if he'd let one stick.

"Nonsense," he said. "Gorsch was the talented one."

She pulled up a stool. Also heavy, but mobile. "Tell me about Gorsch," she said.

"Oh, there's nothing much to tell. We were great friends for many years."

Is he not out of the closet? Caroline thought. How sweet to think that he's keeping something private. How did anyone keep anything private? "Did you cook for him?"

Beverly measured balsamic vinegar into a cup and poured it into a small saucepan, which he set on the stove. "Yes, I cooked for him. Not this sort of thing. Gorsch liked simple stuff. Overcooked meat and potatoes, mostly. But you don't want to hear about that."

"I do want to hear. How did you meet?"

"Are you setting the table or interrogating me?"

"Both," said Caroline. "Are you simmering? Can you come into the dining room with me? I need your opinion."

"I'm reducing, so I suppose I can come in for a moment." He adjusted the heat. "How I despise an electric stove."

They went through to the dining room and Caroline was already cheered by what a difference it made to have the curtains down and the windows open. The room was not dreary at all.

"No plates?" said Beverly.

"They must have better stuff than what's in the kitchen. What's in here, do you think?"

She opened a sticky door to a dark cupboard or closet or pantry. She did not even know the words for these storage places. There were no closets in the bedrooms, but downstairs there were cupboards all over the place. She had learned by now that most of the electricity at Hopewell Cottage was governed irrationally, so she waved a hand in front of her into the dark of the closet and sure enough it hit a string that connected to a lightbulb, which was a nice, regular one, and not a twisted fluorescent. It gave off a dim light.

It wasn't Aladdin's cave, but it was full of treasure. The wooden shelves were filled with crockery. Stacks of dinner plates, luncheon plates, chop plates, bowls. They must have been collected and added to over time, as none of the plates were particularly standard.

"Oh, blue willow pattern," Beverly said, barely loud enough for her to hear.

"What's blue willow pattern?" said Caroline.

Beverly took the plate out of her hand. He held it for a long time. He was barely aware of Caroline next to him until she asked, "Wasn't that the name of Gorsch's big hit?"

He looked at the blue-patterned china: three figures crossing the bridge, the two birds flying, touching wings. "You know the story?"

Of course this exquisite but callow girl would not know the story.

"I don't," said Caroline.

"Two lovers adored each other," Beverly said. "But they were unsuited."

"Sad."

He traced his finger over the crackled glaze. "This is an old one," he said. He flipped the plate over. "You see?"

She looked at the smudged stamp on the back of the plate. "Is that good?"

"England is always good when it comes to china and gardening," said Beverly. "That much they should have taught you in elementary school."

"I was on set."

"No excuse." He turned the plate over again. "The princess grew up in a palace. See the palace? It's hard for me of course because—"

"—you're color-blind."

She mocked but he would not rise to her bait. Not this time. "Indeed. The princess's mother adored her, but as I say, the father was a different matter. The father had chosen someone else for the princess to marry."

"Typical," said Caroline. Beverly did not smile.

"But the princess knew she was not cut out for a life with a suitor of her father's choosing. She loved another, but he was not welcome. Not welcome at all." He concentrated on not allowing his hand to shake.

"Who did the princess love?" Caroline's low voice.

"She loved a boy."

"The wrong boy?"

"Very much the wrong boy."

"Where are they on this plate?" Beverly watched her scan the willow-pattern plate for the two lovers.

"You won't find them there," he said. "They tried to escape the father's wrath by sailing away in that boat. But the father and his two younger, *loyal* sons were ever in pursuit."

"Not a very nice family," Caroline said.

"The gods showed them mercy, and turned them into birds," Beverly finished. "They mated for life."

"What a beautiful story," she said, her eyes tracing the image on the plate. "It must be quite ancient."

"It was made up," said Beverly, "by the china maker. To sell plates."

"No!"

"It was. A beautiful ruse. But it bore some similarity to . . ."

"Someone close to you?"

"A little, yes." He touched the bridge of his nose.

"You mated for life?" asked Caroline.

"Gorsch made a song of it. The story's in the verse, not the chorus, so not everyone knows it. 'Blue Willow.'"

"I know that song," she said. She sang in a quiet voice:

Two lovers,
Their flight of innocent grace.
One palace,
A vast impregnable place.

Gorsch would have written songs for this voice, Beverly thought. He closed his eyes and listened to her sing. She had pitched it just right.

Father, brothers
All intent on breaking the pair.
Willow tree blows skyward
As the birds float on air
Blue willow . . .

She didn't sing the chorus. Beverly let her last note fade to silence.

"My sauce will be reduced to nothing if I don't get in the kitchen. You might do better to lay those plates out than to stare at them."

Caroline leaned close. "Before you go."

This time, when she kissed his cheek, he didn't brush her away.

"I don't know if I told everyone," Rose said that night when they sat down to Beverly's superb chicken with balsamic peaches, "but our cottage owner, Robert SanSouci, is coming up for a day or so on Monday. I hope it's okay."

Rose had gotten into the habit of being the salad maker, and tonight she'd used soft Boston lettuce from the farmers market and basil from the window boxes on the dock. Instead of corn they had blueberry scones—frozen from the specialty store they'd discovered in Dorset Harbor—slathered with butter. Caroline got Max to lay in the wine (no more chardonnay, foreign or domestic), so they were drinking something brilliant that Rose didn't recognize. Jon was taking Ethan for a sunset cruise on the Whaler, so it was just the four of them.

"Robert SanSouci is coming?" said Caroline. "Is there room for him?"

"There's tons of room," said Lottie. "No one's even in the boys' dorm. That has to have six beds at least."

"He can have Kenneth Lumley's room," said Beverly. None of them actually believed in Kenneth Lumley by this point, but it was said in all seriousness.

"That's very generous of you, Beverly," said Lottie. "I think it would be nice for Rose to have someone up here. You don't mind, do you, Caroline?"

"He's not really coming up here for me," Rose said. "He was passing by."

"Nobody passes by Little Lost Island," said Caroline. "Also, I might have a friend come up next week."

This was news. They were going to have a full cottage.

"Great," said Rose. Everyone will be here but Fred, she thought.

"I'm not cooking for massed thousands," said Beverly.

"We could order in," said Caroline.

"We already order in," said Lottie.

"You actually can get people over to the island to do a lobster bake," said Rose. "There are all kinds of signs in the Harbor."

"I know. Jon took their number. It will be nice to have Robert here. I think he has a little crush on Rose, even though she is a married lady," said Lottie.

"He could add frisson," said Beverly.

"Just as long as he doesn't make himself too much at home," said Caroline.

CHAPTER TWENTY-ONE

*T*hat night, after dinner had been eaten and Jon had done the dishes—very helpfully, he thought—Rose told them the story of Max in the library.

It was cold enough to make a fire that night and Jon was the designated fire expert. Except that he wasn't actually that great at it. "Is this the flue? Is it open or shut?"

"It should be open," Lottie said. They were both looking up the chimney. "What did he say exactly?"

"He said, 'In case Meredith was talking, Kitty dumped me.' And then he left."

Jon wasn't really following the conversation. Something about librarians and the handyman. "Is there any kindling?"

"Caroline brought in a bunch of sticks before it started raining," Rose said.

"Very prescient of her," said Jon.

"Or just very smart," said Lottie. "Caroline is the smart one—isn't that funny? You don't think of movie stars as smart."

"Lottie, you must learn not to say everything that comes into your head," said Beverly, but not unkindly. "It will be the undoing of you."

"She's come undone," said Lottie. "I know that from somewhere. So what do you think was the reason, Rose? What's Kitty like?"

"I don't know. I don't even know who she is. Her friend seemed nice enough."

"We have kindling, but what about wood?" asked Jon. "Is this fire really worth it?"

"A fire is always worth it," said Lottie. "You'll make a gorgeous one, Jon, I know." She was so nice to him up here. Was she always this nice, and he just didn't notice?

"The firewood is in a pile under the back stairs outside," said Beverly. "You must have seen it."

Jon had not noticed. He wound his way through the narrow hallway into the kitchen and out the door to the back side of the cottage. The air was wet and cold and the night was black. The clouds that had brought the afternoon rain must have been still overhead because Jon could not see the moon or the stars. He took a deep breath. The lights from the house threw some light his way, but not much. No wonder everyone carries flashlights in their pockets around this island. He needed a flashlight. Maybe I can get one of those headlights that people wear camping, he thought. They're so cool but I'd feel like an idiot in one back home. Here all that gear actually made sense. He and Ethan could have matching headlamps. Dad and lad.

Jon felt tears prick his eyes. Seriously? I'm crying about Ethan wearing a headlamp? This place is going to wreck me.

There was a wood carrier right next to the pile and Jon stacked it full. He'd take in a huge pile and then they wouldn't need to get any more for a few days. He'd be a hero.

The wood was heavy and awkward and it took him a while to get it back to the living room—or the east sitting room, as Caroline had started to call it. She had disappeared from their little cluster again that night. She fixed up the house during the day and holed up in her room at night. She wasn't a joiner.

Jon hoped that they would have stopped talking about that poor guy Max by the time he got back. Relationships are tough, for sure. But not as tough for him up here, where it wasn't real life.

"Oh, Jon, do you need help?" said Rose.

"Primitive. Man. Make. Fire," said Jon. He dropped the firewood with a huge clatter.

"Down, boy," said Beverly.

Caroline was not about to let on about the third-floor hot spot, where she got to carry on with Mike McGowan. It was such a relief to be online again—albeit very slowly and crankily. She must have been picking up a neighbor's wireless, or some faint signal from the mainland. Whatever it was, she was happy for it. Although it made her a little sick at the same time.

He was a gawper. He would stare and he would grab—oh, not literally, of course. He'd be much too refined for that. But she would be a conquest for him. She'd give him boasting rights. That's what they all wanted with her. And with it, of course, came her own sense of power.

tell me why you want to see me so badly

you are exquisite.

you are sublime

Guide par ton odeur vers de charmants climats

He was laying it on with a trowel. **Not one I know.**

214

Baudelaire

Keep going

Je vois un port rempli de voiles et de mâts

Okay, that's good.

It's the one about fragrance and charming climates and ports with sails.

Thanks, I got it. Maybe that was a little too barbed. She toned it down. **do you like lobster?**

lobster is mother's milk to me

That was lame for a genius.

Sorry that was lame. I like lobster a lot.

Should she ask him?

you could come up for the lobster bake next Wednesday night

No immediate swoosh. I bet he's all bluster.

I'll be there.

and then if I don't like you you have to go

She didn't even know what he looked like.

Send me a picture.

A pause, then a photo. Black-and-white. Brooding. From the nineteen . . . twenties?

Isn't that Buster Keaton?

She knew it was not.

Maybe.

Bring your boater hat. But if I say you can't stay here . . .

. . . then I'll drive 500 miles, have a single claw, and drive back.

Wednesday at 6ish on the west shore. Ask anyone

just in time for the mosquitoes

I'll be bitten to shreds

She knew he'd want to write, "Before or after I'm with you?" and if he did she might rescind the invitation.

I'll cover you with calamine.

nite

nite

She moved away from the wireless space. It was like an electric fence—get too close and you'll burn. She was burned.

But why on earth have someone up here? He'll tell the papers; it will be fodder for the bloggers; the publicists will make it into a story for *next* year's Oscar race, except that she wouldn't be in next year's Oscar race. He probably had a wife and three kids—she'd be cast as the home wrecker even if nothing got wrecked but her own damaged heart. The only thing he had going in his favor was that he didn't want to be discovered either. She wondered again who he was. People said Michael Chabon for sure. Neil Gaiman had come up. Didn't those guys have wives who were both super hotties, though?

Oh well, everyone likes to cheat.

Isadora Osgood Saunderson wouldn't have cheated on her earnest, ardent, bearded young scholar, would she? Caroline went back to the picture album that she'd looked at so many times up on that attic floor. There must be other pictures of her when she's older, Caroline thought. Did she marry him? Were they in love their whole lives?

Too bad she hadn't kept a diary. But most of those diaries back then were pretty restrained—chronicles of daily tasks and accomplishments, not of feelings.

She held up Isadora's dress in front of the mirror for the umpteenth time. It made her feel bad this time, like she was cheating on Isadora herself.

One thing was for sure: she was not going to let Mike McGowan up here in the attic. This was her place. No one could come here unless they were worthy. And Mike was already not worthy. She heard an explosion of laughter from downstairs in the east sitting room. The cottage smelled like firewood. It would have been nice to join them tonight, Caroline thought. Instead of texting.

She looked down at her phone. There was one last message.

it'll be a blue moon.

CHAPTER TWENTY-TWO

*B*right and early Monday morning, Robert arrived on the island on the eleven a.m. ferry.

As he wound his way up the hill toward Hopewell, he reminded himself that, other than the cottage—which was, admittedly, staggering good fortune—he was not much of a prize. Too thin, too nerdy, too much a product of the seventeenth century, even though he was only thirty-three. But with his two older parents having been so distant, as a boy he'd filled himself with stories. *Tarzan* was a favorite, then science fiction, and then somewhere in the spring of his junior year in high school his elderly parents took him to an all-Bach harpsichord and lute recital at Chapel Hill and he was smitten. He taught himself guitar when all the other kids were playing soccer, and then it was a short hop from there to the much coveted lute. Actually not such a short hop—lutes were not much in supply in North Carolina, but a very kind music teacher, who may or may not have had designs on Robert, put the antique instrument into his hands and he was transported. The ravishing sound of the strings, the resonance of the large body, the sheer woodenness of it—not to mention its antiquity and the vast diversity of the repertoire. Guitars were his friends but the lute was his love.

What would Rose think about falling in love with a lutenist? It could happen, couldn't it? Someone who looked like Helga could love him. Lots of people could have loved him if he weren't such an oddball.

And he *was* an oddball. Several girlfriends had told him as much. His great love in college, Maeve, was the first to say so. Maeve, second youngest of a large brood of Catholics, may never have encountered anyone who could be called poorly socialized, but that's what he'd be labeled if he took one of those personality quizzes. But he was also all the good things that came with that: fiercely loyal, intensely devoted, and, because he thought so little of himself, dedicated to making his lovers have a superb time in bed.

Robert had the geek's capacity for the study of detail, and he applied an almost academic rigor to the female body. He liked women of all stripes and, for an unassuming fellow, had rabid fantasies about what he might do with just about anyone in bed.

All that said, he was loath to make the first move. Loath to speak up on his own behalf. Unwilling to sell himself. That's why he let the cottage do it for him.

Oh, it was a cheap ploy, he knew. There was barely a soul alive who could go to Hopewell Cottage and not fall in love with it. He'd tried this before, God knows, and a couple of summers ago it almost worked. But that woman—Arlene, bad name—turned out to be in love only with the cottage and not with him at all. And in fact, she wasn't really in love with the cottage as it was. She wanted to add a satellite dish and rip up the kitchen. That was it for her.

Robert hadn't taken any of them up to the third floor. He told them all it was just filled with mildewed crap that he needed to get rid of eventually. Not even Arlene had been up there, and he had spent half of June and all of July with her there. (She was a teacher—long summers.) She loved the turret room on the south side of the cottage, the one with the rose prints, although she didn't like the prints and brought books of wallpaper samples from as far away as Camden, along with other ideas. They could have been good ideas if she had been the right person. He just wished she had liked him as much as she did the house. Or the idea of the house.

But she hadn't, and eventually he had ended it, awkwardly of course. Now he was foolishly doing the same thing again this year. Life presents us with the same lesson over and over again until we learn it, one of Robert's wiser friends always said. Here we go with the same old lesson.

And then there she was.

Robert was startled by how much more striking Rose was here on Little Lost than she was even when he'd first seen her. She belonged in this landscape.

"Robert? Is that you? I didn't think we were expecting you till later."

"No, I'm here." Stupid thing to say. Obviously he was here.

"Nice to see you again. I was just on my way to town but I think I may have gotten the ferry times wrong."

"The ten thirty has pulled out," said Robert. At least he could be helpful about island things. Rose's stoic Wyeth face got more stoic. "But let me take you over in the Whaler. Is it tied up on this side?" He hadn't noticed it when the ferry tied up at the wharf, such was his determination to see the woman who was now next to him. Lovely though she was in this warm August light, she was less happy to see him than he'd fantasized she would be. Of course what he fantasized was not likely to happen in the middle of the path to the ferry at ten forty in the morning. Worse luck.

"Forgive me, I'm so distracted," said Rose. "I have a Skype date with my kids and I'm getting a little frantic. My sister set it up—she's with them for the month. Or they're with her for a month. I have to get to the library. I can't have missed the ferry, can I? Lottie blew a fuse last night and all the clocks went out."

Robert would have spoken sooner but he was far too distressed at hearing that she had children to respond. If she had children, did it mean she had a husband? And if she had a husband, where was he? Here?

"Why didn't you tell me?"

"That I had a Skype date?"

He composed himself. "Oh, no, sorry. No, why didn't you tell me you needed a lift across to the mainland? I'll take you. Unless you want to run up to the cottage and get your husband? There's room in the Whaler for all of us."

"Oh, thank you so much. Can we go down to the dock right now? I don't want to miss them. I miss them so much already."

"Yes, yes, of course. I can take you right into town by boat. We'll get there quicker than by car. I'll make sure you talk to your kids."

"Oh, thank you, Robert!" Her face lit up. I'm her hero. He pressed his suit as they walked fast down to the dock. "How nice for you and your husband to have this holiday away from the children." Rose did not reply. Was he here or not?

"This boat! I was so scared of it the first day we got here, and then I jumped out of it to rescue a hat!"

"That sounds dramatic," said Robert.

"It was!" Rose smiled. What a terrific smile. "It's a lot less threatening now."

"It's a good old tub," he said. "Not much for the open seas but it will get you to Dorset Harbor in no time. Craft fair at the Dorset Green on Mondays, which means traffic. Could you untie?"

"I think so."

It wasn't completely fair of him to ask her to untie when he could as easily have done it himself, but this way he got that satisfying rear view of her as she undid the bow knot without much difficulty. "You're getting to be a sailor yourself," he said.

"My husband always says the elegance of a knot is in the untying, not in the tying," she said. "This must have been an elegantly tied knot if it was easy for *me* to undo. We'll get there by eleven thirty, won't we?"

Robert pulled the cord twice and the engine caught. "We'll be there in half an hour," he said. "Less." He maneuvered the boat around the lobster pots and gave it plenty of gas once they were out of the no-wake zone. It wasn't easy to talk over the drone of the motor, so he didn't try. Rose was looking out over the bow as if she were a figure-head. She called back to him, "I reserved the computer terminal at the library from eleven thirty to twelve. They're usually good about it, aren't they? They seem nice there. I don't want to miss the kids." There was a catch in her voice. All at once, Robert pictured himself with an instant family: two children (what kind? how old?) and perhaps another one or two to round out their happy home. They could populate the dormitory room with loads of kids and their friends. They could field a baseball team, if only he knew how many people were on a baseball team.

Was the husband here?

"I think they're doing well at my sister's. And they should be—all that space! But I haven't heard anything for the past four days and it's kind of killing me. When I see them I want to go back to them. But when I'm here I'm here."

They skirted around the channel marker that would lead them into Dorset Harbor. He wanted her to keep talking, even though he could hear only about one word out of three over the sound of the outboard. He was piecing it together. Kids with sister. Husband possibly not here, so Robert was in with a chance.

"We'll tie up at the public dock. There's usually a space there." He slowed the engine. "See if you can spot an empty cleat and then just loop the rope around it."

"Don't go in too fast!" said Rose. "I'm not good at this."

"Any slower and we will be in neutral. In fact"—he put the engine in neutral—"now we are in neutral. You hop off and I'll tie up. See?" He looked at the clock tower in the white clapboard Congregationalist church that was Dorset Harbor's architectural prize. "It's not even eleven now. You have tons of time."

"Will you come with me?" Rose smiled at him. "I'm not sure how to get to the library from down here."

"I'll show you." He took another chance. "How nice for you to see your husband and kids, even by Skype."

"My kids, yes, not my husband," said Rose. "I mean, he won't be there."

"He's not at his sister's?"

"My sister's. No, he's at home. At home in Brooklyn."

That was all it took for him to be back in bed with her, in the turret room with the roses that conjured her name. "Here's the library," said Robert. "I'll wait."

The twins were having a blast.

"*Mommy!* I can see you!" Ben shoved Bea out of the frame but Bea fought back. She was learning. Maybe it helped not to have Mommy intervene. Something to think about, Rose. "*Mommy!* You're in the computer!"

Rose was crying with relief and love and missing them. "I'm here, you guys! Oh, you look so good. You have *blue lips*. What have you been eating?"

Here proceeded a long conversation, if you could call it that, about the many different FrozFruits Aunt Isobel had offered them while they were staying with her. They were mostly making faces at themselves in the Skype frame, but that was fine. It was all fine. "Are you having fun? A lot of fun?"

Isobel had gone all out, of course, and there was a bouncy castle in her backyard for the weekend, and all the kids from the neighborhood were coming over to play. "Don't worry! I'm having it catered!" she said as she squeezed in the frame. "This is great for them. They're living on FrozFruits. It's brutal here. How's Maine?"

"Maine's great. Are they okay? Are they sleeping? Is Ben hitting?" Or biting, she didn't add.

"He's hitting enough to be noticed. But there are big kids here, don't forget. They outweigh him!"

"I could come back if it gets to be too much."

"HIIIIII MOMMMMMMMMMMY!"

"Hi my sweet pea sweet Bea!"

"I made Ben cry!"

She couldn't say, "That's good," but she applauded Bea's gumption. "Well, try not to make him cry, but I'm glad you two are playing together."

Ben began doing something that was making screeching noises in the background. "I'm moving the chair!" She loved the way he said it: *chay-o.* "Watch me moving the chair!"

They were having a ball and Fred and Isobel had arranged it all.

She had an urge to talk to him, to see him in front of her. To have him next to her in bed at night and wake up with him there.

"I'm really fine with them here, Rose. Fred could go up and see you. What's it like up there? Where are you, anyway?"

"We're Down East!" It was such a funny expression for being so far north they could practically swim to Nova Scotia. "On an island off the coast. In a cottage. Maybe the kids will come here someday." She was feeling expansive. "Maybe you'll all come here someday."

"Rose, they need me out in the yard to break up a fight. Talk to you in a couple of days?"

"Okay—same time Wednesday. No, Thursday. Wednesday's the lobster bake."

"It's just a parade of clichés up there. Are you catching your own lobsters?"

"Not yet! Tell them I send my love."

Isobel waved and the picture froze. Rose closed her eyes, took a breath, and let her shoulders fall.

"Are you over and out?" Robert's voice behind her startled her. "Were they wonderful?"

She smiled broadly. "They were! They're great. They're actually doing okay without me."

"And you are thriving?" he said. He hoped he made the question sound funny.

She grinned. "You sound like a doctor."

"I give you not only a clean bill of health, but an excellent prognosis."

"Oh, and what is that?" she asked. It was fun to flirt.

"My prognosis is that you will enjoy a rich and healthy life if you and your darling children come up to Maine once a year from now till death—"

She cut him off. "Now till death? Yikes." Had he been going to say, "Now till death do us part?" She barely knew him. A little crush was okay but she wasn't ready for a proposal.

He was making an effort to gather his wits back together. "Well, let's just say I hope you come up here for many years."

He was amusing, if a little professorial and Ichabod Craney for her taste. "I don't think we've even found every room in the place yet. We keep discovering new ones. I told the others you were coming and they said you can have Kenneth Lumley's room." She smiled again. They already had Hopewell Cottage in-jokes. "If you stay till Wednesday you can join us for the lobster bake. Lottie's husband, Jon, thinks he has someone lined up to come over and make it all happen."

"He's having it *done* for just the six of you? That's not very Hopewell."

"What *is* very Hopewell?"

"To do it ourselves!"

"Do you think we can manage? There are only"—she counted—"seven of us. And one is three years old. Is that enough?" Rose had no idea what a lobster bake entailed. Lottie said you bury the lobsters in the sand, but that seemed fairly unlikely.

"We just need people who are willing to put some muscle into it. I'll be one of them, if you could really see me staying that long."

"Perfect. And Jon can be the other. We're doing it on Wednesday night because it's apparently a full moon."

"It's a blue moon, in fact," Robert said.

"But it's only the middle of the month. That doesn't seem right. Isn't it supposed to be the second full moon of the month?"

"There's some technicality about it this year," Robert said. "I can't remember what." Fred would know, Rose thought. "But Google says it's a blue moon so I believe them."

They didn't spend a whole lot of time in Dorset Harbor, which pleased Robert. He preferred to keep away from town. They left the library, went back down to the dock, and looked for their Whaler. It had been moved by another boater, with a larger craft.

"Do they just do that? Move boats?" asked Rose.

"It's the law of the sea," said Robert.

"Or the law of the jungle."

Robert untied this time and started up the engine. The ride back to Little Lost was smooth, as the tide had just turned. The clouds looked a little ominous, so Robert concentrated on getting them back quickly. He was pleased that, for a musician, he was pretty good with boats.

They were easy in each other's company and quiet on the path back up to the cottage. The ominous clouds had quickly blown over and the sun looked like it was going to make a comeback.

"I think that cottage needs a lot of people in it, doesn't it?" Rose remarked. "Otherwise it could be kind of a lonely old barn."

"A lonely old barn, yes," said Robert. She was so right. "But it doesn't always have to be that way." He looked at her again with his soulful eyes. "You really do look like Helga," he told her. "The Andrew Wyeth woman. I didn't need to stop at a museum to see her. She's here."

"You've had too much sun," said Rose, who knew she looked exactly like Helga. "Time for you to meet the others."

CHAPTER TWENTY-THREE

"What's that box, Beverly? Want me to open it up?"

Jon was at the point of taking the box right out of the suitcase before Beverly could stop him.

"That's not letters," Beverly said. "That's mine."

"Not to worry," Jon said, and Beverly was pleased that he used that more old-fashioned phrase. But this box was nothing but worries. This box was all he had left of his dearest friend.

Beverly slept little, even here where the night was so inky black and so deeply quiet. When he'd opened his eyes this morning he'd looked to the sky to see if there was even the smallest glint of light in the east. That, or a single bird in song, would be enough to tell him that the night was over. He did not enjoy sleeping alone.

The porch of his turret room stretched around the side of the house—the cottage—so he could see the dawn break from there. He had taken the old coffeepot back up to his room, so he made a cup of coffee, used the bathroom (without flushing—noises were very loud this time of morning), and went outside to watch the dawn.

He took Possum with him.

Possum was in the box—well, the remains of Possum. The *cre-mains* of Possum, as the awful people told him when they gave him what was left of Possum after they had killed him. The vet had killed him, after all. He had still been living some kind of life before Beverly broke down and took him to the pet hospital downtown. He had thought Possum would come out better, but he came out dead. And now he was in this box.

Gorsch would have known what to do. Damn Gorsch for leaving everything to me.

Gorsch had truly left everything to him—the houses, the money, the music rights. Beverly was a very rich man, no doubt. But Gorsch had also been good at *facing* things, making the right decisions. And now he had left that to Beverly too.

The wretchedly noisy lobster boats began their assault on his senses. Their motors were as loud as any garbage truck lumbering down Madison. And their music! Radios playing at top volume as the lobstermen yelled over the sound. They weren't even the craggily handsome lobstermen of those television programs that Beverly flipped through too late at night when he couldn't sleep. He couldn't see them properly from up here at the cottage, but he could tell by the way they moved that they were not his type. Brawny, though.

Beverly had never thought much about how a lobster got to a plate, but Jon had explained that all those buoys in the harbor were actually painted different colors, and each color was the mark of a different lobsterman. Another occupation that's out for me, Beverly thought. If 12 percent of those lobstermen are color-blind, they must be pulling up the wrong lobsters.

That's what the buoys were attached to. Traps, down there on the seafloor. The traps were complicated affairs—Beverly had seen them in stacks on floats in the water, in driveways on land, in piles on wharves; they were everywhere. Lottie had looked it up in the library. Apparently there was bait in one compartment and then for some reason of physics that she had not taken in, the lobster would get caught in another compartment where it would wait till it was pulled up and taken out by the lobsterman. There was some complication about size and tail notching that Beverly had not paid attention to. He was more interested in eating lobsters than in hearing about their capture.

He liked that they were about the freshest thing you could eat. Alive one minute, hot and steaming the next. They didn't have nerve endings, anyway.

Possum had shrunk to almost nothing by the end. Everyone in Beverly's life was always dying, first when they were all young and now when they were all old. And all he could do about it was watch the sunrise.

"Good morning, Beverly!" He was startled by Lottie's bright voice. She was like one of these birds: a little too energetic but not unwelcome. "I know this is your private balcony but I wanted to share the sunrise with somebody and you're the only one up. Do you want some company?"

Of course he didn't want company.

She looked at the box. "Oh no, Beverly. It's Possum, isn't it?"

How did this woman know things? She came nearer. Don't touch that box, he willed. Do not touch Possum.

But she didn't touch Possum. She knelt down at his side and took his hand.

"Shall we sit here with Possum for a bit and watch the sunrise?"

It was a question that did not need an answer. They sat with Possum as a solitary lobster boat churned its way across the channel and the buoy bells sounded, Beverly with Possum in his lap, and the deep and lasting impression of Lottie's hand on his.

Rose had promised Meredith she would finish the book reorganization in the library. Robert did not notice when she slipped out of the cottage and headed to the east shore. She was relieved that she had managed to shake him for a bit. Yesterday, just after he arrived, he had shown her the other two springhouses on the island; the meadow hidden on the far side of the west shore; the old stone wall built far before the leisure class made their way in steamboats to Little Lost. And yesterday evening as she read, wrapped in a blanket, in a green rope hammock, he picked up his guitar just before sunset and played (hauntingly) from the porch. She was flattered by his attention, and rueful. Right time, right place; wrong guy.

She heard the banging before she went through the library door. There was Max, building new shelves.

"Morning," said Max.

"Morning," said Rose.

She got to work. There really were a lot of good books here. It must have been heartbreaking to see so many of them wrecked by the leak. She leafed through the sticky pages of an old one on Maine seabirds. It made her want to see a puffin.

She and Max worked in comfortable silence, other than the hammering. She salvaged quite a few more Maine volumes, and she was ready to start shelving when suddenly the door banged open. The girl who walked in was wild-eyed. She spotted Rose. "Is Max here?" she said. It was almost an accusation. Rose looked at her blankly. "Oh, sorry," said the girl. "Where are my manners? Kitty van Straaten." She extended her hand.

The hammer banged. Hard.

"Max!" The handshake didn't happen. This girl Kitty headed straight for Max. She was going to either throw him down on the floor of the library and ravish him or hit him with the hammer. Rose shrank back.

Max kept hammering.

"Max, stop! I need to talk to you!"

He didn't stop.

"We can't talk if you keep doing that. Don't keep doing that!"

He kept doing it.

Kitty was so angry she was shaking. I know you're furious but please don't mess up my books, Rose thought. She didn't mess up Rose's books. Instead, she swept up Max's brown paper bag of nails, tore it open, and threw the bag across the floor. Hundreds and hundreds of nails went everywhere.

Then she left.

The hammering stopped. Rose wasn't sure whether to stay or go. Max started picking up the nails, one by one.

"You from New York?" he asked.

It seemed an irrelevant question under the circumstances. "Yes— Brooklyn," she said. "Let me help." She started sweeping up the nails with her hands.

"I'll do that," he said. "There's a lot of rich bastards down there, aren't there?"

That was a little bit of a shock. Did he think she was a rich bastard?

"Some."

"Good, then she'll have her pick," said Max. "Or she'll just end up with one they pick *for* her."

Rose didn't say anything for a while. Kitty must live in New York,

Rose thought. Max was picking up the nails deliberately, one by one. "Wouldn't want to miss one, since the islanders are paying for these."

Whoa.

Rose wanted to put her arms around him. "Love's hard," she said.

Max said nothing.

Rose left the library a little while after that, her books unshelved. She thought about Max and his problems, and about her own, too. The attentions of Robert SanSouci, rather than leading Rose away from her husband, drew her to him. She wasn't what Robert thought she was: she loved the cottage, but she didn't want to move in there with him, as he seemed to think she did. She missed the twins desperately, and she missed Fred. She just wanted things to be simple and easy again. She wanted to connect with him without always putting the twins first.

Not to mention, he would love to be here for the lobster bake.

She got up very early the next morning, with the crows. It was too early to go down to the ferry, so she listened to them argue for a while. Ben would have liked hearing them. They were loud. She wondered what they were saying, because they were definitely saying something.

She was fully awake now. The crows might as well have been inside the house, they were so noisy. Maybe they were telling her to go down to the seven thirty ferry and drive into town to send Fred an e-mail to come up in time for the lobster bake tonight. There was a lot one could read into a series of caws.

Rose crept out of bed and went down the hall to the bathroom. Beverly was usually awake at dawn—she could hear him padding about his turret room—but she could easily avoid seeing him. Only Lottie could deal with Beverly in the morning. She slipped some clothes on, not even thinking about a shower or coffee, and went into the kitchen. She had gone to bed early last night, when the kitchen was still a mess from dinner. Now it had all been cleaned up. Was it the fairies? Or possibly Jon?

There was a note on the kitchen table in what she thought must be Jon's handwriting. It was an invitation, or a command:

You are cordially invited
to attend
a celebration of the life of
POSSUM
on Sunday, the twenty-third of August,
at three o'clock in the afternoon.
Please RSVP below.

Jon and Lottie had already signed up. Caroline, too. Rose smiled, and signed her name with the stubby pencil next to the invitation. It turns out Jon was a good guy, even though from the way Lottie had described him before they got to Maine, she'd thought he would be a monster. Not a monster, but an unfeeling prick. He certainly had the capacity to be an unfeeling prick—ambitious lawyer, status conscious; plus, he was tall—but he was more like a kid than a grown man. He followed Lottie around like a Labrador. He and Lottie were having fun and Ethan was easy to have in the cottage. The place needed kids. Ethan spent all day with a passel of island boys and girls and was too exhausted to wake during the night. Plus, Jon seemed to like doing dishes. As she headed out the back door she noticed some changes to the cottage decor. Now the multitude of dusty pillows on the windowsill in the little west sitting room had been removed too—gone with the curtains, Rose supposed. Without the clutter of the motley cushions, the deep amber of the old wood shone in the morning light.

Rose was relieved that she got out of the house without seeing any of her fellow housemates, especially Robert. She took a deep breath of the spicy, clean air. In the stillness of the morning, she could see the spiderwebs of the night before, the dew on the grass. There were a few other islanders heading down to the early boat. Some of them she had met at the hat party and to those she nodded hello. There was a garrulous group of trim older women in shorts and running shoes going over to the mainland for their early morning walk.

"Can you join us for our walk?" one of them asked. Rose could not remember her name.

"Thank you. Not today," Rose said.

"Maybe tomorrow," said the walker. "We'd love to have you."

Rose was touched by the unerring politeness and genuine generosity of these tough old New England birds—not just the early morning walkers, but the much older women who were taking boats back and forth, hauling carts of groceries up and down hills. It was like a conveyer belt: towheaded kids to harried blond parents to ash gray tennis-playing grandmothers. Did they just go on forever?

"I don't see why renters would want to walk with you, Susan." This was said by an imposing woman sitting in a corner of the ferry. She wore crisp white pants and a cotton sweater, with pearls. Was this the woman who'd stolen Caroline's strawberry-rhubarb pie? "She won't know anyone you're talking about. And she'll be leaving before you know it." Rose took her place inconspicuously on the ferry's upper deck. There always had to be a bad fairy in the mix, and this lady was it.

The woman called Susan untied the ferry from the dock and it backed out into the channel. Max was not driving it today. It was a high school kid who did the seven thirty run: Warren.

The water was glassy and the wind was still, and they were over on the mainland before Rose could really settle into any thoughts, except that she had yet to see a seal. She got off, walked up to the car, was massively relieved that she had remembered to leave the car keys in her bag, and drove into town before she lost her resolve.

Fred really should have e-mailed her by now. Maybe he'd decided to surprise her, and was already on his way. She looked at her phone as she drove—no bars till she was right down in Dorset Harbor. There were only a few cars parked in the lot near the library, so she had her pick of spaces. She turned in to a spot that faced the water, still not quite over the fact that there was always a parking space, and almost always a parking space with a killer view.

Under the portico of the library she checked her phone. No texts and no messages from Fred. Never mind—she wanted him here, Lottie saw him here, he would love it here, they would be themselves here. It took her six drafts, then she texted:

Hi sweetheart. It's me. Could you come up to Maine? Maybe today even? If you start now, you'll be here in time for the lobster bake tonight. Hopewell Cottage, Little Lost Island, Maine. Love you, Rosie xx

CHAPTER TWENTY-FOUR

*T*he little notebook that held several generations' worth of recommendations for putting together the perfect lobster bake was on the mantelpiece, where it had lain for many years. Robert leafed through it. The handwriting was familiar to him, not because it evoked any member of his own family, but because he had looked in the book so many times thinking how marvelous it would be if he ever had a cottageful of friends who together might make an event like this occur.

And now he did.

Robert had taken the Whaler into the Harbor very early that morning to get the supplies they would need. He'd taken his orders right from the notebook; his father's cousin was apparently the authority. Robert recognized the name signed at the end of the entry titled "Lobster Bake for Hopewell Cottage—USE THIS ONE. July 1993."

He did not have any recollection of having met Jim Sprague, but he had every confidence that Jim Sprague had known what he was doing. He had used Jim Sprague's shopping list as his own that morning:

Lobsters—one each unless they're soft-shell, and in that case up to two each

Corn—people say they can only eat one ear but get at least two apiece

Potatoes—Chris brings new potatoes down from his root cellar, so use those if you can. Otherwise get them at the market. Half a pound apiece.

Onions—Deeda is no fan of onions and says they're not traditional but people eat them so get one apiece.

Steamers—nowadays you're supposed to check the red tide levels with the Coast Guard but we just rake them up at Harrop Point Beach.

Robert had got the potatoes and corn from the farm stand in Dorset. He grudgingly bought onions, too, though like Deeda (another cousin?) he didn't think they belonged. He had remembered butter, too, which Jim Sprague had not included in the ingredients list but which featured later in the narrative. Or recipe, rather.

The fog had already burned off, and the radio—and the sky—told him the good weather would hold all day. After reading the booklet over and over last night, he figured he could just about do the whole thing by himself, but it would be so much better if they joined in and did it together.

This was about Rose, of course.

Rose was married, yes. And she came with kids, whom, granted, he had yet to meet. So it was complicated. But she had filled the cottage with her friends and changed the look and feel of it and everything now seemed possible. It could be like this every summer. He could take possession of the place. The lobster bake would be the place to start.

He imagined Jon would be the one to help on this. He was a guy who'd like to show off. They could show off together—Jon for Lottie; Robert for Rose. Robert put the feisty lobsters in the fridge and left the other food in the cart on the back boardwalk. He wondered if Jon was up yet.

Robert made coffee with the new pot Jon had bought in the Harbor; he liked being up with the birds. It was something he rarely did in New York (no birds). In Maine he woke up and smelled the coffee.

He took the coffeepot out onto the front porch and consulted the lobster bake notebook again. There were a lot of opinions as to how to go about this ritual. Many people had weighed in on the issue. Men, mostly, from the look of the handwriting. There were instructions for an all-island affair—150 lobsters! Three hundred ears of corn! That was not what he was after today. An intimate cottage lobster bake: just enough to impress. He flipped through the pages.

Start early. Don't leave it all till late in the day because for one thing you'll be tired and for another you won't get the fire hot enough and that's the whole trick of it. Hopewell has the best spot for a bake right down on the little beach with the sea glass. Pick a day when the wind is from the south so you don't get the bugs blowing in from the mainland. A day with just about no wind is good too. The fire can blow.

"Will this be a mistake?" Robert said aloud.

"Will what be a mistake?" Jon asked. He had padded onto the porch without Robert's noticing.

"The lobster bake."

"We're doing it ourselves, right?"

"I thought we'd give it a try," said Robert. "My ancestors had a lot of ideas on the subject. I've done it once or twice here but I didn't know there was an instruction book at the time." He'd tried one for a bunch of early-music people the first year he came up to the house. They had pretty much winged it, and the fire hadn't been hot enough, so nothing got thoroughly steamed. They ended up boiling the corn on the stove and ditching the sandy potatoes.

The ill-suited Arlene insisted he do a lobster bake for her friends from the city, but when they were attacked by mosquitoes that bit through even their black leggings, Robert ended up bringing everything inside for what was ultimately a rather somber meal.

"Everybody's going to have ideas on the subject," said Jon. "Even if they've never done this before. What do they say in there?"

Robert handed him the book. "This part I've done," he said. "I picked up the lobsters in town this morning. And the other food too. Then he says to start early. It's only eight thirty, so I think we're good so far."

"What about the wind?" asked Jon.

"I don't think we're getting much wind today. The water was pretty still this morning."

"'Dig yourself a pit on the beach above the high tide mark. You don't want to start your fire and then worry about the water coming too close to it,'" Jon read. "Smart. 'Be generous with the pit. You'll be digging in sand so it won't be much work. Two foot by four foot should do it for a cottage crowd.' This whole thing is, like, a day's work."

"We're doing work?" asked Rose.

Robert wasn't prepared for this new version of Rose. She was glowing. Had she been up for a morning swim? Or a run? She looked exhilarated, and Jon told her so, flashing his signature smile her way.

Why don't I have a smile like that? Robert wondered. His was so tentative, reserved.

"What have you been up to this early in the morning?" Jon asked.

Rose sat on the swing glider and beamed at them both. "I've been on a secret mission," she said, "more or less because Lottie said I had to. Let's hope she's right. I think she might be." She smiled at Robert, her pale Wyeth eyes bright. "What are you two plotting out here?"

"We're plotting the lobster bake," said Jon. "It's a gigantic amount of work."

"An activity for all of us," said Robert.

"We have to dig pits and make fires and throw seaweed on top of burning coals or something."

"It's going to be a production," Robert added.

"I love a production," said Rose, and she touched him gently on the shoulder. He wanted to feel it all through his body but he only felt it on his shoulder. "Weren't you going to show me the old bathhouses today, Robert? I want to see as much of the island as I can." She seemed to be hugging an idea close to her—Robert continued to hope that it was to stay here on the island. To get to know it, intimately, and to stay forever, with him.

Rose should love this event, Robert thought. He didn't have Jon's smile and he wasn't her husband, obviously, but he had this cottage and he knew (vaguely) how to put together a lobster bake. He imagined her eyes shining as he raked the embers of the fire. "You can do anything, Robert," she'd say. In his dreams.

"We need a galvanized tub," she said. She was now reading the directions too. "'Next year I would start the fire at two p.m. and cook the pot until the seaweed on top has changed color to the ochre yellow color it gets when it's cooked.' Whoever wrote this wasn't color-blind."

"Do we have all this stuff?" Jon asked Robert. "A tarp? Seaweed? You have to soak the tarp in water."

"The tub is under the house. The tarp, too. They should be, at least. If they're not, the whole thing is off. I should have checked." He wished Jon would go away and he and Rose could plan this together. "There's a diagram here, I think." He flipped the pages. "Here you go."

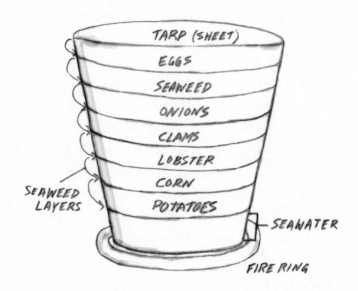

TARP (SHEET)
EGGS
SEAWEED
ONIONS
CLAMS
LOBSTER
CORN
POTATOES

SEAWEED LAYERS

— SEAWATER

FIRE RING

"'If you put eggs on top and they cook, check the tub after one hour!!' What does that even mean?"

"It's a test for doneness," said Robert. "If the eggs are hard-boiled, the whole meal is cooked. But I actually think it's easier just to let it steam for an hour and twenty minutes or so. At the end you put a pot of butter on the very top. It melts fast."

Jon had continued to flip through the lobster bake notebook. "I think we need to start hunting and gathering now. This is a lot of shit."

Robert wanted Jon's help but he didn't want him to take charge. "I suggest we look around under the cottage and get all the stuff together. I already checked the tide chart on the dock, and low tide is at five thirty-seven tonight."

"We'll need to eat early, though, so we can get to Caroline's play. Eight o'clock curtain."

Robert had yet to meet Caroline. He didn't give her too much thought. Rose had described her as an out-of-work actress. He sympathized: the life of a performer was not completely in one's own control. She was probably the brassy type who sang show tunes with too much vibrato and did a lot of stretching.

"Everything will be cooked to perfection by five thirty. And we'll have plenty of beach. The water has been going way out the past couple of days."

"That's because it's a full moon," said Jon.

"A blue moon," said Rose.

CHAPTER TWENTY-FIVE

*T*he whole day was devoted to the lobster bake. Lottie and Jon ended up digging the pit just after noon, when the tide started to go out. Robert brought the wood down to the beach. Rose was about to shuck the corn when he sweetly told her it was better to leave the husks on.

It was nice to have Robert as an admirer, even if she felt more like his big sister than like a potential lover. He needed someone to adore, that was clear.

They did everything Jim Sprague told them to do; he was almost like another participant in the preparations. Beverly cut the onions. Rose scrubbed Chris's potatoes (even though they weren't really Chris's potatoes). Jon carried the charred galvanized tub down to the beach, along with the tarp, all under the cottage as Robert had said they would be. Ethan collected seaweed. Lottie even managed to find the two bricks Jim said they had to have to support the tub.

If Fred comes up tonight for this, it will be almost too perfect, Rose thought. She didn't want to get her hopes up too high.

Caroline was absent most of the day at her play rehearsal with the kids. She wouldn't let anyone know what they were up to, but from the costumes she'd collected around the cottage, Rose surmised it was something *Peter Pan*–ish.

"Were those in your room?" Rose asked. "Our dressers were completely empty. We checked."

"I just found them in the cottage," Caroline said vaguely. "I'm sorry I can't help more. I'm heading out to the Little Lost Opera House."

"Is there an opera house, too? I thought you were doing this at the assembly room."

"We are. But we're calling it the opera house tonight," Caroline said. "I'll be back down for my lobster. I can't believe they have the fire going already." From the porch, the smell of the woodsmoke was strong. "I *adore* a wood fire."

"Robert at work," said Rose.

"Lottie says he's mad about you. He's doing this whole *production* for you."

"Unfortunately, I'm married. And he's not my type. Too tweedy."

"I like tweedy," said Caroline.

"He thought I was the one who feng-shui'd the living room. I told him that was you," Rose said. "He's not a gawper, by the way. He didn't even know who you were. I said you were an actor and he asked if you were out of work. I told him I thought you just had this island play on your plate for the moment. He was very sympathetic. He's a musician, so I'm sure he knows about being out of work. He liked that the dining room was brighter too."

"I'll meet him at the lobster bake and take a bow," said Caroline.

Robert looked for the old key for the door to the third floor. He wanted to go up there without using the trapdoor in the out-of-work actress's room. Caroline. He found the iron key where it always was, under the admittedly ugly hooked rug made from scraps by one of his more frugal relatives. He didn't have the heart to get rid of any of the ugly stuff in the cottage, and there was quite a bit of it. Even after ten seasons of ownership, he still felt more like a cottage caretaker than like a cottage owner. Robert was devoted to Hopewell, it was true, but it did feel pretty cavernous when he was there on his own. By the end of the first long September he'd spent in the house, he had quit the first two floors altogether and established himself on the top floor. He put his bed against the biggest window. He had a chair for reading and he stashed his collection of lesser-loved guitars and lutes on the walls. He was not much of a handyman but even he could hammer a couple of nails into the soft wood of the walls to hang up his collection. He unstrung most of them when the season was over, but the humidity here was good for them—even in the winter there was always moisture in the air.

He had yet to go through the many trunks and boxes and photos and papers that he'd inherited with the house. There would be time enough for that.

He could be happy here with Rose, her Helga face across from his every morning, her two kids, the boy kind and gentle, the girl rambunctious and naughty, playing on the porch. Rose herself would have time to do whatever she liked. (Robert wasn't sure what that was yet—gardening? Crossword puzzles?) And here they would grow old, looking at each other in the firelight, making plans for the future.

Even to him that fantasy sounded anemic.

He thought he had a pair of work boots up on the third floor; they were much more suited to the heavy work on the beach than his

Converses, bought on a nostalgic whim some years ago, without the knowledge that they were hip. Then.

He took the stairs to the second floor two at a time. They had gathered all the spruce and oak and birch they could. This would either be another unmitigated disaster or a giant success.

The door on the north wall of the boys' dorm was still blocked by a low trunk, bright blue, from the seventies. The last time Robert looked through it he'd made a mental note to clean it out. It was filled with cottage ephemera that had clung on for years. Tin trucks and loud neon plastic sand buckets were most prominent. So many things in this cottage needed cleaning out. You could spend a lifetime doing it all. Like painting the Golden Gate Bridge.

The lock opened easily. He wanted to see how his old guitars were holding up but he didn't want to delay too much. Jon would be the type to start the fire without him. He opened the door and went up the staircase. There were the boots, on the landing. Excellent. Socks were right inside—how convenient, if unsanitary. He pulled on the boots, decided the guitars could wait till tomorrow, and closed and locked the door. Then he went back downstairs, out the screen door, and down to the beach.

Rose was right: Whoever had the idea for the "egg timer" did not consider that in order to test the eggs you had to roll them off a steaming hot canvas on a bed of white-hot firewood, peel them, and then decide whether the yolk was fully cooked or not. Surely easier just to say, "Cook for an hour and a half or so." But that was not the Little Lost way.

"I'm burning my skin off!" Lottie cried. "Whose idea was this?"

"My great uncle's," Robert said. "I figured out who he was. He was the tinkerer. The egg idea is brilliant!"

"A timer would have been a lot easier," said Lottie. "Look, this is still runny."

"Then it's not done!" said Robert. "Rose, tell her to stop peeling her egg and be patient."

"Stop peeling the eggs and be patient," said Rose. "And get away from this inferno. Come, take a dip with me." Under her clamdiggers and T-shirt she was wearing the swimsuit that Fred liked—the old Speedo that was so worn and thin that it barely constituted fabric anymore. The fire was hot enough that it made the air ripple. The water might feel good.

"I am not going near that water," said Lottie.

"Have you been out on Forester's Point, Rose?" asked Robert. "You'll feel like the Queen of the Western World from out there. Plus you'll have a fantastic view of the cottage. You should be able to walk the whole way on dry rock—the tides are so low. Come back soon, though. These will be done at *some* point."

Forester's Point was over the rocks and around the bend from Sea Glass Beach, and it was a tricky climb to get there. But even there the smell of the steaming lobsters was almost too good to believe: salty, briny, sweet, sharp, pungent, hot. The sun was getting lower in the sky and her shadow here at the edge of the water was almost impossibly long. She raised her hands to make it longer still. Little Lost is making me a bigger person, she thought.

No one could see her here now, but Rose imagined how she would look from the cottage, silhouetted against the sky. I'm sure Robert wants me to see the cottage from another vantage point so I'll be smitten, she thought. I'm already smitten with Hopewell, just not with him.

She climbed to the end of the point, doing her best not to lose her footing. She imagined them calling from the beach, "Come back soon, Rose!" But she didn't want to come back. She got to the end of the point, dry and smooth and hot from the setting sun. She stretched out in the late sunlight. She was the Queen of the Western World.

CHAPTER TWENTY-SIX

*F*red was not finding it easy to get over to Little Lost Island, and the natives did not seem particularly friendly. Or maybe that was because Fred himself was not being particularly friendly. In fact, he was fucking furious. It had taken him three hours to go seventy miles on the Maine–New Hampshire border, so he had to push it hard to get up to Dorset. Now he only had twelve minutes to make the damn ferry and the GPS didn't work here and the directions seemed completely bogus. He made three desperate three-point turns before he even found the road to Big Lost and now that he was almost there he was behind a classic little old lady driver who would not go more than 27 in a 30-mph zone.

"Fuck *you*, Maine lady!" he said and hit the steering wheel. If he missed this ferry he would be furious at himself. He had driven more than ten hours in a hot car stupidly without even knowing if Caroline Dester would give a shit if he was there or not. She might not even be on the fucking island when he got there. What if he didn't find the lobster bake? What if she had gone back to New York? Can I honk at this lady? Go, woman—*go*, for fuck's sake.

Five fifty-four.

He had six minutes left to make a ferry he had driven ten hours to catch. Was it even possible to be this stupid?

The old lady car put on her blinker.

Turn, damn you.

She slowed way down, looked both ways before she turned, right, and finally got off the road. All the signs read, SLOW DOWN, 25 MPH ZONE MEANS YOU, but Fred didn't give a shit. I don't even know if I'm on the right road anymore, he said to himself as he gunned the engine to 40. If the ferry landing is not at the end of this road I will just swim across.

The ferry landing was at the end of the road.

He swung into a space, grabbed his bag from the passenger seat, and ran wildly in the direction of the water. His watch said six o'clock. "Shit!"

Then he heard a boat motor and the toot of a horn. "Get on if you're gettin' on." At the end of the dock was an excruciatingly adorable ferry, motor running, ready to untie.

"Little Lost Island?" asked Fred. What if he was at the wrong place?

"Yup," said the ferry driver. Not much more than a kid. Could he get them across? "Get on."

Fred took the couple of steps onto the boat and simultaneously it pulled away from the dock. There were only a few other people on it, all of whom seemed to know each other. They said nothing to Fred.

Had he rolled up the windows? Had he locked the car? He didn't know, and at this point he didn't care. He was on the ferry to the island, where a person he barely knew would or would not be. Jesus, what an idiot. He should have been writing. He should have been bonding with the kids. My wife goes away for four weeks and I act like

I'm fifteen. Could I just get a hotel room in Bangor or whatever the hell town is nearby and go home in the morning?

But the die was cast and the Rubicon was crossed. Only it wasn't the Rubicon; it was this incredibly sweet spit of water that the ferry was now cutting through. He was on the *Eleventh Hour*; he was headed to Hopewell.

He approached the ferry driver. Ferry pilot. "Hey."

The boy nodded. Here was a Mainer.

Fred spoke up over the whine of the engine. "I'm headed to the west shore. Do you know it?"

"Yep."

"Can I walk there from where the ferry lands?"

"You're going to have to. No cars on the island."

Fred hadn't even asked Caroline how to get to the beach. Or to meet him at the dock. More imbecility. It was hard, though, to feel too foolish on this boat, with the salt air coming at him and the late sun slanting on the windows of the boat. "Could you give me directions?" Before the ferryman could say, "I could," in that Maine way, Fred added, "I'd like directions, please."

"I'll show you once we're out. Almost there."

It was amazing the difference it made to take a boat to a place. Little Lost Island was not more than ten minutes in the boat from Big Lost Island, but since the former was that much smaller and that much farther out at sea than the latter, it felt considerably more lost than its larger neighbor. Traveling over water was so easy, really. No lights or lanes, just buoys and channel markers to keep you from running aground. There were a few sailboats out, catching the evening breeze as it came up out of the west. He had resisted the temptation to check his messages since he'd left Brooklyn that morning. If

Caroline had told him to call off the trip, it was too late. And if Rose had sent him something loving, it would undo all his resolve.

He checked his phone. It was dead.

"Ha!" Fred said. "Perfect."

Rose's e-mails had been brief—apparently she couldn't get much service—but it sounded like she was enjoying herself. She said she was making new friends, which was good. She didn't mention her writing. Her life had gotten so narrow when the twins were born. She'd had to put all her energy into Ben right from the start. As soon as they got the first part of the book advance, he'd wanted to hire a nanny or an au pair so Rose could write too, but she'd felt like she had to do it all. "When he's ready, Fred, we can hire somebody." But Ben was never ready. Actually, Rose was never ready. Fred felt that she wanted to get Ben to some mythical point of goodness and control before she handed him off to anyone else. But Ben was Ben and he wasn't going to change. Fred was not surprised that Patience was semibooting him from preschool. They'd figure something else out. Maybe this was the shock they needed to make some changes. Rose needed to finish her dissertation or just write something. She needed to be away from the kids. He actually could not believe she had managed to stay away from them for so long already. He'd thought she'd be back within a week, even though he'd told her she should stay away for at least two. Here it was, more than three weeks, and she was still up in Maine. He deliberately had not stopped for a lobster roll in Kennebunkport or Freeport just in case he ran into her. That would take some explaining.

What if this whole Caroline Dester thing was fake—some minion of a film studio leading him on? Then he'd get up here and find, what? The press? A mocking intern? It honestly didn't seem likely. Those texts he'd gotten from her even sounded like her voice. He closed his eyes and heard that voice again. He hoped she would speak French to him.

The ferry motor slowed, then reversed, as they approached the dock. One of the passengers jumped out and tied the boat up. The ferry driver cut the engine, the boat emptied out, and Fred stood waiting for the promised directions to the west shore. He didn't want to have to ask again.

"Go up the dock here, take the path right in front of you. It's the steepest but the quickest. Follow along to the big red cottage on your right, take the path alongside that one, and before you get to Grundys' there's a path to the west shore. Can't miss it."

Fred was pretty sure he could miss it.

"They're all down the beach. Lobster bake. Maybe they saved a lobster for you." He turned and left. Fred started up the dock and found the path. It was pretty steep, but it felt good to walk after ten hours in the car. Even with air-conditioning, it had been a hot, sticky ride. Fred wondered if he could persuade Caroline to take a sunset dive into the water. It was probably freezing, but it would feel so good after that drive. She looked more than hot in a bikini—there were plenty of pictures online. He liked to imagine her in one of those old, worn-out bathing suits that starlets never wear.

He kept hiking up the path. This place was well hidden—a good getaway from the paparazzi, although they seemed to have cooled off since poor Caroline did not get her Oscar. That must have hurt. He would write her an Oscar-winning part in this new book. Ha. Not possible. There are no Oscar-winning action heroes, and especially no Oscar-winning roles for the decorative foils to action heroes. Maybe he'd go back to one of his short stories, to give her something meaty. MACARTHUR WINNER INSPIRED BY DICK TO WRITE ROLE FOR

INGENUE. That would be an unusual headline in *Poets & Writers*. Although dick is the inspiration for a lot of great fiction.

An old barn of a cottage loomed up in front of him. This was where the ferry kid had said to do something—follow along it. There was only one way to do that. He was in less good shape than he thought he was. And he was getting sweatier by the minute. This cottage had better have running water. He'd be damned if he was going to show up to meet Caroline Dester looking like this.

"Holy shit."

The cottage that emerged in front of him on the path was enormous. Really huge. This was a summer place to reckon with. He liked it right away. It looked simple, even if it was gigantic. Shingle-style.

Fred took the steps two at a time and peered in the screen door to the cool interior. "Hello?"

The place felt empty, though there might have been a family of four living upstairs and he wouldn't have found them for days. He didn't want to go inside—what if this wasn't even the place? Somebody else could be living here, for all he knew. And the kid had said they were all down at the beach. Wasn't the whole island basically a beach?

He could smell briny woodsmoke in the air. The lobster bake. He'd been to clambakes, but never a lobster bake. Could he just waltz up and join in? Why not? He walked around the porch to see if he could tell what direction it was coming from. If he strained, he could see a few figures on the water's edge. That had to be them.

He dropped his backpack, which had made huge sweat stains all over his shirt. Well, too bad. He was going to join this party, welcome or not.

He started down a worn grassy path that seemed to lead straight to the beach. It did not. Fred was disoriented and a little lost. The path meandered for a while, then stopped altogether. There was nothing for it but to bushwhack through the ferns. He knew he must look ridiculous in his sweat-stained shirt and skinny jeans—not great for this terrain. He had to be close by now.

In fact, he was. Two more steps took him to the edge of the beach. In front of him, silhouetted on the sand, were figures he did not recognize. A bunch of people and none of them was Caroline. Fred watched them for a while from the cover of his ferns. There was a couple with a kid about Bea and Ben's age. The kid was all over the place but keeping a cautious distance from the fire pit, which was letting off an amazing amount of steam. The smell was almost overwhelming—like salt water on fire. Fred breathed it in, deep.

He noticed something on the periphery of his vision. Oh God, right in front of him was Caroline Dester. At sea. On a rock, above the water, leaning back on her elbows, one leg extended. What a goddess! She wasn't as scrawny as some of those movie shots made her look, either. Here, in real life, she looked less like a movie star, more like a human being.

Had she posed out on the point just because she knew he was coming?

"Caroline!"

She didn't answer.

"Caroline!"

He ran down the path and started to climb over the boulders to where she was. They were a combination of enormous rounded stones and jagged volcanic ones. He didn't even stop to take off his stupid shoes till he got to a patch covered with seaweed and slipped onto his knees. "God *damn* it," he said.

When he scrambled up again, there was a hole in his jeans and his shoes were sodden. "Fuck." He had deliberately chosen his one pair of Prada loafers to impress Caroline Dester. They'd bog him down if he didn't take the time to get them off, so he kicked them off where he was, seaweed or no. He took another look at the goddess of the rock: *The Birth of Venus in Maine.* What if she disappeared before he could get at her? "Caroline!" he called. The sea devoured his voice.

He went out farther, with his leg probably bleeding and his shoes being eaten by sand crabs. The waves were pounding here—no wonder she hadn't heard him. But she had to see him soon. She turned and stood up.

He looked at her looking at him. He was facing straight into the sun, so he couldn't see her features. But after two months of watching videos of Caroline Dester he was almost positive this wasn't Caroline Dester. This woman was in a Speedo, not a bikini. She was taller, and she was not in her twenties. She didn't have a movie star body. She had a lush, curvy body that was actually much sexier than a twenty-something body. She started to climb over the rocks toward him. "I can't believe you came," she said.

All at once she was pressed into him and he felt her breath come quickly.

A million sensations came over him at once: shock, surprise, tenderness, shame, love—and those were just the ones he could name.

"Oh my God," he said. "Rose?"

He found her mouth and she tasted of salt and sun.

"Rose. You're the one who's here."

He tightened his hold on her. She was utterly tender and open and all he could think was I have a goddess for a wife and she's here and Jesus Christ I adore her. I forgot that I adore her. He broke away from her long enough to say, "Rosie, darling, I'm sorry. I'm so sorry."

His heart was pounding against her chest. Her skin was hot. He put his hand at the back of her neck and closed his fingers around her hair.

"I've missed you so much, sweetheart. I need you so much." As he said it he realized how true it was.

She pressed her mouth to his and opened it. Her kiss electrified him.

"Can we go to bed?" she asked. They didn't even stop to pick up his shoes.

CHAPTER TWENTY-SEVEN

"*J*on, come figure this out with me," Robert called. "We take the tarp off first and put it on the sand. There's going to be a lot of steam, so watch out."

With a heave, Jon and Robert lifted the soaking tarp off the galvanized tub. The steam came at them like a typhoon. "Let it blow off! Let it blow off!" called Jon. "Keep Ethan away!"

"He is away!" Lottie called back.

They spread the hot tarp out on the sand.

"Ready?" asked Robert. Lottie had thought to bring oven mitts, thank God. He really was not much of a Mainer, despite the work boots. Anyone who knew what he was doing would have a pair of work gloves in his pocket. At all times.

"Okay, heave!" said Jon.

They lifted the tub, Robert trying not to show how much heavier it was than he'd thought. "Put it on the sand and then we'll tip it over!" said Jon, who suddenly seemed to know more about the whole process than Robert did. "Okay, now."

He and Jon dumped the fragrant, steaming, confusing contents of the galvanized tub on the canvas. If there was ever an ad for Maine island life, this would be it.

Where was Rose?

He had proposed the lobster bake for Rose, and done all that digging and firewood dragging and tending a hot fire for her. At this point, he was almost prepared to admit that Rose did not care about him as much as he cared about her. Or as much as he wanted to care about her.

"Where's Rose?" asked Lottie. "I know you did all this for her, Robert. We are going to enjoy it, but it was meant to be Rose's special moment. But we can't wait for her. She has other things on her mind, I think." She picked out a lobster from the steaming hot seaweed. "That'll be ours, I think, Ethan, don't you?"

"It's a giant *cockroach*! I want the red one!"

"They're all red ones!"

"I want the one that has the most red."

"I hope Caroline makes it down," Beverly said. "She's been up with those monstrous children all day."

"The big-kid play!" said Ethan. "That's not *red*!"

"Yes, it would be very nice if Rose were here," said Robert, not too pitifully, he hoped.

Lottie found another, possibly redder lobster. "Rose is already in love; that's the thing, Robert. You gave her just enough attention so that when she goes home to Fred—or when he comes here—she'll get attention from him, too. Want me to find a lobster for you, Beverly? I know you're color-blind."

"Thank you, Lottie," said Beverly.

"Ethan, see if you can find some corn. But just show me. It's too hot to pick up." She turned to Beverly. "If Caroline doesn't make it down here we can bring her up a plate. She's in intensive rehearsals.

The boys mostly want to play with their fake swords and the girls mostly want to put on costumes. Except for a few of the kids, who wanted to do both."

Robert could not have cared less about the island play. The sun was starting to set and the rushing water was like molten gold behind the black trunks of the spruce trees. Where was Rose?

"Can I get you the crackers, Beverly?" asked Jon. "The shells are harder to break than I thought they would be. Hey, Lotts, Ethan found the corn."

"And the potatoes!" said Ethan. "I found the potatoes, too! They're under the seaweed."

"I can't believe Rose is missing this. Jon, can't you go around to Foster's Rock and get her?"

"Forester's Point," said Robert. He was so disappointed that she hadn't been watching as they tipped the tub onto the tarp—the great moment of triumph!—that he was consoling himself with eating. He slurped a salty clam drenched in butter and then another. Jon sent Ethan over with a beer. Now he knew why people went to all this trouble. Everything tasted like the sea.

"There she is," said Lottie. "Who's with her?"

Robert looked up. Rose—his Rose?—was coming down to the beach with her body pressed tight against a man he didn't recognize. Their bodies were in sync. Their heads leaned toward each other. They had the freshly showered look of the postcoital.

Rose beamed at all of them. "This is my husband, Fred Arbuth-not," she said. "He'll be here for a while." She kissed him.

Robert's heart shattered. "Have a lobster," he said.

He didn't know, precisely, how he got through the rest of the meal. The next clams he ate were sandy, the potatoes underdone, and the corn starchy. Lottie and Jon and Ethan were a tight little unit;

Rose and Fred were practically intertwined; and Beverly was cranky because Caroline the actress had failed to appear. He was tempted to say he'd never felt more alone, but unfortunately, he often felt more alone.

He was tired of sitting there eating rubbery food, so he got started cleaning up. No one was helping. He raked the burning embers and dragged the tarp up the beach to the path leading to the cottage. The shells could stay where they were; the tide was coming in and would take them all away. He started picking up the corn husks and gathering the plates they'd brought down when Fred noticed him at last.

"Want a hand?"

I want a hand to connect with your nose and flatten it. "Sure," said Robert. "Maybe you could take the galvanized tub down to the water and rinse it out. Or we can hose it off at the cottage if that's too much trouble."

"No trouble at all," said Fred. Robert hated that this Fred of Rose's was such a good guy.

"I'll help," said Rose. She didn't look like Helga anymore. She looked like what she was: a real woman, with kids and a life; a woman with a husband whom she apparently loved.

I hope you deserve her, Fred, he thought. Bastard.

Together Fred and Rose took the charred tub down to the water's edge. He could hear them laughing at some private joke as they got closer to the water. They filled the tub with salt water and dumped it out a couple of times. Then they kissed.

"Gross!" said Ethan.

All four of them watched as Fred and Rose's kiss went longer and longer. The low sun cast their long shadows on the beach in front of them. They held each other's hands and came back up to the beach.

"I think we got it all cleaned out," said Fred.

"Nicely done," said Robert. Could he poison Fred's coffee tomorrow without harming Rose?

"Sorry we missed you taking this off the flame," Rose said. "I had to show Fred the cottage right away." They grinned at each other. "I don't think we'll make it to the play." She was leading Fred up to the cottage. *His* cottage. "We have to watch the moon rise."

CHAPTER TWENTY-EIGHT

*O*ver at the assembly room, the scene was chaotic. Four of the kids sent notes with their cousins that they'd gone for a nighttime boat ride to look at the huge blue moon and wouldn't be back in time to perform. And Captain Hook was out with food poisoning. He had experimented with eating a dead crab he'd found on the beach and it had not gone down well. Hook's dad, who'd promised he would play piano for them, bowed out too.

The lack of music was too bad, but there could be no show without the lead pirate, so Caroline took Wills by the shoulder. She knelt down and looked him in the eye. "We need you, Wills. You've got to be Captain Hook," she said. Wills was shaking his head, no no no. "You'd be great out there. They'll love you."

"I don't want to be Captain Hook! He's too mean!" Wills was clearly on the point of a meltdown.

Caroline gave a hard look at the girls. "Come on, ladies. We have three Elsas and two Annas. We could do the show with one less princess. And you know it."

"No way," said Lucia. She was their lead Anna.

"You should be Captain Hook, Caroline!" said Sarah. "You're tall! And you can be mean!"

"I am not appearing onstage," said Caroline. "Anywhere. Sorry."

"Caroline!" Lottie had found her way backstage. "We saved you a lobster. Are you all set?"

"We don't have any music and we're missing Captain Hook. Otherwise we're good."

"Yikes."

Reece, frantic, ran over in a panic. "What should I tell everyone?" he asked. "They think the play should start!"

"I better go," said Lottie. "Break a leg. Maybe Robert plays piano. I'll ask him."

"Or we could just cancel the whole thing," Caroline said as Lottie disappeared into the audience.

"There's always an island play," said Paige, her lower lip quivering. "My grampy will kill me if we don't do it."

"You have to be Captain Hook! We *need* you!" The girls were laying it on thick.

There would be photos and videos and hashtags swirling around the interwebs if she did it. OSCAR LOSER SINKS PIRATE PLAY, or a lawsuit from Disney if she so much as uttered a word from *Frozen*. But her publicist would applaud; anything heartwarming that involved kids was a win. CRYBABY CAROLINE MAKES COMEBACK WITH KIDS. DESTER FINDS HERSELF ON LOST ISLAND.

Oh, what the hell, she thought. "All right. I'll do it."

Her troupe of players cheered, and then got to work drawing a mustache on her upper lip, finding something from the costume box that would be vaguely suitable to wear, and testing her on her lines.

"Okay, everybody, get into position! Time to start!" said Jessie.

Reece flashed the lights. "Please take your seats!" he said. *"And be quiet!* It's time for . . . *Frozen Peter Pan!"*

Jessie pulled open the curtain. A piano fanfare started from nowhere. The play began.

With everyone else at the play, Fred and Rose had the cottage to themselves and made good use of it. The blue moon was rising outside their little bedroom, and Fred regarded Rose, asleep next to him. Her pale skin was almost aglow in this shallow light. Her eyes beneath the delicate lids were utterly still, her eyebrows almost invisible from so much sun, bleached completely away. Her shoulders were a little sunburned, as were her breasts—she must be sunbathing topless, he thought. That's nice. Her nipples were so pale they were almost translucent. He remembered how painful nursing had been for her, with tiny Bea and Ben latched on almost constantly for months. Ben hadn't wanted to feed at all, and Bea's first tooth had given her mastitis.

He kissed one breast very softly, then the other.

The scar from the C-section was a lot fainter now, but he knew she was still self-conscious about it. Hence that old red Speedo that she clung to. Women should bear these scars like warriors do. They should show them off and boast.

He loved that she had the body of a mother. It was a much more interesting body now than she'd had when they were young. Not that he hadn't been interested in her body then; on the contrary. But now she bore their history. That worry line between her eyebrows—that appeared while Ben had his endless colic. The wrinkles beginning to show at the creases of her eyes were from good times: Swings on the playground. Her first published poem. The weekend they spent in New Orleans.

On her left arm were the freckles that always appeared in that exact spot: a cluster right above her wrist, then a pause, then a scattering up to her elbow.

I love my wife, he thought.

Rose opened her eyes. "Penny for your thoughts," she said.

"I love my wife."

"Liar."

"Okay, I was thinking of how much more I love your body now than I did when I first met you."

"Now I know you're lying," said Rose, though she was smiling.

"You think so?" he said, and rolled on top of her.

She grinned. "Guess not."

The piano was not Robert's favorite instrument—the thing was so mechanical—but Lottie told him that the whole show would fall apart if there was no music, so he reluctantly sat down at the bench. There was some sheet music provided for a couple of the songs, but that was it. He started the play with a cheesy fanfare and imagined he could get away with a few well-placed chords to go with the action, but from the first moment Captain Hook stepped onstage, the game was suddenly elevated. When she spoke, her voice sent a thrill through his body from the back of his neck to the soles of his feet.

He was not much of a keyboardist but he played to impress her and took his cues from whatever she did onstage. He was the silent movie pianist to her swashbuckling adventurer. When she didn't have the audience in stitches she had them fearing for their lives. She made the kids seem like professionals. She made him feel like he would do anything for her.

At the end of the show the audience demanded an encore of the dreaded song about following your dreams or letting things go or whatever it was about, and in the final chorus Robert took it up a half step so the girls could really milk it. Then the curtain rang down and the play was over.

A triumph.

The kids poured off the stage and into the arms of their parents, who'd been determined to be pleased by anything they saw but were genuinely delighted at this. Robert began to pack up the music. He looked for Caroline but could not find her in the crowd. A few of the islanders he knew gave him a pat on the back and said, "Good job." He waited for Caroline to come over and tell him he had been magnificent, that he had saved the show, that they made a great duo, but when he did spot her, she was surrounded by kids who wanted a group selfie, so she was not about to notice him.

He gave her a few minutes, just to be sure she'd have a chance to find him if she was looking. Then she went backstage and he was forgotten.

Figures.

Ah well, the walk back to the cottage might be restorative. He turned off the lights as he walked out of the assembly room and turned onto a shortcut to Hopewell. The air had that almost-fall chill; there was the sharp tang of woodsmoke on the breeze; the crickets were deafening; the sky was cloudless. The high, brilliant moon was in its full glory. The path was wide enough for two. He was one.

"Robert!"

Was that the voice? A flashlight wavered on the path behind him. It must be in the hands of someone who didn't know the path well. Someone who needed another person to walk with. Someone who had recently been a pirate?

He turned and shaded his eyes against the light. "Um, can you put that down a little?" He hated to ask, but she was practically blinding him. "Caroline." The thrill of saying this new name.

She lowered the flashlight and he could see her outlined by the moonlight, which made her luminous, which even he recognized was a cliché.

"You saved the show," said Caroline. "Thank you. I'm Caroline Dester."

"*You* saved the show, I think." The more he heard that name, the more he thought he knew her from somewhere. "Do I know you from somewhere?"

"I don't think so," she said. "Every time you're at the cottage, I'm not. Does this path lead back home?"

Home! A thrum of possibilities shot through his body.

"Straight to Hopewell. I don't think we even need the flashlight, do we? The moon is so bright."

They could see their shadows as they walked. "I thought you played guitar," said Caroline.

"I mostly play guitar, but I can noodle around on the piano if absolutely necessary. My own instrument is the lute." So nerdy! Would she run away?

"I'd like to hear a lute sometime," she said.

"Anytime." He hoped he sounded nonchalant.

They walked in silence for a while, the soft tones of the buoy bells in the distance. There was the tiniest trace of a mustache still on her face.

"Do we have to go straight back?" asked Caroline. "It's such a pretty night. I haven't seen the island in moonlight. Where does this path go?"

She was leading them along a dirt path that would take them to the east side of the island if they followed it all the way. "We'll be able to see the moon on Horseshoe Beach if we take that one," he said.

"Then let's take that one."

Even Robert could not have predicted this. Just a couple of hours ago he was gutted by the appearance of Rose's husband. Now he was in the moonlight, on his island, with this exquisite woman, who wanted to keep walking with him and who called his cottage home.

She stumbled. Take care of her, you fool! "Careful, there are a lot of roots to watch out for here. Do you want the flashlight?"

"No, my eyes are used to the dark now. It's quieter this way."

He knew exactly what she meant.

"Watch out on the rocks here too. It's a couple of steps onto the beach. There."

Neither of them spoke as they regarded the moonlight on the water, a wide swath of silver white light on the sleepy waves. It was cold down here on the water's edge. Caroline rubbed her hands over her arms. Why hadn't he thought to bring her a sweater?

"Cold?" he asked.

"No." She was looking out to sea. "I'm good."

Robert wanted to take her hand and almost reached for it. But she didn't need his help to steady herself on a flat beach, so there was no excuse. As he was wondering what kind of excuse he could make up, Caroline said, "You made this all possible."

"What?" he asked.

"Not the moon and the beach. But the cottage. And the sign. The whole month of August. It was all your idea, and it's working. Every one of us is happy here."

They stood in silence till he saw her shiver. "I can't stand that you're cold," he said. "Shall we go back to the cottage?"

"Okay," said Caroline. "But let's take the long way."

They found a lot to talk about as they wound back along the path on the island's periphery to Hopewell. Robert's image of Caroline Dester as an out-of-work actress evaporated when she used the phrases "talk-show appearances" and "my favorite assistant director." He was glad he never read *People* magazine or looked at celebrity websites. He would have been far too intimidated by Caroline Dester to play piano for her island production.

"I hope you don't mind me pushing around the furniture in the cottage," she said. "It just needed a fresh eye, I think."

"Absolutely," he said. He wanted to say, I not only like your eye, I am blown away by every single thing about you, from the top of your moonlit hair to your crooked little toe. Can I kiss you, please?

"You haven't even seen what Beverly and I did in the little garden off the kitchen," said Caroline. They weren't far from Hopewell now and Robert wanted to delay going in for as long as he could.

"Show it to me now," he said.

"It's dark."

"Show it to me in the moonlight, and then again tomorrow, in the sun. How about that?"

They walked over to where Caroline and Beverly had begun working. "We thought Hopewell Cottage needed a kitchen garden," she told him, "so we planted herbs."

He closed his eyes and breathed in their scent. "I'm getting something," he said. "Basil?"

"Basil for one." She leaned down and picked a few leaves off one of the plants. She rubbed them together right under his nose.

"Oh! Lavender," he said.

"I love lavender."

I'll bathe you in it, he thought.

She plucked another. "How about this one?"

"Easy. Thyme." Could he lick her finger?

"Try again." She stepped even closer. He could smell the thyme but more powerfully he could smell her own scent: roses, honey, lime.

"Thyme," he said again. "Oh, but you're right, there's something else in there. *Lemon* thyme," he said.

"Got it," she said. "Here's a tricky one." She crushed some leaves between the palms of her hands, then opened them in front of Robert's face.

I love you, he thought. "Isn't that oregano?" he said.

"Marjoram," said Caroline. "Beverly prefers it to oregano. More subtle, he says. He was so bossy about what we could put in this garden and what we couldn't." She looked up at the cottage. Robert saw her take notice of the light on in one of the turret rooms. "I don't want Beverly worrying about me. We should go in."

She turned toward the back stairs of the cottage and he followed. The Hopewell kitchen, with its pile of lobster crackers, dirty silverware, and wineglasses in the sink, was spectacularly unromantic. He should have made his move out there in the herb garden.

"That was really fun," said Caroline. "Really beautiful, actually. Thanks, Robert."

"Oh. Yes. Thanks."

She hesitated for a moment. "I'll see you in the morning."

"Right. See you in the morning."

Robert went up to the boys' dorm room, where he had been staying since he'd got here. What an idiot not to have offered her a drink or made a fire or done *something*. The lost moment of all time.

He ran the water hard in the bathroom as he brushed his teeth con brio. Who cared if he woke up the place? He climbed unhappily into bed but after two minutes he knew he wouldn't sleep, and not because of the light of the moon. He needed to be in his own space to think about everything that had gone on tonight. This dorm room was not home for him.

Carefully, quietly, he moved the trunk away from the door to the third floor. If he could just look out his own windows onto the sea he could maybe straighten out his head. Were any of his feelings genuine? Or did he just fall in love with every single woman who liked this island, this house?

He crept up the stairs to his own beloved room. No need for the brash overhead light; not with this moon.

There was Caroline, sitting on the old horsehair couch, a lute in her arms.

"That's not how you hold it," he told her.

"Then show me," she said.

The End
of August

CHAPTER TWENTY-NINE

red's heart was pounding from climbing this cliff. At the top were Rose and the kids, and he had to get there before school started. The cliff kept getting higher and garbage trucks were rolling by, which meant they'd all be late for school. He was almost there in time to rescue them when he looked up and saw Caroline Dester pushing Bea's stroller. He shouted and shouted, "Where's Rose?" and then he lost his footing and he started to fall—

He awoke with a jolt, pulse racing. He sat up and oriented himself in the room. Thin gray light was coming in from the window. Rose was asleep beside him. He was at the cottage where Rose was staying for the month of August. And, in the light of day, to his complete horror and distress, he realized that Caroline Dester might be staying here too.

He tried to piece it all together. Rose was sharing the cottage with the other woman from Park Slope, Lottie. Fine. Lottie's husband was here, and their kid. The guy who owned this place was named Robert. And there was an older man with a woman's name.

But Caroline Dester had specifically said she was on Little Lost Island. Was Caroline here too? His mind exploded a little.

He got up as quietly as he could but the bed creaked and the floorboards creaked. Rose turned to him and half-opened her eyes.

"I have to pee," Fred whispered.

He grabbed a blanket from the bed and wrapped it around his waist. It gave him enough yardage to conceal his jeans, which he swept up on the way out of the room. In his jeans was his phone. And in his phone were the messages from Caroline. He could scroll through them again to see if she'd said the name of the place she was staying. And then delete them all. Permanently. If I have any luck at all, he thought, she will be at some other massive cottage on this island and I will never see her. Just do not be staying here. Please.

His phone was dead. Shit.

He thought it through as he peed. If she's here, I find her, tell her it was all a gigantic mistake, and beg her not to tell Rose. What a pussy. Or I just deny it all. If he told Rose the truth now it would crush the fragile thing they'd just built up again last night. And he wanted to rebuild it. The Caroline thing—which wasn't even a thing—was what a teenager did, not a grown man with a wife he loved. It wasn't worthy of him and it wasn't worthy of Rose.

He would get to Caroline Dester before she got to Rose. He had no idea how. He just hoped the fates were with him.

Rose was out of bed when he got back to the room. Her skin was so pretty in this early light. "Rose, can I tell you something?"

"I know. You love me," Rose said, and kissed him. "You have made that amply clear. But now I'm starving and I think all that noise from the kitchen means somebody is making us breakfast. Let's go see. And *then* back to bed."

Fred followed Rose down the hall to the kitchen. The source of the clattering was the older man. What was his name?

"Good morning, Beverly," said Rose.

"Hello, Rose," said Beverly. "I'm cleaning up. The kitchen was left a shambles last night but I've still managed to produce some lemon muffins. They're in the oven."

"I thought I smelled something baking," she said. "You're the best." She smiled at Fred. "I make the downstairs coffee," she told him. "Beverly keeps taking his pot upstairs so he doesn't have to share with anyone."

"You're lucky I'm going deaf, or I would have heard that," said Beverly.

Fred laughed, a little too hard.

"Rose, can you set the table?" asked Beverly. "We all had a late night last night and I suspect many of you young people have worked up an appetite." He looked in the oven, the homey smell of the baking almost putting Fred at ease. Nothing truly bad could happen here. "The muffins will be out of the oven soon. I'm just about to put the bacon on. And perhaps it won't tax you too much to scramble some eggs?"

"I can scramble eggs," said Fred. It would give him something to do. But first he had to find out if Caroline Dester was here. He went to the base of the stairs and looked up.

"They're in the refrigerator," Beverly said. "But did you want a tour first?"

"Nope, no," said Fred. Better not act too jumpy. "Just getting my bearings." Take the plunge. "Where does everyone sleep in this place?"

Rose started the coffee and got out a couple of mugs. "This can be yours," she said, holding one out to him. "The jokey lobster pot one.

And here are the eggs." She handed him the container. "They're from the market boat."

"Great. So, how did you divide up the rooms?"

"Oh, right," Rose said. "Lottie and Jon sleep down here on this floor. Ethan, too. Beverly chose one of the turret rooms, didn't you, Beverly?"

"And a lovely room it is, too," he said.

"Robert's in the dorm room."

"We think," said Beverly. "I suspect there were some shenanigans last night."

"Shenanigans! What a hip word for you, Beverly."

"It's a very old word, and appropriate in this case."

"Ooh," said Rose, "what does that mean? Did I miss something?"

Still no mention of Caroline Dester. Maybe, Fred, maybe you will have a narrow escape.

"Good morning, Beverly," said Lottie as she came into the kitchen. "Hello, Rose and husband Fred. I didn't think you two would be up for ages."

"Fred got up at dawn with a bad dream and I couldn't get back to sleep. So here we are."

"The bacon smells so good, Beverly," said Jon. "Should I make another pot of coffee?"

"I think so," said Lottie. "Then there'll be enough for all of us."

"Rose, you missed the play last night," Lottie said. "Robert played piano! I think he was completely smitten with our Captain Hook."

"You can drain the bacon on paper bags," said Beverly. "Lottie, I can't open the oven with you there."

"Robert and Captain Hook! Were those the shenanigans, Beverly?" said Rose.

"I wouldn't know," said Beverly. "Although it seems to me this cottage has been enlivened. How are those eggs coming, Fred? I don't think you've cracked a single one."

"I'll get on it," said Fred. "Sorry."

Someone was clattering down the stairs. Either it was Robert or it was Captain Hook or it was Caroline Dester. He smashed an egg onto the rim of the bowl.

"Hello, all!"

It was Robert, their host. Solo.

"Good morning, Robert," said Lottie. "Good night?"

"Very good night," he said. He was blushing furiously. Even Fred in his distress noticed that.

"We're just about ready," said Beverly.

"I put out the willow plates in your honor," said Rose. "Let's sit down."

Jon finished cooking the bacon, Lottie made the toast, Fred scorched the eggs, and they sat down at the table.

"Here's to Hopewell," said Jon, raising his coffee mug to Robert.

They all did the same. "To Hopewell," said Rose.

"Am I missing something?"

The voice of a goddess struck Fred's skull like a baseball bat. His mug fell out of his hand and spilled half its contents all over the table.

"Oh, God. Sorry, sorry," said Fred. He stood up and shook his head violently in Caroline's direction. "What a mistake. Sorry. I'm Fred. Fred Arbuthnot."

"It's okay, Fred," Rose said. "Not a big deal. You caught it fast. This is my husband, Caroline. Fred."

"Fred?" asked Caroline. Her brow wrinkled just the tiniest bit.

Why did I send her that picture? Vanity, vanity! "I'm Fred. Fred Arbuthnot." Don't call me Mike McGowan. Please do not call me Mike McGowan. "Rose's husband." His eyes implored her. Truly. Please.

The two of them looked at each other for a moment.

"*Enchantée*," said Caroline.

And then she didn't give him a second glance.

"Pass the bacon, Lottie," she said. "I'm starving."

Thursday morning's breakfast lasted for hours. Robert finally had what he had spent so many years imagining at this place: actual friends around the table who liked each other. A woman he could barely keep his hands off. A future that would not be alone.

He and Caroline spent practically all day Thursday and Friday in bed. He didn't know there were so many things you could do with a lute. Friday night they were all ravenous, and Beverly had prepared a feast of bouillabaisse, green salad, crisp French bread, and a lemon tart for dessert. On Saturday Caroline said she wanted to know all the secrets of the island, so he took her to the tiny museum in the back of the tearoom, which entranced her. By the time she started in on her third scrapbook (Island Tennis, 1922–1927), even he was antsy.

"Let me stay here a minute, Robert. I know you've seen it all before but I can't get enough of these photos."

Reluctantly, he left her. He kissed her good-bye and thought, I should really just drape myself around her shoulders like a cat. Instead, he walked back to the cottage. The wind was really gusting now. The sky was looking grim. The rain was going to start soon.

When he got to the cottage, Rose was collecting her bag and looking a little harried. "Robert, I'm almost beginning to think you need Wi-Fi here," she said. "Or at least a landline that calls long distance. I feel like I haven't talked to the kids in ages. And now Fred's here too, so we need to know they're okay. I think I can make the two thirty ferry if I hurry."

"The wind is really bad out there," said Robert.

"I know. I can't do FaceTime here and I promised. Do you think the ferry is even running?"

"The ferry always runs."

Robert hated to see Rose head across to the other side with the weather being so bad. But he also hated to invite her up to his third floor—his and Caroline's third floor.

"It'll be choppy. I hope I don't throw up. See you in a couple of hours. Fred's writing at the library, but he should be back soon."

Robert's better nature took over. "You can skip the two thirty ferry," he said. "There's a hot spot in the cottage."

"You're kidding. There is?" She put her bag down. "We tried everywhere the first week we got here. Where is it?"

"It's on the third floor. Come on, I'll show you." Caroline will forgive me. I hope.

"Oh, that is so great, Robert," said Rose. "Lottie wanted me to take Jon's phone and hers into the Harbor if I went so I could pick up their messages. We can kill three birds with one stone. Four, if I recharge Fred's phone. Let me get it."

Robert instantly regretted telling Rose about the hot spot. We'll be invaded by technology and our peace will be destroyed. Or maybe she'll just call home.

"I haven't even been up to the third floor," she said. "How do you get up there? Is it the attic?"

"The stairs are hidden," he said. "They're in the boys' dorm. And the door is usually locked. Caroline, however, found a way."

"Very Caroline," said Rose. She grabbed Fred's phone from their room while Robert waited to take her upstairs.

"Oh, Robert. No wonder you like it up here," she said when she got upstairs. "So cozy. Are these all your guitars?"

"Yes, and the lutes." He was so very glad he had not played his lute for Rose. Only for Caroline. He shivered at the thought of her. He wanted to get back to her fast. But he didn't want to leave Rose alone here. This was his place with Caroline, now. "If you stand right here and face the window, you can get a signal. See if it works."

It worked.

"Oh, great!" said Rose. "This makes life so much easier. Robert, could you plug in Fred's phone somewhere?" she handed it to him. "I'll use his if this one cuts out. He's Verizon; I'm AT&T." She started dialing.

Robert dutifully went over to one of the two outlets on this floor and plugged in Fred's phone. Rose was soon talking to her sister. His precious third floor had now been invaded, but he knew Caroline would have done the same.

"Isobel, we want to bring them up here," Rose said into the phone. My God, was she talking about the twins? She hadn't even asked! Though of course it was still *her* rental at this point. The lines have blurred, Robert thought.

There followed a long and pretty nonsensical FaceTime conversation between Rose and the children about Maine, superpowers, and Labradoodles. When they had finally said their good-byes, Robert ushered her downstairs. They were back in the boys' dorm when he remembered Fred's phone. "Let me just get it for you," he said. He ran back upstairs and unplugged it. The phone lit up.

"Oh, thanks, Robert," said Rose. "I know he's dying to hear from his editor. I'll take it over to him. I may even take a peek so I can prepare him." She grabbed a slicker, gave him a wave, and was gone.

Robert was deliberating over whether to take a bottle of wine to the museum to see what that might lead to when he heard Lottie and Jon and Ethan clatter back to the cottage.

"Hello, Robert!" said Lottie. "We are having the great debate. Let me get Ethan in the bath. See what Robert thinks, Jon."

"What I think of what?" asked Robert.

"I'm thinking," said Jon, "that I should quit my job."

"Quitting is usually a good idea," said Robert. He had quit a lot of things. "Why would you quit your job, though?"

"First, I hate it," Jon said. "And second, I think I could make a living working for Beverly Fisher. He asked me about it again, on the way back from the play. Lottie loves the guy and now I do too."

"He seems to need a lot of help. Musicians get screwed if no one's looking out for them."

"His partner Gorsch left everything in great shape but Beverly's just let it go downhill since the poor guy died," Jon said. "And he doesn't like the new management team. I guess his old advisers hung on till Gorsch wasn't around anymore."

Lottie emerged from the bathroom and spotted the two phones on the kitchen table. "I guess Rose didn't take them into the Harbor?"

"No, but I think you'll find your messages have downloaded," said Robert.

She checked her phone. "They have! How did that happen?"

"If I told you, I'd have to kill you."

"Seriously?"

"No, there's a hot spot on the third floor." Everybody might as well know now.

"Are you okay in there, Ethan?" asked Lottie.

"I'm okay!" Ethan called.

"Turn off the water when it gets too full."

"Don't come in!"

"Robert, you didn't tell Jon if you think he should quit his job," said Lottie.

"I'm hardly qualified—"

"Just go with your gut," Lottie said. "We need an objective opinion."

Robert thought about it. "Would you have enough to live on? While you get started?"

"I guess I'd ask Beverly for a retainer and we'd live on that. We're already fucked in terms of finances anyway. Preschool costs the earth."

"Does it?" asked Robert. He would have to learn about children now.

"I am totally going to do it," Jon said. "Leap and the net will appear."

Lottie's face lit up. "Oh, Jon, I am so proud of you." They really were a pretty tight couple. This, Robert thought, is love.

Jon said, "Fuck 'em. They owe me a shitload of vacation pay. I haven't taken a break since I got there."

"Except for this pneumonia," said Lottie, "which has gone on a long time." She handed him the phone and he typed furiously.

"I'm still not on the network, so I'm reduced to sending from my Gmail," Jon said. "I don't even know who my boss is right now; there's been so much turnover."

Robert was impressed with Jon's determination. He had never quit a nine-to-five job because he had never had one. He always pictured the workplace as something between a neighborhood bar and a penal colony.

"And . . . Send." Jon pushed the button with a flourish. Lottie gave him an enormous hug. Then he collapsed onto a chair. "Oh, Christ, Lottie, what have I done?"

She plopped herself in his lap. "I think you've done the right thing, Jon. I really do. And it won't actually send till you're in cell phone range, if you want to change your mind."

"No, I quit," said Jon. "Let's take it up to Robert's hot spot and really send it, Lottie." He looked down at the phone. "I should listen to these voice mails, though," he said. "There are four messages from some new number. It could be my mom about my stepdad. Maybe they're at the hospital?"

Jon pressed the voice mail button. "Oh," he said to Lottie. "It's my new boss."

"Justin?" she asked.

"Carla," he said.

Lottie's face went pale.

Jon kept listening, his face intent. "Christ."

Lottie held her breath. "Are you going back there?" she asked.

"Nope." He swiped the message away. "She fired me."

"Lucky you quit then," said Robert.

Rose found herself running. She couldn't stop running.

"You *shit*! You *asshole*!" She screamed into the rain. "*I hate you!*" Her throat was raw. She wanted to kill herself. She would have thrown the phone onto the rocks and smashed it into shards if she hadn't had to keep it to confront him.

"You made me such a fucking *fool*. What a fucking *dupe* I am!"

She retched. The rain ran down her back and into her bones.

She didn't know where she was going. She wanted to be home with the twins and away from this awful place. But home meant Fred. And this place meant Fred. Could she just lie down on the wet grass and let the rain wash her away?

She kept walking, sliding on the grass and stumbling on the rocks. The boardwalk was treacherous. The paths were drenched in rain and filled with mud. She didn't know how far she had gone or where she was going when she realized she was standing at the back of the library. Where Fred was *writing*. So smug in the knowledge that she, his stupid duped Rose, loved him no matter what. Her breath came in heaves.

She walked in through the screen door and slammed it shut.

Fred was the only one there, computer on, earbuds in. He didn't even look up.

Rose walked over to him and slapped his computer off the table. "You *shit!*"

He looked up. "Jesus, Rose! What the fuck?" Then he could see that her whole body was trembling.

She pummeled his chest. "Did you sleep with her?"

"What are you talking about?"

"*Did you sleep with her?*"

He backed away. "No, I didn't sleep with her."

"So you know what I'm talking about! You didn't sleep with her?"

"I told you, no."

"Do *not* lie to me!"

"I'm not lying to you." He took her by the arm.

"Don't *touch* me!"

"I didn't sleep with her. I didn't even know her! It was just texting, Rose."

"You quoted *Rimbaud* to her! The same *lines*, Fred!"

"I don't know much French."

She pounded on his shoulders again. "Are you sleeping with her now? Because you know she's putting out for Robert SanSouci, too."

"Rose, don't be horrible."

"Don't *me* be horrible? After this?" She dug furiously in her pocket and threw his cell phone on the table.

"*You* moved out! You left me and came up here."

"On *vacation!* Don't you *dare* blame your infidelity on me."

"Rose!" He stood up suddenly. His chair fell behind him. He picked it up and for a moment she thought he might haul it across the room. "It was not infidelity. It didn't happen. And it wasn't real."

"I don't want to be on this island with you. I don't want to be anywhere with you."

"You think this is enough to break us up."

He said it like it was a statement. She wanted to say yes I do. She shook her head and said, "I don't know."

He took an enormous breath and let it out very slowly. "Okay. Great. But I don't want to give up on us, Rose. I love you. It's just not more complicated than that. I love you, Rosie, and I want to be with you. I do."

If he says that one more time I'll believe him and I don't want to believe him.

She put her head down on the long polished table and closed her eyes. "Just go, Fred. Please just go."

The next morning, Fred was gone. Caroline was hanging on by a thread—she had moved into the turret room and hardly came out. Lottie and Jon's little boy was no longer sleeping through the night. The cottage was a wreck and so was Beverly.

He woke on Sunday morning with a headache. No one would remember that they had promised to take care of Possum that afternoon. He was sure of it.

Beverly regarded the box of cremains. He didn't want to be carrying around this box anymore. He made himself coffee and went out to his private porch. Lottie was already there.

"At least *we're* not fighting, Beverly," she said. She looked at what he had in his arms. "There's dear Possum."

"What was Possum, yes."

"I thought we would all be together for Possum's service in the woods, but even I don't see that now." She looked down at Beverly's box. "I don't suppose you want to be carrying around that box anymore. It's not very nice for Possum to be in there, always portable. He needs a final resting place."

"Gorsch needs one too." This was a risk, telling her this. What would she think of him now? A selfish old queen who could only hold on to the remains of his cat, and not of his own life partner?

Lottie did not seem shocked. "He doesn't have one?"

"I didn't know what was happening. People just told me what to do when Gorsch—when he stopped living. I couldn't go into the place where they do the cremation. I couldn't. And then it's days before you get these things, the ashes, for a *human being*. Can you imagine such barbarity? Gorsch refused to be buried. He didn't want me traipsing out to Queens to lay grocery-store flowers on his grave. He said he would have been buried in our back garden in the country place but apparently they don't let you plant bodies in the ground anymore, unless it's a bona fide cemetery. So I gave them away."

He wasn't making a whole lot of sense, even to himself, but Lottie didn't comment. She just drank her coffee. If she so much as glanced at him he would stop talking. She didn't.

"I gave away Gorsch's ashes." Poor good, strong, brilliant, funny Sam Gorsch. In a box. "I didn't know what to do. I couldn't have it in the house or near me. I couldn't touch the ashes. There are bones!" Lottie nodded. She's letting me get it all out. I don't have to say anything more. He went on. "So I called his agent. Imagine. I called his agent and said, here, you take care of them. His niece and nephews asked me, what did you do with Sam's ashes, and I was too ashamed to tell them. How ridiculous would that sound? I said I had spread some of them in front of the Brill Building at dawn and the rest on

Fire Island at sunset. What a lie! They're at ICM. In an urn in a conference room. Or a filing cabinet!"

Beverly couldn't stop the tears that were leaking from his eyes.
He had let Sam down so terribly. But Sam would understand. Sam
was the strong one. Sam let him get away with everything. Why had
Sam had to go first?

"I don't think he much minds where his ashes are," said Lottie.

"He would mind that Possum was still in a box," said Beverly. His
voice was suddenly ferocious. He couldn't help himself. "That's not
how we treated Possum!"

"We'll be good to Possum."

"Possum would have liked it here too. So many *birds*."

"It really is a little bit of heaven," she said. "Even if no one else
shows up, you and I will take care of Possum, and Jon will help you
with your darling Gorsch. Would that work?"

Beverly could only nod.

"Jon is good at that sort of thing. He'll get the box back for you
without a fuss."

"I'm a useless old man."

"You're certainly not useless and you're far from old. You just
need help with all that paperwork. When we get back to the city we'll
get it all straightened out."

Beverly didn't like to think about going back to the city. "Everything will change once we're back."

Lottie sighed. "Everything has already changed, after the blue
moon. I did think we'd be forever friends. I almost still do. It may
take some years to get us back on track, but it will start with you and
me and Jon and your sweet Gorsch."

"He wasn't that sweet. He was like acid when he wanted to be.
That's why . . ."

"I imagine that's why you cared for him so very much," said Lottie.

"I loved him." There, he'd said it. "I was his special love."

He picked up the box of Possum's ashes and found himself stroking the top of it. "Possum would like it here. In the shade, though. Not in the sun. And not on the beach."

"Robert told me the spot he thought would be nice for Possum. And maybe Rose has written a poem."

"I doubt it," said Beverly. "I've barely seen Rose these past several days. She's driven Caroline into seclusion." He knew it wasn't fair as he said it, but the cottage was so empty without Caroline's presence and he had to blame someone. He turned his attention back to the box. "I put a note on the kitchen table to remind them to meet us at Cathedral Woods at three. I even drew them a map."

Jon came up the stairs to Beverly's little porch. "May I join you?"

"Of course," said Beverly. His mind flashed back to Lottie at the beginning of their month there. She'd said he would want them with him in his private rooms. And now he did.

"Are you thinking back to the old days? When you took this turret before any of us came up?"

"I'd do it again in a heartbeat," said Beverly.

"This will be your room whenever you come up," said Lottie. "I see it."

"Lottie and her visions," Jon said. "The amazing thing is that they pretty much come true."

"I don't see it," said Beverly. "Robert SanSouci is a nice enough young man, but he won't have me staying here every summer, I can tell you that."

"Caroline adores you, and that's enough," said Lottie.

"Oh, Lottie," Jon said, "even you can't think that this Caroline-

Robert moment is going to survive the week. She's not even speaking to him. I can't figure out why she hasn't gone home."

"She still has some clothes in the wash," said Lottie. "And anwyay, I think she's already fallen in love with Robert."

"Even if she takes him back she'll crush his heart," said Jon.

"She won't! Robert wants someone who needs the cottage. Caroline needs Robert to worship her."

"Caroline has millions of people worshipping her."

"But she needs *one* person. To worship *her*."

"It doesn't make a whole lot of sense to me," said Beverly, "but no harm in letting you entertain yourself with the idea. I don't think anyone else is going to appear for Possum's great event this afternoon. You two will have to do."

Robert sat morosely cradling his lute on the horsehair settee on his beloved third floor. But his beloved third floor was no longer beloved. He had been betrayed.

Caroline and Fred Arbuthnot! It was so disgusting. Even if she'd thought Fred Arbuthnot was Mike McGowan and he wasn't married to Rose. And even though she was texting him before she'd *met* Robert.

He strummed the first mournful notes of "Dueil Angoisseux," the perfect sad-guy-with-a-lute song, except it was about a woman being left in the lurch by a man. So he stopped. Had he left Caroline? Or had she left him?

Robert wasn't even sure where she was at this point. Some of her clothes were still here on the bed. He swept up her precious thin tissue of a T-shirt and held it to his nose. It smelled of woodsmoke and herbs and just a little bit of sweat, which made him crazy. He had been so angry when she'd told him the story. She'd expected him to laugh and protect her from the wrath of Rose and he had been furious and hurt instead. For no good reason!

Then he told her he needed space. Even when he said it he knew it was (a) a cliché and (b) not even true! He actually wanted to take her to bed and experiment with his guitar this time but he thought he should be hurt, so he acted hurt and now she was gone.

He played more of the sad-guy song, with his own lyrics. "I let her go-o. I really let her run and go-o," he sang. It was an abomination to treat such beautiful music this way.

He put the lute down.

Go find her, you idiot. Maybe she hasn't left yet. That's got to mean something.

He got to his feet and starting pacing.

I need to find her. Now. Was she still on the island, or had she left for home without telling anyone? He didn't have a cell number for her. Fred had that. Bastard! He wasn't about to ask Fred for Caroline's number. He took out his phone and stepped over toward the window to get a signal. Max would know if she'd been on the ferry. So awful to chase after her like this! He couldn't do it.

He punched Max's number. Pick up. Pick up.

"Yep?"

"Max, it's Robert up at Hopewell." It was humiliating to have to call about one's own girlfriend, if he could dare call her that. "Max, you haven't by any chance seen Caroline on the ferry today, have you?"

"Not today."

Don't always be so exasperating! "When did you see her, Max? This is important!"

"She left on the seven-thirty a couple of days ago. I was running it myself."

Robert felt ice run through his whole body. I've lost her.

"But she came back on the six," Max added. "Did the same thing the next day. She hasn't been on the ferry since, far as I know."

The blood rushed back to his head. "Then she's on the island."

"Sounds like it," said Max.

Robert ended the call. Maybe I'm in with a chance.

Caroline couldn't figure out why she was still hanging around Little Lost. The day after the shit hit the fan she found herself on the seven-thirty ferry, heading back to the city.

"Untie if we're going," Max had said.

The engine was already running and her bags were packed and onboard. She'd unwound the rope from the cleat. She had gotten the hang of cleats, at least, if not of knots.

Max had steered the ferry away from the dock and opened up the throttle. She thought she'd heard him say something.

"What?" she'd asked.

"He's not a bad guy."

"Thanks, I'll figure this out on my own."

"Suit yourself."

Caroline knew Robert was not a bad guy. He was actually a great guy. She could already tell that he adored her, and not as a screen goddess. He'd barely seen her movies. When he took her to bed and kissed her so ardently, he was not kissing a movie star. He was kissing her.

When she'd gotten off the ferry and into the parking lot, she discovered she didn't have her keys.

She'd spent the day walking around Big Lost Island and trying to find houses she thought she'd like more than Hopewell. There were none. She'd taken the six o'clock back and had no supper, even though Beverly had made paella.

The next day she caught the early ferry again, and this time she left her wallet behind. Clearly Dr. Freud was trying to tell her something.

Now it was the day of Possum's life celebration, and she didn't want to let Beverly down by not showing up. She'd avoid Robert and Rose during the ceremony, stay just till it ended, and then she'd go. If she didn't have her wallet and keys, she'd hitchhike.

Caroline didn't want to be in the cottage, and she was sick of riding the ferry back and forth, so to kill time she wandered up to the assembly room, the scene of her triumph as Captain Hook. She hadn't even checked to see whether any photos had gotten out or if they were making fun of her online. She'd had a blast that night. Robert's music had really helped.

She sat down at the piano. Another beautiful piece of wood covered in old paint. But the yellow was cheery, and matched the notes' tinny sound, so it all seemed to work.

She had lost what little piano skills she'd been taught at St. Andrew's. Mostly she could play "Für Elise," "Chopsticks," and a mean bass on "Heart and Soul." She started on that now. She gave it a bluesy beat that echoed around the room.

She heard the screen door slam and knew instantly who was there. It would have been a real movie moment if Robert hadn't sneezed to announce his entrance. For a slender guy, he had an enormous sneeze.

Caroline looked over her shoulder. "You," she said. He looked so utterly forlorn and crestfallen she almost forgave him right then. But let him say the first word.

"Oh my God, Caroline, I am so sorry."

She started playing again. This time with a lot of drama. Keep him on the line.

He came closer. "I was an utter fool and idiot."

She shrugged her shoulders.

He hovered next to the piano bench. "What I'm trying to tell you is I think I've fallen—"

"Say it with music," she said.

He put all he had into "Heart and Soul."

"Someone lead the way, before I lose my nerve." Jon, Lottie, and Ethan were neatly dressed and ready on the porch at three o'clock. Rose had also appeared, silent and gloomy. Beverly was mistrustful of this instant family, but they were doing what family does: rallying round.

They took the boardwalk that led past the chapel and up to Cathedral Woods. Ethan ran ahead with Jon. Beverly's legs had grown stronger from all this walking, but still, it was a long way and he took it slowly. Rose and Lottie kept pace with him. No one spoke.

"This will do, won't it, Beverly?" Lottie asked. They had come to a spot where the spruce trees were particularly high. It did look a little like a cathedral.

"Yes, this is where Robert thought we should be," Lottie said. They gathered around Beverly as Jon struggled to open the box. He took out his key chain and gingerly tore open the packing tape. He was mercifully gentle. Inside the box was a somber canvas bag, which Jon handed to Beverly.

"Poor old Possum," Beverly said. There was silence. They don't expect me to speak, I hope. I won't be speaking.

The silence hung.

Then Rose spoke up. At first he wasn't even sure what she was talking about or to whom she was speaking or why. All he registered was her saying that losing things was not a disaster. Ha!

Was this a eulogy or just an observation? Beverly couldn't tell, but at least Rose's sudden declaiming meant he didn't have to say anything. He spilled some of the ashes out of the sack and onto the ground. There was no wind, which was a mercy. He did not want to touch the ashes or to have them touch him. What if he felt fur? Or a bone?

Rose's voice, though not Caroline's, was strong and deep. It was poetry she was reciting, he was sure of it. He closed his eyes and let her words wash over him. On she went, about losing things. And people. And places.

Gorsch would have liked it up here in Maine. He would so have enjoyed those lads who sang, from the hat party. Doubtless he would have invited one of them back to bed with him—and the poor boy would have had to accept: an invitation from the great Sam Gorsch! Who would not take him up on it? Gorsch would have had a whale of a time showing the lad his member. Half of Gorsch's success, Beverly thought, could be laid at the feet of his enormous dick. He smiled. Then he started listening to Rose again.

Now she had moved on to losing houses and keys. As if keys mattered! At least Jon is now going to take over the upkeep of all those houses we have, he thought. Jon seems so eager to do all the things I don't want to do at all. What will I do with myself instead, though? Lottie says we'll all stay friends. I doubt it.

Rose had not stopped.

She keeps saying that one line, Beverly thought, about the art of losing. Is it really in the poem that many times? What a lazy writer. He hoped it was not Rose who had written the poem, though her voice, now raw, was having an effect on him. And on the others. Between the soaring trees and the slanting light and the ashes and the birds and the ragged circle they had formed it was hard to resist the waves of sentiment. Sentiment or real feeling.

I lost my husband, Beverly thought. It has been a disaster.

When Rose finished speaking at last, there was silence for a while. Jon may actually have been crying.

"Now can I get gelato?" asked Ethan. That helped.

Then Beverly saw two figures at the edge of the circle of trees. His darling Caroline, and Robert. Had they patched things up? Rose walked away.

"We stayed at the edges," said Caroline. "But we came. Robert is forgiven."

"Thank you," said Beverly.

"He must have been a very good companion," said Caroline. "Possum, I mean."

"They were both very good companions," said Beverly. "And now one of them is laid to rest. The other one, my darling Sammy"—there, he'd said his name now, his true name—"Lottie said you'd help me, Jon. Will you?" He was suddenly almost panic-stricken that Sam wasn't taken care of.

"Of course," said Jon. "Do you want to stay here and talk about Possum?"

"I have talked and talked about Possum," said Beverly. "I think we can talk about other things." He looked for Rose. "Did she write that poem herself, do you think?" he asked. "Rose, I mean. It was so repetitive, but it made sense. I wonder if she always writes that way, saying the same thing over and over."

"I actually don't think she wrote it," said Caroline.

"It's Elizabeth Bishop," said Caroline and Robert together.

Lottie turned to Caroline. "Now Beverly must come here all the time, every summer, to visit."

"I think that's up to Robert," said Caroline.

"I think that's up to you," said Robert. He took her arm.

"Everyone's coupling off," said Beverly. "Rose!" he called. "I need a little help getting back to the cottage. Could you possibly give me your arm?" He was making Rose and Caroline get near each other and they both knew it. He gave Caroline his left arm and offered Rose his right.

Rose reluctantly took it. "You're trying to get me back into the fold," she said. "Hi, Caroline."

"Bah," said Beverly. "In case it helps, what Gorsch and I did to each other over umpteen years was much worse than this little hiccup of yours."

"I don't think it will make a difference," said Rose, "but tell us about it anyway."

After the cat funeral, Ethan ran off with the island kids, what few were left. A lot of them had already headed back home for school. The adults watched as he played soccer in the field next to the tennis courts. Robert and Caroline had organized a picnic. It made for the perfect funeral repast.

"Happy?" said Jon, coming up next to Lottie, very close.

"I'm happy," she said, with a sigh.

"What's the matter?"

"I'm sorry about Rose and Fred. Otherwise I am perfectly happy."

"The magic will wear off, though, once we get home. It's not like this in real life."

"But we'll have had it. We'll know it's possible. That's a lot." She gave him a kiss. "Why are all those hot blazer boys clustering around Beverly?"

"Hot blazer boys?"

"They're all in blue blazers and they all are very cute. What are they up to?"

The clear note of a pitch pipe sounded. It was the singing group who had been at the hat party all that long time ago—at least it seemed a long time ago.

"You know what fans we are of Sam Gorsch," one of them said. He wore a lavender shirt. "So when we heard you were on the island, and we learned a little about you, we taught ourselves this song. Carl wrote the harmonies. They're a little different than you're probably used to. Plus, we made it a lot more upbeat. Times have changed."

Beverly looked over at Lottie. "You'll have to check with my musical executors," he said.

"Permission granted," said Jon. "And we'll waive the fee."

The lead singer blew the pitch pipe again, nodded to a snappy internal beat, mouthed, "One-two-three-four," and they began to sing.

Two lovers,
Their flight of innocent grace.
One palace,
A vast impregnable place.
Father, brothers
All intent on breaking the pair.
Willow tree blows skyward
As the birds float on air
Blue willow . . .

When they were done, they held the last note a long time. Then they broke with a yelp. Everyone clapped. Beverly beamed. He turned to Caroline. "Say what you will about that dreadful world we'll go back to when all this is over," he said, "but times have changed indeed."

CHAPTER THIRTY

*H*opewell Cottage was to be filled to the rafters for the last week of August, quite literally. The stray cat at last found Beverly's saucer of goodies and was coming around regularly for left-over grilled swordfish. Fred arranged with Rose that he would fly up with the kids to Boston on the last Tuesday of the month, rent a car, and bring them over on the ferry.

Rose met them at the dock. The kids went wild when they saw her. "Mama! Mommyyyyyy!"

They threw themselves at her and she had to stop herself from toppling over.

"Mommy's crying!"

"I'm crying because I'm so happy to see you."

"That's crazy! You're crazy, Mom."

"I know. I know I'm crazy." She looked at Fred. "Thank you, Fred. Thanks for bringing them." She wiped her nose on Bea's shoulder. "I'm sorry," she said.

"Here take this." He gave her a bandanna. He always had a clean bandanna. It made her cry more. "I wanted them to see you up here. I'm sorry, too. I was a shit."

"Bad word! Bad word, Daddy!" Bea was thrilled to catch him.

Ben had already found the single scariest item on the dock. "Ben! Do not touch that hook!" Fred sprang after him. "Don't touch anything. And let's get out of the way of the other people."

Rose hadn't even noticed that their homecoming was blocking the gangway for the rest of the ferry passengers. "Come on, guys, let's move for a second. Bea, what did you do to your hair?"

"Aunt Isobel let me make it *purple*! But not all the way."

"Thank God for that. Are you taller than Ben now?"

"Nobody's taller than me!"

"Max said he'd take me back to the car," Fred said, "I'm on the six o'clock shuttle from Boston so I've got to get going."

"Wait," Rose said. "You can't stay? Even for a little?"

"Mom, watch me jump!" said Ben.

"No jumping! Come here, Ben." She grabbed him by the back of the life jacket.

"Do you want me to stay?"

At that moment, on that dock, with the kids and the water and the boats and the sunlight, she didn't want him out of her life. Their life. "I want you to be home when we get home on the weekend. Back home to Brooklyn. Is that okay?"

"That's good, Rose. Really good."

"I gotta take this thing *off*, Mom!" Bea said. She was unbuckling her life vest.

"Life jackets on till we're off the dock."

"Come say good-bye, kids," Fred said. "I'll see you in a few days."

"Bye, Dad," Bea said and blew him a kiss. Ben had already strewn his life jacket on the dock and had commandeered a wheelbarrow up on the path to the cottages.

Max had started up the ferry engine. "I better go. I'll be home, Rosie. Come home soon," Fred said.

The ferry cast off. If Bea hadn't been clinging to her leg and Ben hadn't been in danger of tipping himself over in a wheelbarrow, she might have jumped onto the boat too.

She watched it leave, and waved. Fred waved back.

"Don't worry, Mommy," Bea said. "Daddy's okay."

"Thanks, you," said Rose. She buried her face in Bea's now half-purple hair. "Let's go see the others. I'll take you up in the wheelbarrow. Ben! Be careful!"

To her great surprise, Rose felt much better about Caroline once her kids were there, especially since Bea took such a shine to her and because Robert let Ben bash away on a very old guitar. It was hard not to like someone who obviously liked her kids. At night Ethan and Ben and Bea, plus assorted island kids who had been demanding sleepovers, slept in the boys' dormitory, like a den of puppies. Caroline told them stories in her thrilling voice, and Robert sang medieval lullabies accompanied by his lute.

"Better than Hogwarts," Lottie said.

Beverly spent his last week on the island coaxing the cat, whom he'd named Abigail, onto the lawn of the cottage and from there to the porch. Even if he wasn't ready to have a pet yet, she was comforting to have around. Rose learned from another parent that Abigail was one of a litter of cats that had been born under mysterious circumstances. Her mama cat, presumed dead early in the season, had actually been hiding out in the old boathouse and had had enough company there to give birth in early June. "So the pedigree is impeccable," said Beverly. "Little Lost Islanders through and through."

Once Abigail was willing to be touched, Jon took her (kicking and screaming) to the vet in the Harbor, who fixed her up with shots and pronounced her healthy.

"We can't leave her here over the winter, can we?" said Beverly as they took the ferry back to the island. "She wouldn't survive alone."

"No, I don't think she would," said Jon, and that was settled.

Robert had emerged from the third floor long enough to arrange for someone to close up the cottage when they all left on Saturday. The end of the summer.

"We better go home soon, Mommy," Ethan said. "Ben and I have to start being friends at home too. I told him he could go to my school."

"And I want to take care of Abigail! She needs me!" said Bea.

"Oh, so this is how it happens," said Rose. "Children and animals."

"They always upstage one," said Caroline.

"No one upstages you," said Robert.

"Someone, please stop him," said Jon.

"Oh not yet, not yet," said Caroline.

"Turns out," Robert said, "she likes the gawpers."

"Only if they're you," Caroline said.

August 31 was their last day. Robert said they were all welcome to stay longer, but Labor Day loomed, so there was school to get back to and co-op shifts to make up, and books to turn in and movie scripts to read. The weather urged them home too. It was as if the island were conspiring in the end of the season: the night came much earlier; the fog didn't lift in the morning; some of the leaves on the trees were starting to turn red. The pull of real life was strong and, by now, almost welcome. Not that they were tired of the magic of Hopewell Cottage; just that they wanted to take some of it back with them, and try it on for size at home.

The trash and bottles gathered, the food all out of the fridge, the laundry mostly done, the duffle bags dragged out to the island truck—they were ready. Fred and Jon got into the back with the kids and the bags. Robert squeezed next to Warren, Max's second in command. Rose and Lottie and Caroline would walk down with Beverly, who toted Abigail in a snazzy little cat carrier they'd found at an antique store.

"One picture of us all!" said Lottie. "Before we disappear to the four winds!"

"Can you take it, Warren?" Robert asked.

Warren agreed.

"We should take it on the cottage steps," said Robert.

"On the truck! On the truck!" said Ben.

"On the truck!" repeated Ethan.

"On the truck it is," said Robert. They gathered around the flatbed, the Roses, the Carolines, the Lotties, and Beverly with his Abigail.

"Say cheese!" said Warren. They said cheese; the picture was taken. Warren started up the motor. "Meet you at the dock!" said Robert, and the truck rumbled downhill.

Caroline, Beverly, Lottie, and Rose remained in the quiet left behind by the truck's noisy engine. They stood in front of the cottage for a moment, all of them lost in thought. With all the windows closed and the porch empty of towels and books and swept clean, it looked so serene.

"There are about a thousand things I didn't do," said Rose.

"We never went to Bar Harbor," said Lottie.

"Or climbed Cadillac Mountain," said Rose. "And we didn't get to

Monhegan. I didn't finish my dissertation. Or even make a start. But I will."

"Did we have lobster rolls?" asked Caroline. Beverly couldn't pinpoint exactly when Rose and Caroline had started speaking to each other again, but he was glad they had. "Oh, right—way back at the beginning of the month. It seems like that happened last year. Beverly's the only one who accomplished what he came to do."

"But we will accomplish what we need to do. I see it."

"You know what, Lottie?" Rose said. "I actually see it too."

"It's yours now," Lottie said to Caroline. "Hopewell Cottage."

"It's hardly mine," said Caroline, as she put a hand on the stair railing. "But I do like Robert a lot."

"Yes, we've picked that up," said Beverly. "My room was directly under your love nest, and I'm not completely deaf."

"Let's cut some of those flowers," said Caroline, changing the subject, "to take home with us. A little piece of the island. Zinnias, right?"

"Zinnias, indeed. Pretty," said Beverly.

"To go with our sea glass and shells and smelly seaweed," said Rose. "We are taking practically a metric ton of the island back with the twins."

"A little more won't hurt," said Caroline. She dug in her shorts and found Robert's pocketknife. She smiled. "Remember when we looked at these the first day, Beverly?" She bent over and started cutting. "The red ones are gone but there are new ones now. Orange."

"Orange?" said Beverly. "I would have called them persimmon."

September

CHAPTER THIRTY-ONE

*T*he East Seventeenth Street place felt so small and so dark and dirty when Robert got home. His bags and shoes and fleeces from Maine crowded the front entryway. He'd need to get that food into the fridge. And some of the shirts were damp and would have to be taken out of their plastic bags, pronto.

But not yet.

Robert went over to his pigeonhole desk, which took up too much space in his living room/dining room/kitchen. It was the one thing he had taken from Hopewell for his apartment, a little piece of Little Lost in the big city.

He reached into one of the cubbies. Not there. Tried another. Aha.

He drew out a stack of index cards. "The Rule of Robert's Sign," he said. And he tore them into very small pieces, one by one.